D0059225

Dame Ngaio's last book

Alleyn and Others...

A man dies with his hand on a radio dial. A disguised aristocrat finds murder at the opening night at a play. A cryptogram causes death in an English churchyard. These are the short cases of Scotland Yard's Inspector Roderick Alleyn, who with his lovely wife, the celebrated painter Agatha Troy, charmed his way through more than thirty novels.

Here for the first time in one volume is the collected short fiction of Dame Ngaio Marsh. In addition to the "lost" cases of Rory Alleyn, this book contains Marsh's own account of the creation of her detective as well as four urbane crime tales with settings ranging from an elegant London restaurant to the outback of the author's native New Zealand. It concludes with a real find; a previously unpublished script written for British television. The teleplay is a courtroom drama about a spinster charged with murdering an apoplectic major. (The accused was originally portrayed by Joan Hickson, who would later find acclaim as Agatha Christie's Miss Marple.)

The Collected Short Fiction of Ngaio Marsh is filled with the wit, clever plotting, and careful characterizations that are synonymous with its author.

This paperback also contains a recently discovered story which may be Dame Ngaio's first published fiction. The work has never before appeared in the U.S., and elsewhere has been out of print for sixty years. The tale, entitled "The Figure Quoted," concerns a lovely and unashamedly naked lady in an appropriately unconventional situation.

ALLEYN
and OTHERS

the collected short fiction of
Ngaio Marsh

Edited and with an introduction by
Douglas G. Greene

From the collection of
Janette E. Horst
1921 - 2000

INTERNATIONAL POLYGONICS, LTD.
NEW YORK CITY

Alleyn and Others

ISBN 1-55882-028-0

The following appeared in the hardcover edition:
Library of Congress Cataloging-in-Publication Data

Marsh, Ngaio, 1899-1982
[Novels]
The Collected Short Fiction of Ngaio Marsh/ edited
and with an introduction by Douglas G. Greene.
p.cm.

1. Crime and criminals—Literary collections.
2. Detective and mystery stories, New Zealand.
I. Greene, Douglas G. II. Title.

PR9639.3.M27A6 1989
823—dc20   89-39751
                                                              CIP

First published as *The Collected Short Fiction of Ngaio Marsh*
by IPL in 1989

Printed and manufactured in the United States of America.

10 9 8 7 6 5 4 3 2 1

Table of Contents

Introduction

Literate. Polished. Witty. Urbane. These words describe the traditional English mystery and, above all, the novels of Dame Ngaio Marsh (1899–1982). Paradoxically, Marsh was born and reared far from England and had little interest in detective fiction as a form. "These are not the sort of books I buy to read," she said of the works of other mystery novelists. Her real interests were painting and the theater. But perhaps all of this is not so surprising: she brought to her writing the clearsightedness of an outsider—an outsider who could view a scene as a painter and plot with the dramatic sense of a playwright.

Edith Ngaio Marsh was born in Christchurch, New Zealand. Her father came from England, but her mother was from a family that was basically colonial, having come to New Zealand by way of the West Indies. Marsh explained to an interviewer many years later that in New Zealand European children often receive native names, and Ngaio —the name by which she was known all her life—can mean either "light on the water" or "little tree bug" in the Maori language. Other sources say that it is the name of a native flowering tree. Whatever the case, Marsh found whenever she was outside New Zealand that her name was constantly mispronounced "Ner-gy-oh," rather than the correct "Nye-oh." At the age of fifteen, she entered art school and planned a career as a painter. While a student, she attended a performance of Allan Wilkie's Shakespeare Company, and sent him a playscript called *The Medallion.* Wilkie did not produce the play, but he was so impressed that for two years Marsh worked for his company.

In 1928 when she was almost thirty, Marsh went to London with friends around whom she would base the Lampreys, a family that would be featured in many of her stories. For a while, she wrote syndicated articles for publication back in New Zealand and, as she later recalled, began "to develop some appreciation, at least, for cadence and the balance of words." She and one of the Lampreys decided to open a shop called Touch and Go to sell various handcrafts—decorated trays, bowls, lampshades, and even "funny rhymes for bathroom and lavatory doors."

While trying to keep the shop going, Marsh filled in odd moments in writing her first book, a detective novel called *A Man Lay Dead.* Details of its composition and the invention of Inspector Roderick Alleyn are given in Marsh's essay, "Roderick Alleyn," which begins this book. Shortly after finishing the manuscript, she had to return to New Zealand to attend her mother's ultimately fatal illness, but her English agent arranged for the book to be published in 1934. In later years, Marsh grew disenchanted with *A Man Lay Dead.* In her autobiography, *Black Beech and Honeydew,* she remarked that "I don't think that before or since . . . I have ever written with less trouble and certainly with less distinction." "It wasn't very good," she said to an interviewer, "and sometimes [I] wish it could be withdrawn. I don't like the title even. It sounds awfully like 'A Man–Laid Egg.' " To modern readers Alleyn seems something of a twit on his first appearance, as is evident from his very first words: "You've guessed my boyish secret. I've been given a murder to solve—aren't I a lucky little detective?" And the solution—involving the murderer sliding down a bannister toward the victim—does not have the subtlety of her later books. *Enter a Murderer* (1935), written in New Zealand while Marsh was keeping house for her father, was a marked improvement, perhaps because it was based on her first love, the theater, but Alleyn still talks like one of the "bright young things" of the 1920s. His first words in this book are: "Perhaps he knew me. I'm as famous as anything, you know. . . . An actor in his dressing-room will thrill me to mincement. I shall sit and goggle at him, I promise you." Though in each successive book Marsh gradually deepened his character, Alleyn does not become truly believable until he meets his future wife, the painter Agatha Troy, in *Artists in Crime* (1938).

Marsh said that she got the idea of writing a detective story while reading a novel by Agatha Christie or Dorothy L. Sayers. I suspect it was one of Sayers's Lord Peter Wimsey novels, for Sayers's influence is manifest throughout Marsh's early books. Sayers had developed a formula that soon was used by many other writers. Her cases are solved by Lord Peter Wimsey, an aristocratic amateur sleuth who collects books and who fills his talk with obscure quotations. He is assisted by his man, Bunter, and by Inspector Parker, a competent but unimaginative Scotland Yard official. Other writers who used the bright amateur/stolid professional combination included Miles Burton, Max Afford, Rupert Penny, Margery Allingham, John Dickson Carr, Ianthe Jerrold, and H. C. Bailey. Ngaio Marsh varied the formula, but only slightly. Roderick Alleyn is a professional, but he begins as a literary cousin to Lord Peter. Alleyn is the scion of an old aristocratic family, and his mother, Lady Alleyn, seems almost a clone of Lord Peter's mother, the Dowager Duchess of Denver. Even in Marsh's middle-period novels, such as *A Wreath for Rivera* (1949), Alleyn addresses his assistant, Inspector Fox, in Wimsey-like language: "Fox, my cabbage, my rare edition, my *objet d'art*, my own especial bit of bijouterie." Fox himself is not only much like Parker and other Scotland Yard detectives who assist aristocratic sleuths, but he also shares some characteristics with Wimsey's servant, Bunter. He is especially good at obtaining information below stairs, in the servants' quarters. And like Wimsey, Alleyn falls in love with a suspect in one of his cases and marries her in a later novel.

Whenever the matter came up, Marsh said that she did not follow Sayers in falling in love with her detective. I think that she did. Or at any rate, she identified with Alleyn's wife: "People who know me very well see me in her. Agatha Troy's tastes are mine and of course she's a painter and I started off as a painter." And viewing Alleyn through Troy's eyes made him much less the effete aristocrat that he often seemed to be in the early novels. By the time that Marsh brought him to New Zealand to help the local authorities in *Colour Scheme* (1943) and *Died in the Wool* (1945), Alleyn has gained sensitivity and sympathy. Though he may have emerged from Lord Peter Wimsey, he had become the spiritual ancestor of Ruth Rendell's Wexford and P. D. James's Dalgliesh.

The fact that Alleyn is a policeman has led some scholars to write that "in most cases he relies on routine police procedure." In fact, although Alleyn has fingerprint experts and photographers who investigate the scene of the crime, technical matters are rarely described and the solutions are almost never discovered by such means. Marsh's books are part of the Golden Age tradition, in which crimes are solved by clues given to the reader and the murders are frequently bizarre. In Marsh's books, bodies are hidden in bales of wool, and victims are dispatched by guns lurking inside pianos, by lethal wine bottles, and by poisoned darts. Although not particularly interested in the form of detective fiction, she nonetheless followed it almost religiously. She explained that "the mechanics in a detective novel may be shamelessly contrived but the writing need not be so nor, with one exception, need the characterisation. About the guilty person, of course, endless duplicity is practised." In 1981, I wrote to Ngaio Marsh about research I was doing into the life of another mystery novelist. I received a friendly letter in which—as an aside—she mentioned that "at the moment I am deeply involved with a very elaborate case that I have funked until now. It has become more and more elaborate and the un-knotting of clues has never been one of my talents." Some current writers who share Marsh's difficulties in handling clues have solved the problem by ignoring clues altogether. It says much for Marsh's adherence to the form that she was willing to struggle with clueing, and she produced books as well structured and as fair to the reader as any of the Golden Age.

Much has been made of the influence of the stage on Marsh's detective stories. Many of her novels are centered on a theatrical company, including *Enter a Murderer* (1935), *Vintage Murder* (1937), *Night at the Vulcan* (1951), *Killer Dolphin* (1966), and *Light Thickens* (1982); and some of her nontheatrical novels, such as *Death at the Bar* (1940), feature actors as major characters. More significantly, Marsh sets a scene much in the way of a playwright. In the interviews that play so large a part in Alleyn's investigations, she clearly visualizes where each character is standing or sitting in relation to the props—the furniture and other objects in the room. Her painter's eye is also involved, for she describes the setting vividly yet without making it more than the backdrop for the people. Some scholars go even further. LeRoy Panek, in *Watteau's Shepherds, The Detective Novel in Britain* (1979), analyzes the structure of her novels according to the Aristotelian rules for Greek drama. If this is going too far, there is no denying that she creates her stories with a feeling for dramatic interest, for placing of the climax, and for directing her characters in a way that is more the style of a playwright than a novelist. Although there are exceptions, we learn about Marsh's characters not by what they tell us of themselves—the soliloquy had gone out of fashion by the time that Marsh began to write—but by how they relate to one another. In short, Marsh treats the reader as though he or she were a part of an audience at a play.

Marsh's stories are related to a specific kind of play, the comedy of manners. The best works in this form are written by people who are in one way or another outsiders. As a New Zealander, Ngaio Marsh did not think—as Christie sometimes did—that the English class structure was the best of all possible worlds. I think that *Death in a White Tie* (1938) is the best of her early books, not because of the crime and solution but because of its sensitive discussion of the social expectations that produced the "season" of debutante balls. In the novel, poor but presentable women are hired to sponsor girls, including one who has an unhappy time in entering what amounts to a marriage market. Marsh comments that "she was not so very plain but only rather disastrously uneventful." Troy sums up the situation: "There's something so blasted cruel and barbaric about this season game." Another character, one who approves of the system, also gains an insight into what it really means:

It took [Lord Robert] some time to get round the ballroom and as he edged past dancing couples and over the feet of sitting chaperones he suddenly felt as if an intruder had thrust open all the windows of this neat little world and let in a flood of uncompromising light. In this cruel light he saw the people he liked best and they were changed and belittled. . . . He was plunged into a violent depression that had a sort of nightmare-ish quality. How many of these women were what he still thought of as "virtuous?" And the debutantes? They had gone back to chaperones and were guided and guarded by women, many of whose private lives would look ugly in this flood of hard light that had been let in on Lord Robert's world. The girls were sheltered by a convention for three months but at the same time they heard all sorts of things that would have horrified and bewildered his sister Mildred at their age. And he wondered if the Victorian and Edwardian eras had been no more than freakish incidents in the history of society and if their proprieties had been as artificial as the paint on a modern woman's lips. This idea seemed abominable to Lord Robert and he felt old and lonely for the first time in his life.

Those who argue that the detective story had to give way to the crime novel sometimes say that the classical, fair-play form did not allow commentary on society or on people. The above passage shows that it is less the form than the talent of the writer that makes for insights.

This volume contains all of Ngaio Marsh's known uncollected fiction as well as a few related pieces. Following Marsh's essays on the creations of Roderick and Troy Alleyn, the book reprints the three short stories about Alleyn originally published in periodicals over the space of thirty-four years. "Death on the Air," which first appeared in a British magazine in 1939, is a typical closed-circle detective story of the period with a clever murder device and a cleverly hidden murderer. "I Can Find My Way Out," published in 1946, is Marsh's only short story with a theatrical setting, and it contains her bow to one of the most famous detectival plot devices, murder in a locked room. "Chapter and Verse," from 1973, has a plot that could easily have been expanded into a full-length novel, and like the previous story is redolent of the Golden Age of Detection. The remaining tales are urbane studies of crime. The short-short "The Hand in the Sand" (1953) is Marsh's only venture into writing about true crime. "The Cupid Mirror" (1972) and "A Fool About Money" (1974) are completely different from each other except in one way—they conclude with a victory over a totally exasperating person. "Morepork" (1978), Marsh's final and probably best short story, tells of an odd trial in the forests of New Zealand. The book concludes with *Evil Liver*, a previously unpublished telescript produced in 1975, in which the viewer (or reader) must act as detective.

In assembling this book, I have become indebted to

many people: Robert C. S. Adey, Margaret Lewis, Barry Pike, and Collin Southern helped to locate material. I am also grateful to Tony Medawar, researcher extraordinaire, whose investigation into the production of *Evil Liver* was invaluable. Granada Television Limited kindly allowed us to print Marsh's telescript. Phyllis Westberg of the Harold Ober Company, American agents for the Marsh estate, was unfailingly helpful. Publishers normally are expected to act only as publishers, but Hugh Abramson of International Polygonics took a personal interest in this work and the result is a far better book than the editor could have produced alone.

Douglas G. Greene
Norfolk, Virginia
April 1989

ADDENDA

After the publication of the first edition of this book, a long-forgotten short story by Ngaio Marsh came to light. "The Figure Quoted" is probably her first published fiction and originated in her hometown newspaper, *The Christchurch Sun*, Christmas 1927; it was reprinted in O. N. Gillespie's anthology, *New Zealand Short Stories* (London: Dent, 1930). It is not a detective story or a crime story—at least, I don't think so—but it is one of the most intriguing mystery tales that she ever wrote. We have added it to the end of this collection.

Another important discovery was made by Rowan Gibbs and Richard Williams in *Ngaio Marsh: A Bibliography* (Scunthorpe, South Humberside: Dragonby Press, 1990). Ngaio Marsh was born in 1895, not 1899 as all other authorities have reported. Her parents, who were apparently dilatory sorts, waited until she was four years old before registering her birth, and as an adult Marsh preferred not to correct the error.

Douglas G. Greene
November 1990

ESSAYS

Roderick Alleyn

He was born with the rank of Detective-Inspector, C.I.D., on a very wet Saturday afternoon in a basement flat off Sloane Square, in London. The year was 1931.

All day, rain splashed up from the feet of passersby going to and fro, at eye-level, outside my water-streaked windows. It fanned out from under the tires of cars, cascaded down the steps to my door and flooded the area. "Remorseless" was the word for it and its sound was, beyond all expression, dreary. In view of what was about to take place, the setting was, in fact, almost too good to be true.

I read a detective story borrowed from a dim little lending-library in a stationer's shop across the way. Either a Christie or a Sayers, I think it was. By four o'clock, when the afternoon was already darkening, I had finished it, and still the rain came down. I remember that I made up the London coal-fire of those days and looked down at it, idly wondering if I had it in me to write something in the genre. That was the season, in England, when the Murder Game was popular at weekend parties. Someone was slipped a card saying he or she was the "murderer." He or she then chose a moment to select a "victim," and there was a subsequent "trial." I thought it might be an idea for a whodunit—they were already called that—if a real corpse was found instead of a phony one. Luckily for me, as it turned out, I wasn't aware until much later that a French practitioner had been struck with the same notion.

I played about with this idea. I tinkered with the fire and with an emergent character who might have been engendered in its sulky entrails: a solver of crimes.

The room had grown quite dark when I pulled on a mackintosh, took an umbrella, plunged up the basement steps and beat my way through rain-fractured lamplight to the stationer's shop. It smelt of damp newsprint, cheap magazines, and wet people. I bought six exercise books, a pencil and pencil sharpener and splashed back to the flat.

Then with an odd sensation of giving myself some sort of treat, I thought more specifically about the character who already had begun to take shape.

In the crime fiction of that time, the solver was often a person of more-or-less eccentric habit with a collection of easily identifiable mannerisms. This, of course, was in the tradition of Sherlock Holmes. Agatha Christie's splendid M. Poirot had his moustaches, his passion for orderly arrangements, his frequent references to "grey cells." Dorothy L. Sayers's Lord Peter Wimsey could be, as I now am inclined to think, excruciatingly facetious. Nice Reggie Fortune said—and author H. C. Bailey had him say it very often— "My dear chap! Oh, my dear chap!" and across the Atlantic there was Philo Vance, who spoke a strange language that his author, S. S. Van Dine, had the nerve to attribute, in part, to Balliol College, Oxford.

Faced with this assembly of celebrated eccentrics, I decided, on that long-distant wet afternoon, that my best chance lay in comparative normality: in the invention of a man with a background resembling that of the friends I had made in England, and that I had better not tie mannerisms, like labels, round his neck. (I can see now that with my earlier books I did not altogether succeed in this respect.)

I thought that my detective would be a professional policeman but, in some ways, atypical: an attractive, civilized man with whom it would be pleasant to talk but much less pleasant to fall out.

He began to solidify.

From the beginning I discovered that I knew quite a lot about him. Indeed, I rather think that, even if I had not fallen so casually into the practice of crime-writing and had taken to a more serious form, he would still have arrived and found himself in an altogether different setting.

He was tall and thin with an accidental elegance about him and fastidious enough to make one wonder at his choice of profession. He was a compassionate man. He had a cockeyed sense of humor, dependent largely upon understatement, but for all his unemphatic, rather apologetic ways, he could be a formidable person of considerable authority. As for his background, that settled itself there and then: he was a younger son of a Buckinghamshire family and had his schooling at Eton. His elder brother, whom he regarded as a bit of an ass, was a diplomatist, and his mother, whom he liked, a lady of character.

I remember how pleased I was, early in his career, when one of the reviews called him "that nice chap, Alleyn," because that was how I liked to think of him: a nice chap with more edge to him than met the eye—a good deal more, as I hope it has turned out. The popular press of his early days would refer to him as "the handsome inspector," a practice that caused him acute embarrassment.

On this day of his inception I fiddled about with the idea of writing a tale that would explain why he left the Diplomatic Service for the Police Force, but somehow the idea has never jelled.

His age? Here I must digress. His age would defy the

investigation of an Einstein, and he is not alone in this respect. Hercule Poirot, I have been told, was, by ordinary reckoning, going on 122 when he died. Truth to tell, fictional investigations move in an exclusive space-time continuum where Mr. Bucket in *Bleak House* may be seen going about his police investigations cheek-by-jowl with the most recent fledglings. It is enough to say that on the afternoon of my detective's arrival, I did not concern myself with his age, and I am still of the same mind in that respect.

His arrival had been unexpected and occurred, you might say, out of nothing. One of the questions writers are most often asked about characters in their books is whether they are based upon people in the workaday world—"real people." Some of mine certainly are but they have gone through various mutations and in doing so have moved away from their original begetters. But not this one. He, as far as I can tell, had no begetter apart from his author. He came in without introduction and if, for this reason, there is an element of unreality about him, I can only say that for me, at least, he was and is very real indeed.

Dorothy L. Sayers has been castigated, with some justification perhaps, for falling in love with her Wimsey. To have done so may have been an error in taste and judgment though her ardent fans would never have admitted as much. I can't say I have ever succumbed in this way to my own investigator but I have grown to like him as an old friend. I even dare to think he has developed third-dimensionally in my company. We have traveled widely: in a night express through the North Island of New Zealand, and among the geysers, boiling mud and snow-clad mountains of that country. We have cruised along English canals and walked through the streets and monuments of Rome. His duties have taken us to an island off the coast of Normandy and to the backstage regions of several theatres. He has sailed with a psychopathic homicide from Tilbury to Cape Town and has made arrests in at least three country houses, one hospital, a church, a canal boat and a pub. Small wonder, perhaps, that we have both broadened our outlook under the pressure of these undertakings, none of which was anticipated on that wet afternoon in London.

At his first appearance he was a bachelor and, although responsive to the opposite sex, did not bounce in and out of irresponsible beds when going about his job. Or, if he did, I knew nothing about it. He was, to all intents and purposes, fancy-free and would remain so until, sailing out of Suva in Fiji, he came across Agatha Troy, painting in oils, on the boat-deck of a liner. And that was still some half-dozen books in the future.

There would be consternation shown by editors and publishers when, after another couple of jobs, the lady accepted him. The acceptance would be a *fait accompli*, and from then on I would be dealing with a married investigator, his celebrated wife, and later on, their son.

By a series of coincidences and much against his inclination, it would come about that these two would occasionally get themselves embroiled in his professional duties, but generally speaking he would keep his job out of his family life. He would set about his cases with his regular associate, who is one of his closest friends; Inspector Fox, massive, calm, and plain-thinking, would tramp sedately in. They have been working together for a considerable time, and still allow me to accompany them.

But "on the afternoon in question," all this, as lady crime novelists used to say, "lay in the future." The fire had burnt clear and sent leaping patterns up the walls of my London flat when I turned on the light, opened an exercise book, sharpened my pencil, and began to write. There he was, waiting quietly in the background ready to make his entrance at Chapter IV, page 58, in the first edition.

I had company. It became necessary to give my visitor a name.

Earlier in that week I had visited Dulwich College. This is an English public school, which in any other country would mean a private school. It was founded and very richly endowed by a famous actor in the days of the first Elizabeth. It possesses a splendid picture gallery and a fabulous collection of relics from the Shakespearean-Marlovian theatre: enthralling to me who has a passion for that scene.

My father was an old boy of Dulwich College—an "old Alleynian," as it is called, the name of the Elizabethan actor being Alleyn.

Detective-Inspector Alleyn, C.I.D. ? Yes.

His first name was in doubt for some time, but another visit, this time to friends in the Highlands of Scotland, had familiarized me with some resoundingly-named characters, among them one Roderick (or Rory) MacDonald.

Roderick Alleyn, Detective-Inspector, C.I.D. ?

Yes.

The name, by the way, is pronounced "Allen."

Portrait of Troy

Troy made her entrance with the sixth of the books about Alleyn. In those days, I still painted quite a lot and quite seriously, and was inclined to look upon everything I saw in terms of possible subject matter.

On a voyage out to New Zealand from England, we called at Suva. The day was overcast, still and sultry. The kind of day when sounds have an uncanny clarity, and colour an added sharpness and intensity. The wharf at Suva, as seen from the boat-deck of the *Niagara*, was remarkable in these respects: the acid green of a bale of bananas packed in their own leaves; the tall Fijian with a mop of hair dyed screaming magenta, this colour repeated in the sari of an Indian woman; the slap of bare feet on wet boards and the deep voices that sounded as if they were projected through pipes. All these elements made their impressions, and I felt a great itch for a paint brush between my fingers.

The ship drew away, the wharf receded, and I was left with an unattempted, non-existent picture that is as vivid today as it was then.

I don't think it is overdoing it to say that when I began *Artists in Crime*, it was this feeling of unfulfilment that led me to put another painter on another boat-deck making a sketch of the wharf at Suva and that she made a much better job of it than I ever would have done.

This was Troy. It was in this setting that she and Alleyn first met.

I have always tried to keep the settings of my books as far as possible within the confines of my own experience. Having found Troy and decided that Alleyn was to find her, too, the rest of the book developed in the milieu of a painters' community. It was written before capital punishment was abolished in Great Britain, and Troy shared my own repugnance for that terrible practice: I had talked with a detective-inspector and learnt that there were more men in the force who were for abolition than was commonly supposed. I knew Alleyn would be one of them. He would sense that the shadow of the death penalty lay between himself and Troy. It was not until the end of the next book, *Death in a White Tie*, that they came finally together. In *Death and the Dancing Footman*, they are already married.

My London agent, I remember, was a bit dubious about marrying Alleyn off. There is a school of thought that considers love-interest, where the investigating character is involved, should be kept off-stage in detective fiction or at least handled in a rather gingerly fashion and got rid of with alacrity. Conan Doyle seems to have taken this view.

"To Sherlock Holmes she is always *the* woman," he begins, writing of Irene Adler. But after a couple of sentences expressive of romantic attachment, he knocks that idea sideways by stating that, as far as Holmes was concerned, all emotions (sexual attraction in particular) were "abhorrent to his cold, precise, but admirably balanced mind."

So much for Miss Adler.

An exception to the negative attitude appears in Bentley's classic *Trent's Last Case*, where the devotion of Trent for one of the suspects is a basic ingredient of the investigation. Dorothy L. Sayers, however, turns the whole thing inside out by herself regrettably falling in love with her own creation and making rather an ass of both of them in the process.

Troy came along at a time when thoroughly nice girls

were often called Dulcie, Edith, Cecily, Mona, Madeleine. Even, alas, Gladys. I wanted her to have a plain, rather down-to-earth first name and thought of Agatha—not because of Christie—and a rather odd surname that went well with it, so she became Agatha Troy and always signed her pictures "Troy" and was so addressed by everyone. *Death in a White Tie* might have been called *Siege of Troy.*

Her painting is far from academic but not always non-figurative. One of its most distinguished characteristics is a very subtle sense of movement brought about by the inter-relationships of form and line. Her greatest regret is that she never painted the portrait of Isabella Sommita, which was commissioned in the book I am at present writing. The diva was to have been portrayed with her mouth wide open, letting fly with her celebrated A above high C. It is questionable whether she would have been pleased with the result. It would have been called *Top Note.*

Troy and Alleyn suit each other. Neither impinges upon the other's work without being asked, with the result that in Troy's case she does ask pretty often, sometimes gets argumentative and up-tight over the answer and almost always ends up by following the suggestion. She misses Alleyn very much when they are separated. This is often the case, given the nature of their work, and on such occasions each feels incomplete and they write to each other like lovers.

Perhaps it is advisable, on grounds of credibility, not to make too much of the number of times coincidence mixes Troy up in her husband's cases: a situation that he embraces with mixed feelings. She is a reticent character and as sensitive as a sea-urchin, but she learns to assume and even feel a certain detachment.

"After all," she has said to herself, "I married him and I would be a very boring wife if I spent half my time wincing and showing sensitive."

I like Troy. When I am writing about her, I can see her with her shortish dark hair, thin face and hands. She's absent-minded, shy and funny, and she can paint like nobody's business. I'm always glad when other people like her, too.

THE CASES OF
RODERICK ALLEYN

THE SHORT CASES OF RODERICK ALLEYN

Death on the Air

On the 25th of December at 7:30 a.m. Mr. Septimus
Tonks was found dead beside his wireless set.

It was Emily Parks, an under-housemaid, who discovered
him. She butted open the door and entered, carrying mop,
duster, and carpet-sweeper. At that precise moment she
was greatly startled by a voice that spoke out of the darkness.

"Good morning, everybody," said the voice in superbly
inflected syllables, "and a Merry Christmas!"

Emily yelped, but not loudly, as she immediately realized
what had happened. Mr. Tonks had omitted to turn off his
wireless before going to bed. She drew back the curtains,
revealing a kind of pale murk which was a London Christmas dawn, switched on the light, and saw Septimus.

He was seated in front of the radio. It was a small but
expensive set, specially built for him. Septimus sat in an
armchair, his back to Emily and his body tilted towards the
wireless.

His hands, the fingers curiously bunched, were on the
ledge of the cabinet under the tuning and volume knobs.
His chest rested against the shelf below and his head leaned
on the front panel.

He looked rather as though he was listening intently to
the interior secrets of the wireless. His head was bent so
that Emily could see the bald top with its trail of oiled
hairs. He did not move.

"Beg pardon, sir," gasped Emily. She was again greatly startled. Mr. Tonk's enthusiasm for radio had never before induced him to tune in at seven-thirty in the morning.

"Special Christmas service," the cultured voice was saying. Mr. Tonks sat very still. Emily, in common with the other servants, was terrified of her master. She did not know whether to go or to stay. She gazed wildly at Septimus and realized that he wore a dinner-jacket. The room was now filled with the clamor of pealing bells.

Emily opened her mouth as wide as it would go and screamed and screamed and screamed. . . .

Chase, the butler, was the first to arrive. He was a pale, flabby man but authoritative. He said: "What's the meaning of this outrage?" and then saw Septimus. He went to the armchair, bent down, and looked into his master's face.

He did not lose his head, but said in a loud voice: "My Gawd!" And then to Emily: "Shut your face." By this vulgarism he betrayed his agitation. He seized Emily by the shoulders and thrust her towards the door, where they were met by Mr. Hislop, the secretary, in his dressing-gown. Mr. Hislop said: "Good heavens, Chase, what is the meaning—" and then his voice too was drowned in the clamor of bells and renewed screams.

Chase put his fat white hand over Emily's mouth.

"In the study if you please, sir. An accident. Go to your room, will you, and stop that noise or I'll give you something to make you." This to Emily, who bolted down the hall, where she was received by the rest of the staff who had congregated there.

Chase returned to the study with Mr. Hislop and locked the door. They both looked down at the body of Septimus Tonks. The secretary was the first to speak.

"But—but—he's dead," said little Mr. Hislop.

"I suppose there can't be any doubt," whispered Chase.

"Look at the face. Any doubt! My God!"

Mr. Hislop put out a delicate hand towards the bent head and then drew it back. Chase, less fastidious, touched one of the hard wrists, gripped, and then lifted it. The body at once tipped backwards as if it was made of wood. One of the hands knocked against the butler's face. He sprang back with an oath.

There lay Septimus, his knees and his hands in the air, his terrible face turned up to the light. Chase pointed to the right hand. Two fingers and the thumb were slightly blackened.

Ding, dong, dang, ding.

"For God's sake stop those bells," cried Mr. Hislop. Chase turned off the wall switch. Into the sudden silence came the sound of the door-handle being rattled and Guy Tonk's voice on the other side.

"Hislop! Mr. Hislop! Chase! What's the matter?"

"Just a moment, Mr. Guy." Chase looked at the secretary. "You go, sir."

So it was left to Mr. Hislop to break the news to the family. They listened to his stammering revelation in stupefied silence. It was not until Guy, the eldest of the three children, stood in the study that any practical suggestion was made.

"What has killed him?" asked Guy.

"It's extraordinary," burbled Hislop. "Extraordinary. He looks as if he'd been—"

"Galvanized," said Guy.

"We ought to send for a doctor," suggested Hislop timidly.

"Of course. Will you, Mr. Hislop? Dr. Meadows."

Hislop went to the telephone and Guy returned to his family. Dr. Meadows lived on the other side of the square and arrived in five minutes. He examined the body without moving it. He questioned Chase and Hislop. Chase was very voluble about the burns on the hand. He uttered the word "electrocution" over and over again.

"I had a cousin, sir, that was struck by lightning. As soon as I saw the hand—"

"Yes, yes," said Dr. Meadows. "So you said. I can see the burns for myself."

"Electrocution," repeated Chase. "There'll have to be an inquest."

Dr. Meadows snapped at him, summoned Emily, and then saw the rest of the family—Guy, Arthur, Phillipa, and their mother. They were clustered round a cold grate in the drawing-room. Phillipa was on her knees, trying to light the fire.

"What was it?" asked Arthur as soon as the doctor came in.

"Looks like electric shock. Guy, I'll have a word with you if you please. Phillipa, look after your mother, there's a good child. Coffee with a dash of brandy. Where are those damn maids? Come on, Guy."

Alone with Guy, he said they'd have to send for the police.

"The police!" Guy's dark face turned very pale. "Why? What's it got to do with them?"

"Nothing, as like as not, but they'll have to be notified. I can't give a certificate as things are. If it's electrocution, how did it happen?"

"But the police!" said Guy. "That's simply ghastly. Dr. Meadows, for God's sake couldn't you—?"

"No," said Dr. Meadows, "I couldn't. Sorry, Guy, but there it is."

"But can't we wait a moment? Look at him again. You haven't examined him properly."

"I don't want to move him, that's why. Pull yourself together boy. Look here. I've got a pal in the C.I.D.— Alleyn. He's a gentleman and all that. He'll curse me like a fury, but he'll come if he's in London, and he'll make things easier for you. Go back to your mother. I'll ring Alleyn up."

That was how it came about that Chief Detective Inspector Roderick Alleyn spent his Christmas Day in harness. As a matter of fact he was on duty, and as he pointed out to Dr. Meadows, would have had to turn out and visit his miserable Tonkses in any case. When he did arrive it was with his usual air of remote courtesy. He was accompanied by a tall, thick-set officer—Inspector Fox—and by the divisional police-surgeon. Dr. Meadows took them into the study. Alleyn, in his turn, looked at the horror that had been Septimus.

"Was he like this when he was found?"

"No. I understand he was leaning forward with his hands on the ledge of the cabinet. He must have slumped forward and been propped up by the chair arms and the cabinet."

"Who moved him?"

"Chase, the butler. He said he only meant to raise the arm. *Rigor* is well established."

Alleyn put his hand behind the rigid neck and pushed. The body fell forward into its original position.

"There you are, Curtis," said Alleyn to the divisional surgeon. He turned to Fox. "Get the camera man, will you, Fox?"

The photographer took four shots and departed. Alleyn marked the position of the hands and feet with chalk, made a careful plan of the room and then turned to the doctors.

"Is it electrocution, do you think?"

"Looks like it," said Curtis. "Have to be a p.m. of course."

"Of course. Still, look at the hands. Burns. Thumb and two fingers bunched together and exactly the distance between the two knobs apart. He'd been tuning his hurdy-gurdy."

"By gum," said Inspector Fox, speaking for the first time.

"D'you mean he got a lethal shock from his radio?" asked Dr. Meadows.

"I don't know. I merely conclude he had his hands on the knobs when he died."

"It was still going when the housemaid found him. Chase turned it off and got no shock."

"Yours, partner," said Alleyn, turning to Fox. Fox stooped down to the wall switch.

"Careful," said Alleyn.

"I've got rubber soles," said Fox, and switched it on. The radio hummed, gathered volume, and found itself.

"No-oel, No-o-el," it roared. Fox cut it off and pulled out the wall plug.

"I'd like to have a look inside this set," he said.

"So you shall, old boy, so you shall," rejoined Alleyn. "Before you begin, I think we'd better move the body. Will you see to that, Meadows? Fox, get Bailey, will you? He's out in the car."

Curtis, Hislop, and Meadows carried Septimus Tonks into a spare downstairs room. It was a difficult and horrible business with that contorted body. Dr. Meadows came back alone, mopping his brow, to find Detective-Sergeant Bailey, a fingerprint expert, at work on the wireless cabinet.

"What's all this?" asked Dr. Meadows. "Do you want to find out if he'd been fooling round with the innards?"

"He," said Alleyn, "or—somebody else."

"Umph!" Dr. Meadows looked at the Inspector. "You agree with me, it seems. Do you suspect—?"

"Suspect? I'm the least suspicious man alive. I'm merely being tidy. Well, Bailey?"

"I've got a good one off the chair arm. That'll be the deceased's, won't it, sir?"

"No doubt. We'll check up later. What about the wireless?"

Fox, wearing a glove, pulled off the knob of the volume control.

"Seems to be O.K." said Bailey. "It's a sweet bit of work. Not too bad at all, sir." He turned his torch into the back of the radio, undid a couple of screws underneath the set, and lifted out the works.

"What's the little hole for?" asked Alleyn.

"What's that, sir?" said Fox.

"There's a hole bored through the panel above the knob. About an eighth of an inch in diameter. The rim of the knob hides it. One might easily miss it. Move your torch, Bailey. Yes. There, do you see?"

Fox bent down and uttered a bass growl. A fine needle of light came through the front of the radio.

"That's peculiar, sir," said Bailey from the other side. "I don't get the idea at all."

Alleyn pulled out the tuning knob.

"There's another one there," he murmured. "Yes. Nice clean little holes. Newly bored. Unusual, I take it?"

"Unusual's the word, sir," said Fox.

"Run away, Meadows," said Alleyn.

"Why the devil?" asked Dr. Meadows indignantly. "What are you driving at? Why shouldn't I be here?"

"You ought to be with the sorrowing relatives. Where's your corpse-side manner?"

"I've settled them. What are you up to?"

"Who's being suspicious now?" asked Alleyn mildly. "You may stay for a moment. Tell me about the Tonkses. Who are they? What are they? What sort of a man was Septimus?"

"If you must know, he was a damned unpleasant sort of a man."

"Tell me about him."

Dr. Meadows sat down and lit a cigarette.

"He was a self-made bloke," he said, "as hard as nails and—well, coarse rather than vulgar."

"Like Dr. Johnson perhaps?"

"Not in the least. Don't interrupt. I've known him for twenty-five years. His wife was a neighbor of ours in Dorset. Isabel Foreston. I brought the children into this vale of tears and, by jove, in many ways it's been one for them. It's an extraordinary household. For the last ten years Isabel's condition has been the sort that sends these psycho-jokers dizzy with rapture. I'm only an out of date G.P., and I'd just say she is in an advanced stage of hysterical neurosis. Frightened into fits of her husband."

"I can't understand these holes," grumbled Fox to Bailey.

"Go on, Meadows," said Alleyn.

"I tackled Sep about her eighteen months ago. Told him the trouble was in her mind. He eyed me with a sort of grin on his face and said: 'I'm surprised to learn that my wife has enough mentality to—' But look here, Alleyn, I can't talk about my patients like this. What the devil am I thinking about."

"You know perfectly well it'll go no further unless—"

"Unless what?"

"Unless it has to. Do go on."

But Dr. Meadows hurriedly withdrew behind his professional rectitude. All he would say was that Mr. Tonks had suffered from high blood pressure and a weak heart, that Guy was in his father's city office, that Arthur had wanted to study art and had been told to read for law, and that Phillipa wanted to go on the stage and had been told to do nothing of the sort.

"Bullied his children," commented Alleyn.

"Find out for yourself. I'm off." Dr. Meadows got as far as the door and came back.

"Look here," he said, "I'll tell you one thing. There was a row here last night. I'd asked Hislop, who's a sensible little beggar, to let me know if anything happened to upset Mrs. Sep. Upset her badly, you know. To be indiscreet again, I said he'd better let me know if Sep cut up rough because Isabel and the young had had about as much of that as they could stand. He was drinking pretty heavily. Hislop rang me up at ten-twenty last night to say there'd been a hell of a row; Sep bullying Phips—Phillipa, you know; always call her Phips—in her room. He said Isabel—Mrs. Sep—had gone to bed. I'd had a big day and I didn't want to turn out. I told him to ring again in half an hour if things hadn't quieted down. I told him to keep out of Sep's way and stay in his own room, which is next to Phip's, and see if she was all right when Sep cleared out. Hislop was involved. I won't tell you how. The servants were all out. I said that if I didn't hear from him in half an hour I'd ring again and if there was no answer I'd know they were all in bed and quiet. I did ring, got no answer, and went to bed myself. That's all. I'm off. Curtis knows where to find me. You'll want me for the inquest, I suppose. Goodbye."

When he had gone Alleyn embarked on a systematic prowl round the room. Fox and Bailey were still deeply engrossed with the wireless.

"I don't see how the gentleman could have got a bump-off from the instrument," grumbled Fox. "These control knobs are quite in order. Everything's as it should be. Look here, sir."

He turned on the wall switch and tuned in. There was a prolonged humming.

". . . concludes the program of Christmas carols," said the radio.

"A very nice tone," said Fox approvingly.

"Here's something sir," announced Bailey suddenly.

"Found the sawdust, have you?" said Alleyn.

"Got it in one," said the startled Bailey.

Alleyn peered into the instrument, using the torch. He scooped up two tiny traces of sawdust from under the holes.

"Vantage number one," said Alleyn. He bent down to the wall plug. "Hullo! A two-way adapter. Serves the radio and the radiator. Thought they were illegal. This is a rum business. Let's have another look at those knobs."

He had his look. They were the usual wireless fitments, bakelite knobs fitting snugly to the steel shafts that projected from the front panel.

"As you say," he murmured, "quite in order. Wait a bit." He produced a pocket lens and squinted at one of the shafts. "Ye-es. Do they ever wrap blotting-paper round these objects, Fox?"

"Blotting-paper!" ejaculated Fox. "They do not."

Alleyn scraped at both the shafts with his penknife, holding an envelope underneath. He rose, groaning, and crossed to the desk. "A corner torn off the bottom bit of blotch," he said presently. "No prints on the wireless, I think you said, Bailey?"

"That's right," agreed Bailey morosely.

"There'll be none, or too many, on the blotter, but try, Bailey, try," said Alleyn. He wandered about the room, his eyes on the floor; got as far as the window and stopped.

"Fox!" he said. "A clue. A very palpable clue."

"What is it?" asked Fox.

"The odd wisp of blotting-paper, no less." Alleyn's gaze traveled up the side of the window curtain. "Can I believe my eyes?"

He got a chair, stood on the seat, and with his gloved hand pulled the buttons from the ends of the curtain rod.

"Look at this." He turned to the radio, detached the control knobs, and laid them beside the ones he had removed from the curtain rod.

Ten minutes later Inspector Fox knocked on the drawing-room door and was admitted by Guy Tonks. Phillipa had got the fire going and the family was gathered round it. They looked as though they had not moved or spoken to one another for a long time.

It was Phillipa who spoke first to Fox. "Do you want one of us?" she asked.

"If you please, miss," said Fox. "Inspector Alleyn would like to see Mr. Guy Tonks for a moment, if convenient."

"I'll come," said Guy, and led the way to the study. At the door he paused. "Is he—my father—still—?"

"No, no, sir," said Fox comfortably. "It's all ship-shape in there again."

With a lift of his chin Guy opened the door and went in, followed by Fox. Alleyn was alone, seated at the desk. He rose to his feet.

"You want to speak to me?" asked Guy.

"Yes, if I may. This has all been a great shock to you, of course. Won't you sit down?"

Guy sat in the chair farthest away from the radio.

"What killed my father? Was it a stroke?"

"The doctors are not quite certain. There will have to be a *post-mortem.*"

"Good God! And an inquest?"

"I'm afraid so."

"Horrible!" said Guy violently. "What do they think was the matter? Why the devil do these quacks have to be so mysterious? What killed him?"

"They think an electric shock."

"How did it happen?"

"We don't know. It looks as if he got it from the wireless."

"Surely that's impossible. I thought they were foolproof."

"I believe they are, if left to themselves."

For a second undoubtedly Guy was startled. Then a look of relief came into his eyes. He seemed to relax all over.

"Of course," he said, "he was always monkeying about with it. What had he done?"

"Nothing."

"But you said—if it killed him he must have done something to it."

"If anyone interfered with the set it was put right afterwards."

Guy's lips parted but he did not speak. He had gone very white.

"So you see," said Alleyn, "your father could not have done anything."

"Then it was not the radio that killed him."

"That we hope will be determined by the *post-mortem*."

"I don't know anything about wireless," said Guy suddenly. "I don't understand. This doesn't seem to make sense. Nobody ever touched the thing except my father. He was most particular about it. Nobody went near the wireless."

"I see. He was an enthusiast?"

"Yes, it was his only enthusiasm except—except his business."

"One of my men is a bit of an expert," Alleyn said. "He says this is a remarkably good set. You are not an expert, you say. Is there anyone in the house who is?"

"My young brother was interested at one time. He's given it up. My father wouldn't allow another radio in the house."

"Perhaps he may be able to suggest something."

"But if the thing's all right now—"

"We've got to explore every possibility."

"You speak as if—as—if—"

"I speak as I am bound to speak before there has been an

inquest," said Alleyn. "Had anyone a grudge against your father, Mr. Tonks?"

Up went Guy's chin again. He looked Alleyn squarely in the eyes.

"Almost everyone who knew him," said Guy.

"Is that an exaggeration?"

"No. You think he was murdered, don't you?"

Alleyn suddenly pointed to the desk beside him.

"Have you ever seen those before?" he asked abruptly. Guy stared at two black knobs that lay side by side on an ashtray.

"Those?" he said. "No. What are they?"

"I believe they are the agents of your father's death."

The study door opened and Arthur Tonks came in.

"Guy," he said, "what's happening? We can't stay cooped up together all day. I can't stand it. For God's sake, what happened to him?"

"They think those things killed him," said Guy.

"Those?" For a split second Arthur's glance slewed to the curtain rods. Then, with a characteristic flicker of his eyelids, he looked away again.

"What do you mean?" he asked Alleyn.

"Will you try one of those knobs on the shaft of the volume control?"

"But," said Arthur, "they're metal."

"It's disconnected," said Alleyn.

Arthur picked one of the knobs from the tray, turned to the radio, and fitted the knob over one of the exposed shafts.

"It's too loose," he said quickly, "it would fall off."

"Not if it was packed—with blotting-paper, for instance."

"Where did you find these things?" demanded Arthur.

"I think you recognized them, didn't you? I saw you glance at the curtain rod."

"Of course I recognized them. I did a portrait of Phillipa against those curtains when—he—was away last year. I've painted the damn things."

"Look here," interrupted Guy, "exactly what are you driving at, Mr. Alleyn? If you mean to suggest that my brother—."

"I!" cried Arthur. "What's it got to do with me? Why should you suppose—."

"I found traces of blotting-paper on the shafts and inside the metal knobs," said Alleyn. "It suggested a substitution of the metal knobs for the bakelite ones. It is remarkable, don't you think, that they should so closely resemble one another? If you examine them, of course, you find they are not identical. Still, the difference is scarcely perceptible."

Arthur did not answer this. He was still looking at the wireless.

"I've always wanted to have a look at this set," he said surprisingly.

"You are free to do so now," said Alleyn politely. "We have finished with it for the time being."

"Look here," said Arthur suddenly, "suppose metal knobs were substituted for bakelite ones, it couldn't kill him. He wouldn't get a shock at all. Both the controls are grounded."

"Have you noticed those very small holes drilled through the panel?" asked Alleyn. "Should they be there, do you think?"

Arthur peered at the little steel shafts. "By God, he's right, Guy," he said. "That's how it was done."

"Inspector Fox," said Alleyn, "tells me those holes could be used for conducting wires and that a lead could be taken from the—the transformer, is it?—to one of the knobs."

"And the other connected to earth," said Fox. "It's a job for an expert. He could get three hundred volts or so that way."

"That's not good enough," said Arthur quickly; "there wouldn't be enough current to do any damage—only a few hundredths of an amp."

"I'm not an expert," said Alleyn, "but I'm sure you're right. Why were the holes drilled then? Do you imagine someone wanted to play a practical joke on your father?"

"A practical joke? On *him?*" Arthur gave an unpleasant screech of laughter. "Do you hear that, Guy?"

"Shut up," said Guy. "After all, he is dead."

"It seems almost too good to be true, doesn't it?"

"Don't be a bloody fool, Arthur. Pull yourself together. Can't you see what this means? They think he's been murdered."

"Murdered! They're wrong. None of us had the nerve for that, Mr. Inspector. Look at me. My hands are so shaky they told me I'd never be able to paint. That dates from when I was a kid and he shut me up in the cellars for a night. Look at me. Look at Guy. He's not so vulnerable, but he caved in like the rest of us. We were conditioned to surrender. Do you know—"

"Wait a moment," said Alleyn quietly. "Your brother is quite right, you know. You'd better think before you speak. This may be a case of homicide."

"Thank you, sir," said Guy quickly. "That's extraordinarily decent of you. Arthur's a bit above himself. It's a shock."

"The relief, you mean," said Arthur. "Don't be such an ass. I didn't kill him and they'll find it out soon enough. Nobody killed him. There must be some explanation."

"I suggest that you listen to me," said Alleyn. "I'm going to put several questions to both of you. You need not answer them, but it will be more sensible to do so. I understand no one but your father touched this radio. Did any of you ever come into this room while it was in use?"

"Not unless he wanted to vary the program with a little bullying," said Arthur.

Alleyn turned to Guy, who was glaring at his brother.

"I want to know exactly what happened in this house last night. As far as the doctors can tell us, your father died not less than three and not more than eight hours before he was found. We must try to fix the time as accurately as possible."

"I saw him at about a quarter to nine," began Guy slowly. "I was going out to a supper-party at the Savoy and had come downstairs. He was crossing the hall from the drawing-room to his room."

"Did you see him after a quarter to nine, Mr. Arthur?"

"No. I heard him, though. He was working in here with Hislop. Hislop had asked to go away for Christmas. Quite enough. My father discovered some urgent correspondence. Really, Guy, you know, he was pathological. I'm sure Dr. Meadows thinks so."

"When did you hear him?" asked Alleyn.

"Some time after Guy had gone. I was working on a drawing in my room upstairs. It's above his. I heard him bawling at little Hislop. It must have been before ten o'clock, because I went out to a studio party at ten. I heard him bawling as I crossed the hall."

"And when," said Alleyn, "did you both return?"

"I came home at about twenty past twelve," said Guy immediately. "I can fix the time because we had gone on to Chez Carlo, and they had a midnight stunt there. We left immediately afterwards. I came home in a taxi. The radio was on full blast."

"You heard no voices?"

"None. Just the wireless."

"And you, Mr. Arthur?"

"Lord knows when I got in. After one. The house was in darkness. Not a sound."

"You had your own key?"

"Yes," said Guy. "Each of us has one. They're always left on a hook in the lobby. When I came in I noticed Arthur's was gone."

"What about the others? How did you know it was his?"

"Mother hasn't got one and Phips lost hers weeks ago. Anyway, I knew they were staying in and that it must be Arthur who was out."

"Thank you," said Arthur ironically.

"You didn't look in the study when you came in," Alleyn asked him.

"Good Lord, no," said Arthur as if the suggestion was fantastic. "I say," he said suddenly, "I suppose he was sitting here—dead. That's a queer thought." He laughed nervously. "Just sitting here, behind the door in the dark."

"How do you know it was in the dark?"

"What d'you mean? Of course it was. There was no light under the door."

"I see. Now do you two mind joining your mother again? Perhaps your sister will be kind enough to come in here for a moment. Fox, ask her, will you?"

Fox returned to the drawing-room with Guy and Arthur and remained there, blandly unconscious of any embarrassment his presence might cause the Tonkses. Bailey was already there, ostensibly examining the electric points.

Phillipa went to the study at once. Her first remark was characteristic. "Can I be of any help?" asked Phillipa.

"It's extremely nice of you to put it like that," said Alleyn. "I don't want to worry you for long. I'm sure this discovery has been a shock to you."

"Probably," said Phillipa. Alleyn glanced quickly at her. "I mean," she explained, "that I suppose I must be shocked but I can't feel anything much. I just want to get it all over as soon as possible. And then think. Please tell me what has happened."

Alleyn told her they believed her father had been electrocuted and that the circumstances were unusual and puzzling. He said nothing to suggest that the police suspected murder.

"I don't think I'll be much help," said Phillipa, "but go ahead."

"I want to try to discover who was the last person to see your father or speak to him."

"I should think very likely I was," said Phillipa composedly. "I had a row with him before I went to bed."

"What about?"

"I don't see that it matters."

Alleyn considered this. When he spoke again it was with deliberation.

"Look here," he said, "I think there is very little doubt that your father was killed by an electric shock from his wireless set. As far as I know the circumstances are unique. Radios are normally incapable of giving a lethal shock to anyone. We have examined the cabinet and are inclined to think that its internal arrangements were disturbed last night. Very radically disturbed. Your father may have experimented with it. If anything happened to interrupt or upset him, it is possible that in the excitement of the moment he made some dangerous re-adjustment."

"You don't believe that, do you?" asked Phillipa calmly.

"Since you ask me," said Alleyn, "no."

"I see," said Phillipa; "you think he was murdered, but you're not sure." She had gone very white, but she spoke crisply. "Naturally you want to find out about my row."

"About everything that happened last evening," amended Alleyn.

"What happened was this," said Phillipa; "I came into the hall some time after ten. I'd heard Arthur go out and had looked at the clock at five past. I ran into my father's secretary, Richard Hislop. He turned aside, but not before

I saw . . . not quickly enough. I blurted out: 'You're cry-ing.' We looked at each other. I asked him why he stood it. None of the other secretaries could. He said he had to. He's a widower with two children. There have been doc-tor's bills and things. I needn't tell you about his . . . about his damnable servitude to my father nor about the refinements of cruelty he'd had to put up with. I think my father was mad, really mad, I mean. Richard gabbled it all out to me higgledy-piggledy in a sort of horrified whisper. He's been here two years, but I'd never realized until that moment that we . . . that . . ." A faint flush came into her cheeks. "He's such a funny little man. Not at all the sort I've always thought . . . not good-looking or exciting or anything."

She stopped, looking bewildered.

"Yes?" said Alleyn.

"Well, you see—I suddenly realized I was in love with him. He realized it too. He said: 'Of course, it's quite hope-less, you know. Us, I mean. Laughable, almost.' Then I put my arms round his neck and kissed him. It was very odd, but it seemed quite natural. The point is my father came out of this room into the hall and saw us."

"That was bad luck," said Alleyn.

"Yes, it was. My father really seemed delighted. He al-most licked his lips. Richard's efficiency had irritated my father for a long time. It was difficult to find excuses for being beastly to him. Now, of course . . . He ordered Richard to the study and me to my room. He followed me upstairs. Richard tried to come too, but I asked him not to. My father . . . I needn't tell you what he said. He put the worst possible construction on what he'd seen. He was ab-solutely foul, screaming at me like a madman. He was in-sane. Perhaps it was DTs. He drank terribly, you know. I dare say it's silly of me to tell you all this."

"No," said Alleyn.

"I can't feel anything at all. Not even relief. The boys are frankly relieved. I can't feel afraid either." She stared meditatively at Alleyn. "Innocent people needn't feel afraid, need they?"

"It's an axiom of police investigation," said Alleyn and wondered if indeed she was innocent.

"It just *can't* be murder," said Phillipa. "We were all too much afraid to kill him. I believe he'd win even if you murdered him. He'd hit back somehow." She put her hands to her eyes. "I'm all muddled," she said.

"I think you are more upset than you realize. I'll be as quick as I can. Your father made this scene in your room. You say he screamed. Did anyone hear him?"

"Yes. Mummy did. She came in."

"What happened?"

"I said: 'Go away, darling, it's all right.' I didn't want her to be involved. He nearly killed her with the things he did. Sometimes he'd . . . we never knew what happened between them. It was all secret, like a door shutting quietly as you walk along a passage."

"Did she go away?"

"Not at once. He told her he'd found out that Richard and I were lovers. He said . . . it doesn't matter. I don't want to tell you. She was terrified. He was stabbing at her in some way I couldn't understand. Then, quite suddenly, he told her to go to her own room. She went at once and he followed her. He locked me in. That's the last I saw of him, but I heard him go downstairs later."

"Were you locked in all night?"

"No. Richard Hislop's room is next to mine. He came up and spoke through the wall to me. He wanted to unlock the door, but I said better not in case—he—came back. Then, much later, Guy came home. As he passed my door I tapped on it. The key was in the lock and he turned it."

"Did you tell him what had happened?"

"Just that there'd been a row. He only stayed a moment."

"Can you hear the radio from your room?"

She seemed surprised.

"The wireless? Why, yes. Faintly."

"Did you hear it after your father returned to the study?"

"I don't remember."

"Think. While you lay awake all that long time until your brother came home?"

"I'll try. When he came out and found Richard and me, it was not going. They had been working, you see. No, I can't remember hearing it at all unless—wait a moment. Yes. After he had gone back to the study from mother's room I remember there was a loud crash of static. Very loud. Then I think it was quiet for some time. I fancy I heard it again later. Oh, I've remembered something else. After the static my bedside radiator went out. I suppose there was something wrong with the electric supply. That would account for both, wouldn't it? The heater went on again about ten minutes later."

"And did the radio begin again then, do you think?"

"I don't know. I'm very vague about that. It started again sometime before I went to sleep."

"Thank you very much indeed. I won't bother you any longer now."

"All right," said Phillipa calmly, and went away.

Alleyn sent for Chase and questioned him about the rest of the staff and about the discovery of the body. Emily was summoned and dealt with. When she departed, awe-struck but complacent, Alleyn turned to the butler.

"Chase," he said, "had your master any peculiar habits?"

"Yes, sir."

"In regard to his use of the wireless?"

"I beg pardon, sir. I thought you meant generally speaking."

"Well, then, generally speaking."

"If I may say so, sir, he was a mass of them."

"How long have you been with him?"

"Two months, sir, and due to leave at the end of this week."

"Oh. Why are you leaving?"

Chase produced the classic remark of his kind.

"There are some things," he said, "that flesh and blood will not stand, sir. One of them's being spoke to like Mr. Tonks spoke to his staff."

"Ah. His peculiar habits, in fact?"

"It's my opinion, sir, he was mad. Stark, staring."

"With regard to the radio. Did he tinker with it?"

"I can't say I've ever noticed, sir. I believe he knew quite a lot about wireless."

"When he tuned the thing, had he any particular method? Any characteristic attitude or gesture?"

"I don't think so, sir. I never noticed, and yet I've often come into the room when he was at it. I can seem to see him now, sir."

"Yes, yes," said Alleyn swiftly. "That's what we want. A clear mental picture. How was it now? Like this?"

In a moment he was across the room and seated in Septimus's chair. He swung round to the cabinet and raised his right hand to the tuning control.

"Like this?"

"No, sir," said Chase promptly, "that's not him at all. Both hands it should be."

"Ah." Up went Alleyn's left hand to the volume control. "More like this?"

"Yes, sir," said Chase slowly. "But there's something else and I can't recollect what it was. Something he was always doing. It's in the back of my head. You know, sir. Just on the edge of my memory, as you might say."

"I know."

"It's a kind—something—to do with irritation," said Chase slowly.

"Irritation? His?"

"No. It's no good, sir. I can't get it."

"Perhaps later. Now look here, Chase, what happened to all of you last night? All the servants, I mean."

"We were all out, sir. It being Christmas Eve. The mistress sent for me yesterday morning. She said we could take the evening off as soon as I had taken in Mr. Tonks' grog-tray at nine o'clock. So we went," ended Chase simply.

"When?"

"The rest of the staff got away about nine. I left at ten past, sir, and returned about eleven-twenty. The others were back then, and all in bed. I went straight to bed myself, sir."

"You came in by a back door, I suppose?"

"Yes, sir. We've been talking it over. None of us noticed anything unusual."

"Can you hear the wireless in your part of the house?"

"No, sir."

"Well," said Alleyn, looking up from his notes, "that'll do, thank you."

Before Chase reached the door Fox came in.

"Beg pardon, sir," said Fox, "I just want to take a look at the *Radio Times* on the desk."

He bent over the paper, wetted a gigantic thumb, and turned a page.

"That's it, sir," shouted Chase suddenly. "That's what I tried to think of. That's what he was always doing."

"But what?"

"Licking his fingers, sir. It was a habit," said Chase. "That's what he always did when he sat down to the radio.

I heard Mr. Hislop tell the doctor it nearly drove him demented, the way the master couldn't touch a thing without first licking his fingers."

"Quite so," said Alleyn. "In about ten minutes, ask Mr. Hislop if he will be good enough to come in for a moment. That will be all, thank you, Chase."

"Well, sir," remarked Fox when Chase had gone, "if that's the case and what I think's right, it'd certainly make matters worse."

"Good heavens, Fox, what an elaborate remark. What does it mean?"

"If metal knobs were substituted for bakelite ones and fine wires brought through those holes to make contact, then he'd get a bigger bump if he tuned in with *damp* fingers."

"Yes. And he always used both hands. Fox!"

"Sir."

"Approach the Tonkses again. You haven't left them alone, of course?"

"Bailey's in there making out he's interested in the light switches. He's found the main switchboard under the stairs. There's signs of a blown fuse having been fixed recently. In a cupboard underneath there are odd lengths of flex and so on. Same brand as this on the wireless and the heater."

"Ah, yes. Could the cord from the adapter to the radiator be brought into play?"

"By gum," said Fox, "you're right! That's how it was done, Chief. The heavier flex was cut away from the radiator and shoved through. There was a fire, so he wouldn't want the radiator and wouldn't notice."

"It might have been done that way, certainly, but there's little to prove it. Return to the bereaved Tonkses, my Fox, and ask prettily if any of them remember Septimus's peculiarities when tuning his wireless."

Fox met little Mr. Hislop at the door and left him alone with Alleyn. Phillipa had been right, reflected the Inspector, when she said Richard Hislop was not a noticeable man. He was nondescript. Grey eyes, drab hair; rather pale, rather short, rather insignificant; and yet last night there had flashed up between those two the realization of love. Romantic but rum, thought Alleyn.

"Do sit down," he said. "I want you, if you will, to tell me what happened between you and Mr. Tonks last evening."

"What happened?"

"Yes. You all dined at eight, I understand. Then you and Mr. Tonks came in here?"

"Yes."

"What did you do?"

"He dictated several letters."

"Anything unusual take place?"

"Oh, no."

"Why did you quarrel?"

"Quarrel!" The quiet voice jumped a tone. "We did not quarrel, Mr. Alleyn."

"Perhaps that was the wrong word. What upset you?"

"Phillipa has told you?"

"Yes. She was wise to do so. What was the matter, Mr. Hislop?"

"Apart from the . . . what she told you . . . Mr. Tonks was a difficult man to please. I often irritated him. I did so last night."

"In what way?"

"In almost every way. He shouted at me. I was startled and nervous, clumsy with papers, and making mistakes. I wasn't well. I blundered and then . . . I . . . I broke down. I have always irritated him. My very mannerisms—"

"Had he no irritating mannerisms, himself?"

"He! My God!"

"What were they?"

"I can't think of anything in particular. It doesn't matter does it?"

"Anything to do with the wireless, for instance?"

There was a short silence.

"No," said Hislop.

"Was the radio on in here last night, after dinner?"

"For a little while. Not after—after the incident in the hall. At least, I don't think so. I don't remember."

"What did you do after Miss Phillipa and her father had gone upstairs?"

"I followed and listened outside the door for a moment." He had gone very white and had backed away from the desk.

"And then?"

"I heard someone coming. I remembered Dr. Meadows had told me to ring him up if there was one of the scenes. I returned here and rang him up. He told me to go to my room and listen. If things got any worse I was to telephone again. Otherwise I was to stay in my room. It is next to hers."

"And you did this?" He nodded. "Could you hear what Mr. Tonks said to her?"

"A—a good deal of it."

"What did you hear?"

"He insulted her. Mrs. Tonks was there. I was just thinking of ringing Dr. Meadows up again when she and Mr. Tonks came out and went along the passage. I stayed in my room."

"You did not try to speak to Miss Phillipa?"

"We spoke through the wall. She asked me not to ring Dr. Meadows, but to stay in my room. In a little while, perhaps it was as much as twenty minutes—I really don't know—I heard him come back and go downstairs. I again spoke to Phillipa. She implored me not to do anything and said that she herself would speak to Dr. Meadows in the morning. So I waited a little longer and then went to bed."

"And to sleep?"

"My God, no!"

"Did you hear the wireless again?"

"Yes. At least I heard static."

"Are you an expert on wireless?"

"No. I know the ordinary things. Nothing much."

"How did you come to take this job, Mr. Hislop?"

"I answered an advertisement."

"You are sure you don't remember any particular mannerism of Mr. Tonks's in connection with the radio?"

"No."

"Will you please ask Mrs. Tonks if she will be kind enough to speak to me for a moment?"

"Certainly," said Hislop, and went away.

Septimus's wife came in looking like death. Alleyn got her to sit down and asked her about her movements on the preceding evening. She said she was feeling unwell and dined in her room. She went to bed immediately afterwards. She heard Septimus yelling at Phillipa and went to Phillipa's room. Septimus accused Mr. Hislop and her daughter of "terrible things." She got as far as this and then broke down quietly. Alleyn was very gentle with her. After a little while he learned that Septimus had gone to her room with her and had continued to speak of "terrible things."

"What sort of things?" asked Alleyn.

"He was not responsible," said Isabel. "He did not know what he was saying. I think he had been drinking."

She thought he had remained with her for perhaps a quarter of an hour. Possibly longer. He left her abruptly and she heard him go along the passage, past Phillipa's door, and presumably downstairs. She had stayed awake for a long time. The wireless could not be heard from her room. Alleyn showed her the curtain knobs, but she seemed quite unable to take in their significance. He let her go, summoned Fox, and went over the whole case.

"What's your idea on the show?" he asked when he had finished.

"Well, sir," said Fox, in his stolid way, "on the face of it the young gentlemen have got alibis. We'll have to check them up, of course, and I don't see we can go much further until we have done so."

"For the moment," said Alleyn, "let us suppose Masters Guy and Arthur to be safely established behind cast-iron alibis. What then?"

"Then we've got the young lady, the old lady, the secretary, and the servants."

"Let us parade them. But first let us go over the wireless game. You'll have to watch me here. I gather that the only way in which the radio could be fixed to give Mr. Tonks his quietus is like this: Control knobs removed. Holes bored in front panel with fine drill. Metal knobs substituted and packed with blotting paper to insulate them from metal shafts and make them stay put. Heavier flex from adapter to radiator cut and the ends of the wires pushed through the drilled holes to make contact with the new knobs. Thus we have a positive and negative pole. Mr. Tonks bridges the gap, gets a mighty wallop as the current passes through him to the earth. The switchboard fuse is blown almost immediately. All this is rigged by murderer while Sep was upstairs bullying wife and daughter. Sep revisited study some time after ten-twenty. Whole thing was made ready between ten, when Arthur went out, and the time Sep returned—say, about ten-forty-five. The murderer reappeared, connected radiator with flex, removed wires, changed back knobs, and left the thing tuned in. Now I take it that the burst of static described by Phillipa and

Hislop would be caused by the short-circuit that killed our Septimus?"

"That's right."

"It also affected all the heaters in the house. *Vide* Miss Tonks's radiator."

"Yes. He put all that right again. It would be a simple enough matter for anyone who knew how. He'd just have to fix the fuse on the main switchboard. How long do you say it would take to—what's the horrible word?—to recondition the whole show?"

"M'm," said Fox deeply. "At a guess, sir, fifteen minutes. He'd have to be nippy."

"Yes," agreed Alleyn. "He or she."

"I don't see a female making a success of it," grunted Fox. "Look here, Chief, you know what I'm thinking. Why did Mr. Hislop lie about deceased's habit of licking his thumbs? You say Hislop told you he remembered nothing and Chase says he overheard him saying the trick nearly drove him dippy."

"Exactly," said Alleyn. He was silent for so long that Fox felt moved to utter a discreet cough.

"Eh?" said Alleyn. "Yes, Fox, yes. It'll have to be done." He consulted the telephone directory and dialed a number.

"May I speak to Dr. Meadows? Oh, it's you, is it? Do you remember Mr. Hislop telling you that Septimus Tonks's trick of wetting his fingers nearly drove Hislop demented. Are you there? You don't? Sure? All right. All right. Hislop rang you up at ten-twenty, you said? And you telephoned him? At eleven. Sure of the times? I see. I'd be glad if you'd come round. Can you? Well, do if you can."

He hung up the receiver.

"Get Chase again, will you, Fox?"

Chase, recalled, was most insistent that Mr. Hislop had spoken about it to Dr. Meadows.

"It was when Mr. Hislop had flu, sir. I went up with the

doctor. Mr. Hislop had a high temperature and was talking very excited. He kept on and on, saying the master had guessed his ways had driven him crazy and that the master kept on purposely to aggravate. He said if it went on much longer he'd . . . he didn't know what he was talking about, sir, really."

"What did he say he'd do?"

"Well, sir, he said he'd—he'd do something desperate to the master. But it was only his rambling, sir. I daresay he wouldn't remember anything about it."

"No," said Alleyn, "I daresay he wouldn't." When Chase had gone he said to Fox: "Go and find out about those boys and their alibis. See if they can put you on to a quick means of checking up. Get Master Guy to corroborate Miss Phillipa's statement that she was locked in her room."

Fox had been gone for some time and Alleyn was still busy with his notes when the study door burst open and in came Dr. Meadows.

"Look here, my giddy sleuth-hound," he shouted, "what's all this about Hislop? Who says he disliked Sep's abominable habits?"

"Chase does. And don't bawl at me like that. I'm worried."

"So am I, blast you. What are you driving at? You can't imagine that . . . that poor little broken-down hack is capable of electrocuting anybody, let alone Sep?"

"I have no imagination," said Alleyn wearily.

"I wish to God I hadn't called you in. If the wireless killed Sep, it was because he'd monkeyed with it."

"And put it right after it had killed him?"

Dr. Meadows stared at Alleyn in silence.

"Now," said Alleyn, "you've got to give me a straight answer, Meadows. Did Hislop, while he was semi-delirious, say that this habit of Tonks's made him feel like murdering him?"

"I'd forgotten Chase was there," said Dr. Meadows.

"Yes, you'd forgotten that."

"But even if he did talk wildly, Alleyn, what of it? Damn it, you can't arrest a man on the strength of a remark made in delirium."

"I don't propose to do so. Another motive has come to light."

"You mean—Phips—last night?"

"Did he tell you about that?"

"She whispered something to me this morning. I'm very fond of Phips. My God, are you sure of your grounds?"

"Yes," said Alleyn. "I'm sorry. I think you'd better go, Meadows."

"Are you going to arrest him?"

"I have to do my job."

There was a long silence.

"Yes," said Dr. Meadows at last. "You have to do your job. Goodbye, Alleyn."

Fox returned to say that Guy and Arthur had never left their parties. He had got hold of two of their friends. Guy and Mrs. Tonks confirmed the story of the locked door.

"It's a process of elimination," said Fox. "It must be the secretary. He fixed the radio while deceased was upstairs. He must have dodged back to whisper through the door to Miss Tonks. I suppose he waited somewhere down here until he heard deceased blow himself to blazes and then put everything straight again, leaving the radio turned on."

Alleyn was silent.

"What do we do now, sir?" asked Fox.

"I want to see the hook inside the front-door where they hang their keys."

Fox, looking dazed, followed his superior to the little entrance hall.

"Yes, there they are," said Alleyn. He pointed to a hook with two latchkeys hanging from it. "You could scarcely miss them. Come on, Fox."

Back in the study they found Hislop with Bailey in attendance.

Hislop looked from one Yard man to another.

"I want to know if it's murder."

"We think so," said Alleyn.

"I want you to realize that Phillipa—Miss Tonks—was locked in her room all last night."

"Until her brother came home and unlocked the door," said Alleyn.

"That was too late. He was dead by then."

"How do you know when he died?"

"It must have been when there was that crash of static."

"Mr. Hislop," said Alleyn, "why would you not tell me how much that trick of licking his fingers exasperated you?"

"But—how do you know! I never told anyone."

"You told Dr. Meadows when you were ill."

"I don't remember." He stopped short. His lips trembled. Then, suddenly he began to speak.

"Very well. It's true. For two years he's tortured me. You see, he knew something about me. Two years ago when my wife was dying, I took money from the cash-box in that desk. I paid it back and thought he hadn't noticed. He knew all the time. From then on he had me where he wanted me. He used to sit there like a spider. I'd hand him a paper. He'd wet his thumbs with a clicking noise and a sort of complacent grimace. Click, click. Then he'd thumb the papers. He knew it drove me crazy. He'd look at me and then . . . click, click. And then he'd say something about the cash. He never quite accused me, just hinted. And I was impotent. You think I'm insane. I'm not. I could have murdered him. Often and often I've thought how I'd do it. Now you think I've done it. I haven't. There's the joke of it. I hadn't the pluck. And last night when Phillipa showed me she cared, it was like Heaven—unbelievable. For the first time since I've been here I *didn't* feel like killing him. And last night someone else *did!*"

He stood there trembling and vehement. Fox and Bailey, who had watched him with bewildered concern, turned to Alleyn. He was about to speak when Chase came in. "A note for you, sir," he said to Alleyn. "It came by hand."

Alleyn opened it and glanced at the first few words. He looked up.

"You may go, Mr. Hislop. Now I've got what I expected —what I fished for."

When Hislop had gone they read the letter.

Dear Alleyn,

   Don't arrest Hislop. I did it. Let him go at once if you've arrested him and don't tell Phips you ever suspected him. I was in love with Isabel before she met Sep. I've tried to get her to divorce him, but she wouldn't because of the kids. Damned nonsense, but there's no time to discuss it now. I've got to be quick. He suspected us. He reduced her to a nervous wreck. I was afraid she'd go under altogether. I thought it all out. Some weeks ago I took Phips's key from the hook inside the front door. I had the tools and the flex and wire all ready. I knew where the main switchboard was and the cupboard. I meant to wait until they all went away at the New Year, but last night when Hislop rang me I made up my mind to act at once. He said the boys and servants were out and Phips locked in her room. I told him to stay in his room and to ring me up in half an hour if things hadn't quieted down. He didn't ring up. I did. No answer, so I knew Sep wasn't in his study.

   I came round, let myself in, and listened. All quiet upstairs, but the lamp still on in the study, so I knew he would come down again. He'd said he wanted to get the midnight broadcast from somewhere.

   I locked myself in and got to work. When Sep was away last year, Arthur did one of his modern monstrosities of paintings in the study. He talked about the knobs making good pattern. I noticed then that they were very like the ones on the radio and later on I tried one and saw that it would fit if I packed it up a bit. Well, I did the job just as you worked it out, and it only took twelve minutes. Then I went into the drawing-room and waited.

   He came down from Isabel's room and evidently went straight to the radio. I hadn't thought it would make such a row, and half ex-

pected someone would come down. No one came. I went back, switched off the wireless, mended the fuse in the main switchboard, using my torch. Then I put everything right in the study.

There was no particular hurry. No one would come in while he was there and I got the radio going as soon as possible to suggest he was at it. I knew I'd be called in when they found him. My idea was to tell them he had died of a stroke. I'd been warning Isabel it might happen at any time. As soon as I saw the burned hand I knew that cat wouldn't jump. I'd have tried to get away with it if Chase hadn't gone round bleating about electrocution and burned fingers. Hislop saw the hand. I daren't do anything but report the case to the police, but I thought you'd never twig the knobs. One up to you.

I might have bluffed through if you hadn't suspected Hislop. Can't let you hang the blighter. I'm enclosing a note to Isabel, who won't forgive me, and an official one for you to use. You'll find me in my bedroom upstairs. I'm using cyanide. It's quick.

I'm sorry, Alleyn. I think you knew, didn't you? I've bungled the whole game, but if you will be a super-sleuth . . . Goodbye.

Henry Meadows

I Can Find My Way Out

At half-past six on the night in question, Anthony Gill, unable to eat, keep still, think, speak or act coherently, walked from his rooms to the Jupiter Theatre. He knew that there would be nobody backstage, that there was nothing for him to do in the theatre, that he ought to stay quietly in his rooms and presently dress, dine and arrive at, say, a quarter to eight. But it was as if something shoved him into his clothes, thrust him into the street and compelled him to hurry through the West End to the Jupiter. His mind was overlaid with a thin film of inertia. Odd lines from the play occurred to him, but without any particular significance. He found himself busily reiterating a completely irrelevant sentence: "She has a way of laughing that would make a man's heart turn over."

Piccadilly, Shaftesbury Avenue. "Here I go," he thought, turning into Hawke Street, "towards my play. It's one hour and twenty-nine minutes away. A step a second. It's rushing towards me. Tony's first play. Poor young Tony Gill. Never mind. Try again."

The Jupiter. Neon lights: I CAN FIND MY WAY OUT—*by Anthony Gill.* And in the entrance the bills and photographs. *Coralie Bourne with H. J. Bannington, Barry George and Canning Cumberland.*

Canning Cumberland. The film across his mind split and there was the Thing itself and he would have to think about it. How bad would Canning Cumberland be if he came down drunk? Brilliantly bad, they said. He would bring out all the tricks. Clever actor stuff, scoring off everybody, making a fool of the dramatic balance. "In Mr. Canning Cumberland's hands indifferent dialogue and unconvincing situations seemed almost real." What can you do with a drunken actor?

He stood in the entrance feeling his heart pound and his inside deflate and sicken.

Because, of course, it was a bad play. He was at this moment and for the first time really convinced of it. It was terrible. Only one virtue in it and that was not his doing. It had been suggested to him by Coralie Bourne: "I don't think the play you have sent me will do as it is but it has occurred to me—" It was a brilliant idea. He had rewritten the play round it and almost immediately and quite innocently he had begun to think of it as his own although he had said shyly to Coralie Bourne: "You should appear as joint author." She had quickly, over-emphatically, refused. "It was nothing at all," she said. "If you're to become a dramatist you will learn to get ideas from everywhere. A single situation is nothing. Think of Shakespeare," she added lightly. "Entire plots! Don't be silly." She had said later, and still with the same hurried, nervous air: "Don't go talking to everyone about it. They will think there is more, instead of less, than meets the eye in my small suggestion. Please promise." He promised, thinking he'd made an error in taste when he suggested that Coralie Bourne, so famous an actress, should appear as joint author with an unknown youth. And how right she was, he thought, because, of course, it's going to be a ghastly flop. She'll be sorry she consented to play in it.

Standing in front of the theatre he contemplated nightmare possibilities. What did audiences do when a first play flopped? Did they clap a little, enough to let the curtain rise and quickly fall again on a discomforted group of players? How scanty must the applause be for them to let him off his own appearance? And they were to go on to the Chelsea Arts Ball. A hideous prospect. Thinking he would give anything in the world if he could stop his play, he turned into the foyer. There were lights in the offices and he paused, irresolute, before a board of photographs. Among them, much smaller than the leading players, was Dendra Gay with the eyes looking straight into his. *She had a way of laughing that would make a man's heart turn over.* "Well," he thought, "so I'm in love with her." He turned away from the photograph. A man came out of the office. "Mr. Gill? Telegrams for you."

Anthony took them and as he went out he heard the man call after him: "Very good luck for tonight, sir."

There were queues of people waiting in the side street for the early doors.

At six-thirty Coralie Bourne dialed Canning Cumberland's number and waited.

She heard his voice. "It's me," she said.

"O God! darling, I've been thinking about you." He spoke rapidly, too loudly. "Coral, I've been thinking about Ben. You oughtn't to have given that situation to the boy."

"We've been over it a dozen times, Cann. Why not give it to Tony? Ben will never know." She waited and then said nervously, "Ben's gone, Cann. We'll never see him again."

"I've got a Thing about it. After all, he's your husband."

"No, Cann, no."

"Suppose he turns up. It'd be like him to turn up."

"He won't turn up."

She heard him laugh. "I'm sick of all this," she thought suddenly. "I've had it once too often. I can't stand any more. . . . Cann," she said into the telephone. But he had hung up.

At twenty to seven, Barry George looked at himself in his bathroom mirror. "I've got a better appearance," he thought, "than Cann Cumberland. My head's a good shape, my eyes are bigger and my jaw line's cleaner. I never let a show down. I don't drink. I'm a better actor." He turned his head a little, slewing his eyes to watch the effect. "In the big scene," he thought, "I'm the star. He's the feed. That's the way it's been produced and that's what the author wants. I ought to get the notices."

Past notices came up in his memory. He saw the print, the size of the paragraphs; a long paragraph about Canning Cumberland, a line tacked on the end of it. "Is it unkind to add that Mr. Barry George trotted in the wake of Mr. Cumberland's virtuosity with an air of breathless dependability?" And again: "It is a little hard on Mr. Barry George that he should be obliged to act as foil to this brilliant performance." Worst of all: "Mr. Barry George succeeded in looking tolerably unlike a stooge, an achievement that evidently exhausted his resources."

"Monstrous!" he said loudly to his own image, watching the fine glow of indignation in the eyes. Alcohol, he told himself, did two things to Cann Cumberland. He raised his finger. Nice, expressive hand. An actor's hand. Alcohol destroyed Cumberland's artistic integrity. It also invested him with devilish cunning. Drunk, he would burst the seams of a play, destroy its balance, ruin its form and himself emerge blazing with a showmanship that the audience mistook for genius. "While I," he said aloud, "merely pay my author the compliment of faithful interpretation. Psha!"

He returned to his bedroom, completed his dressing and pulled his hat to the right angle. Once more he thrust his face close to the mirror and looked searchingly at its image. "By God!" he told himself, "he's done it once too often, old boy. Tonight we'll even the score, won't we? By God, we will."

Partly satisfied, and partly ashamed, for the scene, after all, had smacked a little of ham, he took his stick in one hand and a case holding his costume for the Arts Ball in the other, and went down to the theatre.

At ten minutes to seven, H. J. Bannington passed through the gallery queue on his way to the stage door alley, raising his hat and saying: "Thanks so much," to the gratified ladies who let him through. He heard them murmur his name. He walked briskly along the alley, greeted the stage-doorkeeper, passed under a dingy lamp, through an entry and so to the stage. Only working lights were up. The walls of an interior set rose dimly into shadow. Bob Reynolds, the stage-manager, came out through the prompt-entrance. "Hello, old boy," he said, "I've changed the dressing-rooms. You're third on the right: they've moved your things in. Suit you?"

"Better, at least, than a black-hole the size of a W.C. but without its appointments," H.J. said acidly. "I suppose the great Mr. Cumberland still has the star-room?"

"Well, yes, old boy."

"And who pray, is next to him? In the room with the other gas fire?"

"We've put Barry George there, old boy. You know what he's like."

"Only too well, old boy, and the public, I fear, is beginning to find out." H.J. turned into the dressing-room passage. The stage-manager returned to the set where he encountered his assistant. "What's biting *him?*" asked the assistant. "He wanted a dressing-room with a fire." "Only natural," said the A.S.M. nastily. "He started life reading gas meters."

On the right and left of the passage, nearest the stage

end, were two doors, each with its star in tarnished paint. The door on the left was open. H.J. looked in and was greeted with the smell of greasepaint, powder, wet-white, and flowers. A gas fire droned comfortably. Coralie Bourne's dresser was spreading out towels. "Good evening, Katie, my jewel," said H.J. "La Belle not down yet?" "We're on our way," she said.

H.J. hummed stylishly: *"Bella filia del amore,"* and returned to the passage. The star-room on the right was closed but he could hear Cumberland's dresser moving about inside. He went on to the next door, paused, read the card, "Mr. Barry George," warbled a high derisive note, turned in at the third door and switched on the light.

Definitely not a second lead's room. No fire. A wash-basin, however, and opposite mirrors. A stack of telegrams had been placed on the dressing-table. Still singing he reached for them, disclosing a number of bills that had been tactfully laid underneath and a letter, addressed in a flamboyant script.

His voice might have been mechanically produced and arbitrarily switched off, so abruptly did his song end in the middle of a roulade. He let the telegrams fall on the table, took up the letter and tore it open. His face, wretchedly pale, was reflected and endlessly re-reflected in the mirrors.

At nine o'clock the telephone rang. Roderick Alleyn answered it. "This is Sloane 84405. No, you're on the wrong number. *No.*" He hung up and returned to his wife and guest. "That's the fifth time in two hours."

"Do let's ask for a new number."

"We might get next door to something worse."

The telephone rang again. "This is not 84406," Alleyn warned it. "No, I cannot take three large trunks to Victoria Station. No, I am not the Instant All Night Delivery. No."

"They're 84406," Mrs. Alleyn explained to Lord Michael Lamprey. "I suppose it's just faulty dialing, but you can't imagine how angry everyone gets. Why do you want to be a policeman?"

"It's a dull hard job, you know—" Alleyn began.

"Oh," Lord Mike said, stretching his legs and looking critically at his shoes, "I don't for a moment imagine I'll leap immediately into false whiskers and plainclothes. No, no. But I'm revoltingly healthy, sir. Strong as a horse. And I don't think I'm as stupid as you might feel inclined to imagine—"

The telephone rang.

"I say, do let me answer it," Mike suggested and did so.

"Hullo?" he said winningly. He listened, smiling at his hostess. "I'm afraid—" he began. "Here, wait a bit—Yes, but—" His expression became blank and complacent. "May I," he said presently, "repeat your order, sir? Can't be too sure, can we? Call at 11 Harrow Gardens, Sloane Square, for one suitcase to be delivered immediately at the Jupiter Theatre to Mr. Anthony Gill. Very good, sir. Thank you, sir. Collect. Quite."

He replaced the receiver and beamed at the Alleyns.

"What the devil have you been up to?" Alleyn said.

"He just simply wouldn't listen to reason. I tried to tell him."

"But it may be urgent," Mrs. Alleyn ejaculated.

"It couldn't be more urgent, really. It's a suitcase for Tony Gill at the Jupiter."

"Well, then—"

"I was at Eton with the chap," said Mike reminiscently. "He's four years older than I am so of course he was madly important while I was less than the dust. This'll larn him."

"I think you'd better put that order through at once," said Alleyn firmly.

"I rather thought of executing it myself, do you know, sir. It'd be a frightfully neat way of gate-crashing the show, wouldn't it? I did try to get a ticket but the house was sold out."

"If you're going to deliver this case you'd better get a bend on."

"It's clearly an occasion for dressing up though, isn't it? I say," said Mike modestly, "would you think it most frightful cheek if I—well I'd promise to come back and return everything. I mean—"

"Are you suggesting that my clothes look more like a vanman's than yours?"

"I thought you'd have things—"

"For Heaven's sake, Rory," said Mrs. Alleyn, "dress him up and let him go. The great thing is to get that wretched man's suitcase to him."

"I know," said Mike earnestly. "It's most frightfully sweet of you. That's how I feel about it."

Alleyn took him away and shoved him into an old and begrimed raincoat, a cloth cap and a muffler. "You wouldn't deceive a village idiot in a total eclipse," he said, "but out you go."

He watched Mike drive away and returned to his wife.

"What'll happen?" she asked.

"Knowing Mike, I should say he will end up in the front stalls and go on to supper with the leading lady. She, by the way, is Coralie Bourne. Very lovely and twenty years his senior so he'll probably fall in love with her." Alleyn reached for his tobacco jar and paused. "I wonder what's happened to her husband," he said.

"Who was he?"

"An extraordinary chap. Benjamin Vlasnoff. Violent temper. Looked like a bandit. Wrote two very good plays and got run in three times for common assault. She tried to divorce him but it didn't go through. I think he afterwards lit off to Russia." Alleyn yawned. "I believe she had a hell of a time with him," he said.

"All Night Delivery," said Mike in a hoarse voice, touching his cap. "Suitcase. One." "Here you are," said the woman who had answered the door. "Carry it carefully, now, it's not locked and the catch springs out."

"Fanks," said Mike. "Much obliged. Chilly, ain't it?"

He took the suitcase out to the car.

It was a fresh spring night. Sloane Square was threaded with mist and all the lamps had halos round them. It was the kind of night when individual sounds separate themselves from the conglomerate voice of London; hollow sirens spoke imperatively down on the river and a bugle rang out over in Chelsea Barracks; a night, Mike thought, for adventure.

He opened the rear door of the car and heaved the case in. The catch flew open, the lid dropped back and the contents fell out. "Damn!" said Mike and switched on the inside light.

Lying on the floor of the car was a false beard.

It was flaming red and bushy and was mounted on a chinpiece. With it was incorporated a stiffened mustache. There were wire hooks to attach the whole thing behind the ears. Mike laid it carefully on the seat. Next he picked up a wide black hat, then a vast overcoat with a fur collar, finally a pair of black gloves.

Mike whistled meditatively and thrust his hands into the pockets of Alleyn's mackintosh. His right-hand fingers closed on a card. He pulled it out. "Chief Detective-Inspector Alleyn," he read, "C.I.D. New Scotland Yard."

"Honestly," thought Mike exultantly, "this is a gift."

Ten minutes later a car pulled into the curb at the nearest parking place to the Jupiter Theatre. From it emerged a figure carrying a suitcase. It strode rapidly along Hawke Street and turned into the stage-door alley. As it passed under the dirty lamp it paused, and thus murkily lit, resembled an illustration from some Edwardian spy-story. The face was completely shadowed, a black cavern from which there projected a square of scarlet beard, which was the only note of color.

The doorkeeper who was taking the air with a member of stage-staff, moved forward, peering at the stranger.

"Was you wanting something?"

"I'm taking this case in for Mr. Gill."

"He's in front. You can leave it with me."

"I'm so sorry," said the voice behind the beard, "but I promised I'd leave it backstage myself."

"So you will be leaving it. Sorry, sir, but no one's admitted be'ind without a card."

"A card? Very well. Here is a card."

He held it out in his black-gloved hand. The stage-doorkeeper, unwillingly removing his gaze from the beard, took the card and examined it under the light. "Coo!" he said, "what's up, governor?"

"No matter. Say nothing of this."

The figure waved its hand and passed through the door.

" 'Ere!" said the doorkeeper excitedly to the stage-hand, "take a slant at this. That's a plainclothes flattie, that was."

"*Plain* clothes!" said the stage-hand. "Them!"

" 'E's disguised," said the doorkeeper. "That's what it is. 'E's disguised 'isself."

" 'E's bloody well lorst 'isself be'ind them whiskers if you arst me."

Out on the stage someone was saying in a pitched and beautifully articulate voice: "*I've always loathed the view from these windows. However if that's the sort of thing you admire. Turn off the lights, damn you. Look at it.*"

"Watch it, now, watch it," whispered a voice so close to Mike that he jumped. "O.K.," said a second voice somewhere above his head. The lights on the set turned blue. "Kill that working light." "Working light gone."

Curtains in the set were wrenched aside and a window flung open. An actor appeared, leaning out quite close to Mike, seeming to look into his face and saying very distinctly: "God: it's frightful!" Mike backed away towards a passage, lit only from an open door. A great volume of sound broke out beyond the stage. "House lights," said the sharp voice. Mike turned into the passage. As he did so, someone came through the door. He found himself face to face with Coralie Bourne, beautifully dressed and heavily painted.

For a moment she stood quite still; then she made a curious gesture with her right hand, gave a small breathy sound and fell forward at his feet.

Anthony was tearing his program into long strips and dropping them on the floor of the O.P. box. On his right hand, above and below, was the audience; sometimes laughing, sometimes still, sometimes as one corporate being, raising its hands and striking them together. As now; when down on the stage, Canning Cumberland, using a strange voice, and inspired by some inward devil, flung back the window and said: "God: it's frightful!"

"Wrong! Wrong!" Anthony cried inwardly, hating Cumberland, hating Barry George because he let one speech of three words over-ride him, hating the audience because they liked it. The curtain descended with a long sigh on the second act and a sound like heavy rain filled the theatre, swelled prodigiously and continued after the house lights welled up.

"They seem," said a voice behind him, "to be liking your play."

It was Gosset, who owned the Jupiter and had backed the show. Anthony turned on him stammering: "He's destroying it. It should be the other man's scene. He's stealing."

"My boy," said Gosset, "he's an actor."

"He's drunk. It's intolerable."

He felt Gosset's hand on his shoulder.

"People are watching us. You're on show. This is a big thing for you; a first play, and going enormously. Come and have a drink, old boy. I want to introduce you—"

Anthony got up and Gosset, with his arm across his shoulders, flashing smiles, patting him, led him to the back of the box.

"I'm sorry," Anthony said. "I can't. Please let me off. I'm going backstage."

"Much better not, old son." The hand tightened on his shoulder. "Listen, old son—" But Anthony had freed himself and slipped through the pass-door from the box to the stage.

At the foot of the breakneck stairs Dendra Gay stood waiting. "I thought you'd come," she said.

Anthony said: "He's drunk. He's murdering the play."

"It's only one scene, Tony. He finishes early in the next act. It's going colossally."

"But don't you understand—"

"I do. You *know* I do. But you're a success, Tony darling! You can hear it and smell it and feel it in your bones."

"Dendra—" he said uncertainly.

Someone came up and shook his hand and went on shaking it. Flats were being laced together with a slap of rope on canvas. A chandelier ascended into darkness. "Lights," said the stage-manager, and the set was flooded with them. A distant voice began chanting. "Last act, please. Last act."

"Miss Bourne all right?" the stage-manager suddenly demanded.

"She'll be all right. She's not on for ten minutes," said a woman's voice.

"What's the matter with Miss Bourne?" Anthony asked.

"Tony, I must go and so must you. Tony, it's going to be grand. *Please* think so. *Please.*"

"Dendra—" Tony began, but she had gone.

Beyond the curtain, horns and flutes announced the last act.

"Clear please."

The stage hands came off.

"House lights."

"House lights gone."

"Stand by."

And while Anthony still hesitated in the O.P. corner, the curtain rose. Canning Cumberland and H. J. Bannington opened the last act.

As Mike knelt by Coralie Bourne he heard someone enter the passage behind him. He turned and saw, silhouetted against the lighted stage, the actor who had looked at him through a window in the set. The silhouette seemed to repeat the gesture Coralie Bourne had used, and to flatten itself against the wall.

A woman in an apron came out of the open door.

"I say—here!" Mike said.

Three things happened almost simultaneously. The woman cried out and knelt beside him. The man disappeared through a door on the right.

The woman, holding Coralie Bourne in her arms, said violently: "Why have you come back?" Then the passage lights came on. Mike said: "Look here, I'm most frightfully sorry," and took off the broad black hat. The dresser gaped at him, Coralie Bourne made a crescendo sound in her throat and opened her eyes. "Katie?" she said.

"It's all right, my lamb. It's not him, dear. You're all right." The dresser jerked her head at Mike: "Get out of it," she said.

"Yes, of course, I'm most frightfully—" He backed out

of the passage, colliding with a youth who said: "Five minutes, please." The dresser called out: "Tell them she's not well. Tell them to hold the curtain."

"No," said Coralie Bourne strongly. "I'm all right, Katie. Don't say anything. Katie, what was it?"

They disappeared into the room on the left.

Mike stood in the shadow of a stack of scenic flats by the entry into the passage. There was great activity on the stage. He caught a glimpse of Anthony Gill on the far side talking to a girl. The call-boy was speaking to the stage-manager who now shouted into space: "Miss Bourne all right?" The dresser came into the passage and called: "She'll be all right. She's not on for ten minutes." The youth began chanting: "Last act, please." The stage-manager gave a series of orders. A man with an eyeglass and a florid beard came from further down the passage and stood outside the set, bracing his figure and giving little tweaks to his clothes. There was a sound of horns and flutes. Canning Cumberland emerged from the room on the right and on his way to the stage, passed close to Mike, leaving a strong smell of alcohol behind him. The curtain rose.

Behind his shelter, Mike stealthily removed his beard and stuffed it into the pocket of his overcoat.

A group of stage-hands stood nearby. One of them said in a hoarse whisper: "'E's squiffy." "Garn, 'e's going good." "So 'e may be going good. And for why? *Becos* 'e's squiffy."

Ten minutes passed. Mike thought: "This affair has definitely not gone according to plan." He listened. Some kind of tension seemed to be building up on the stage. Canning Cumberland's voice rose on a loud but blurred note. A door in the set opened. "Don't bother to come," Cumberland said. "Goodbye. I can find my way out." The door slammed. Cumberland was standing near Mike. Then, very close, there was a loud explosion. The scenic flats vibrated.

Mike's flesh leapt on his bones and Cumberland went into his dressing-rooms. Mike heard the key turn in the door. The smell of alcohol mingled with the smell of gunpowder. A stage-hand moved to a trestle table and laid a pistol on it. The actor with the eyeglass made an exit. He spoke for a moment to the stage-manager, passed Mike and disappeared in the passage.

Smells. There were all sorts of smells. Subconsciously, still listening to the play, he began to sort them out. Glue. Canvas. Greasepaint. The call-boy tapped on the doors. "Mr. George, please." "Miss Bourne, please." They came out, Coralie Bourne with her dresser. Mike heard her turn a door handle and say something. An indistinguishable voice answered her. Then she and her dresser passed him. The others spoke to her and she nodded and then seemed to withdraw into herself, waiting with her head bent, ready to make her entrance. Presently she drew back, walked swiftly to the door in the set, flung it open and swept on, followed a minute later by Barry George.

Smells. Dust, stale paint, cloth. Gas. Increasingly, the smell of gas.

The group of stage-hands moved away behind the set to the side of the stage. Mike edged out of cover. He could see the prompt-corner. The stage-manager stood there with folded arms, watching the action. Behind him were grouped the players who were not on. Two dressers stood apart, watching. The light from the set caught their faces. Coralie Bourne's voice sent phrases flying like birds into the auditorium.

Mike began peering at the floor. Had he kicked some gas fitting adrift? The call-boy passed him, stared at him over his shoulder and went down the passage, tapping. "Five minutes to the curtain, please. Five minutes." The actor with the elderly make-up followed the call-boy out. "God, what a stink of gas," he whispered. "Chronic, ain't it?" said the call-boy. They stared at Mike and then crossed to the waiting group. The man said something to the stage-manager who tipped his head up, sniffing. He made an impatient gesture and turned back to the prompt-box, reaching over the prompter's head. A bell rang somewhere up in the flies and Mike saw a stage-hand climb to the curtain platform.

The little group near the prompt corner was agitated. They looked back towards the passage entrance. The call-boy nodded and came running back. He knocked on the first door on the right. *"Mr. Cumberland! Mr. Cumberland!* You're on for the call." He rattled the door handle. *"Mr. Cumberland! You're on."*

Mike ran into the passage. The call-boy coughed retchingly and jerked his hand at the door. "Gas!"

"Break it in."

"I'll get Mr. Reynolds."

He was gone. It was a narrow passage. From halfway across the opposite room Mike took a run, head down, shoulder forward, at the door. It gave a little and a sickening increase in the smell caught him in the lungs. A vast storm of noise had broken out and as he took another run he thought: "It's hailing outside."

"Just a minute if *you* please, sir."

It was a stage-hand. He'd got a hammer and screwdriver. He wedged the point of the screwdriver between the lock and the doorpost, drove it home and wrenched. The screws squeaked, the wood splintered and gas poured into the passage. "No winders," coughed the stage-hand.

Mike wound Alleyn's scarf over his mouth and nose. Half-forgotten instructions from anti-gas drill occurred to him. The room looked queer but he could see the man slumped down in the chair quite clearly. He stooped low and ran in.

He was knocking against things as he backed out, lugging the dead weight. His arms tingled. A high insistent voice hummed in his brain. He floated a short distance and came to earth on a concrete floor among several pairs of legs. A long way off, someone said loudly: "I can only thank you for being so kind to what I know, too well, is a very imperfect play." Then the sound of hail began again. There was a heavenly stream of clear air flowing into his mouth and nostrils. "I could eat it," he thought and sat up.

The telephone rang. "Suppose," Mrs. Alleyn suggested, "that this time you ignore it."

"It might be the Yard," Alleyn said, and answered it.

"Is that Chief Detective-Inspector Alleyn's flat? I'm speaking from the Jupiter Theatre. I've rung up to say that the Chief Inspector is here and that he's had a slight mishap. He's all right, but I think it might be as well for someone to drive him home. No need to worry."

"What sort of mishap?" Alleyn asked.

"Er—well—er, he's been a bit gassed."

"*Gassed!* All right. Thanks, I'll come."

"*What* a bore for you darling," said Mrs. Alleyn. "What sort of case is it? Suicide?"

"Masquerading within the meaning of the act, by the sound of it. Mike's in trouble."

"What trouble, for Heaven's sake?"

"Got himself gassed. He's all right. Good night darling. Don't wait up."

When he reached the theatre, the front of the house was in darkness. He made his way down the side alley to the stage-door where he was held up.

"Yard," he said, and produced his official card.

" 'Ere," said the stage-doorkeeper, " 'ow many more of you?"

"The man inside was working for me," said Alleyn and walked in. The doorkeeper followed, protesting.

To the right of the entrance was a large scenic dock from which the double doors had been rolled back. Here Mike was sitting in an armchair, very white about the lips. Three men and two women, all with painted faces, stood near him and behind them a group of stage-hands with Reynolds, the stage-manager, and, apart from these, three men in evening dress. The men looked woodenly shocked. The women had been weeping.

"I'm most frightfully sorry, sir," Mike said. "I've tried to explain. This," he added generally, "is Inspector Alleyn."

"I can't understand all this," said the oldest of the men in evening dress irritably. He turned on the doorkeeper. "You said—"

"I seen 'is card—"

"I know," said Mike, "but you see—"

"This is Lord Michael Lamprey," Alleyn said. "A recruit to the Police Department. What's happened here?"

"Doctor Rankin, would you—?"

The second of the men in evening dress came forward. "All right, Gosset. It's a bad business, Inspector. I've just been saying the police would have to be informed. If you'll come with me—"

Alleyn followed him through a door onto the stage proper. It was dimly lit. A trestle table had been set up in the centre and on it, covered with a sheet, was an unmistakable shape. The smell of gas, strong everywhere, hung heavily about the table.

"Who is it?"

"Canning Cumberland. He'd locked the door of his dressing-room. There's a gas fire. Your young friend dragged him out, very pluckily, but it was no go. I was in front. Gosset, the manager, had asked me to supper. It's a perfectly clear case of suicide as you'll see."

"I'd better look at the room. Anybody been in?"

"God, no. It was a job to clear it. They turned the gas off

at the main. There's no window. They had to open the double doors at the back of the stage and a small outside door at the end of the passage. It may be possible to get in now."

He led the way to the dressing-room passage. "Pretty thick, still," he said. "It's the first room on the right. They burst the lock. You'd better keep down near the floor."

The powerful lights over the mirror were on and the room still had its look of occupation. The gas fire was against the left hand wall. Alleyn squatted down by it. The tap was still turned on, its face lying parallel with the floor. The top of the heater, the tap itself, and the carpet near it, were covered with a creamish powder. On the end of the dressing-table shelf nearest to the stove was a box of this powder. Further along the shelf, greasepaints were set out in a row beneath the mirror. Then came a wash basin and in front of this an overturned chair. Alleyn could see the track of heels, across the pile of the carpet, to the door immediately opposite. Beside the wash basin was a quart bottle of whiskey, three parts empty, and a tumbler. Alleyn had had about enough and returned to the passage.

"Perfectly clear," the hovering doctor said again, "Isn't it?"

"I'll see the other rooms, I think."

The one next to Cumberland's was like his in reverse, but smaller. The heater was back to back with Cumberland's. The dressing-shelf was set out with much the same assortment of greasepaints. The tap of this heater, too, was turned on. It was of precisely the same make as the other and Alleyn, less embarrassed here by fumes, was able to make a longer examination. It was a common enough type of gas fire. The lead-in was from a pipe through a flexible metallic tube with a rubber connection. There were two taps, one in the pipe and one at the junction of the tube with the heater itself. Alleyn disconnected the tube and examined the connection. It was perfectly sound, a close fit and stained red at the end. Alleyn noticed a wiry thread of some reddish stuff resembling packing that still clung to it. The nozzle and tap were brass, the tap pulling over when it was turned on, to lie in a parallel plane with the floor. No powder had been scattered about here.

He glanced round the room, returned to the door and read the card: "Mr. Barry George."

The doctor followed him into the rooms opposite these, on the left-hand side of the passage. They were a repetition in design of the two he had already seen but were hung with women's clothes and had a more elaborate assortment of greasepaint and cosmetics.

There was a mass of flowers in the star-room. Alleyn read the cards. One in particular caught his eye: "From Anthony Gill to say a most inadequate 'thank you' for the great idea." A vase of red roses stood before the mirror: "To your greatest triumph, Coralie darling. C.C." In Miss Gay's room there were only two bouquets, one from the management and one "From Anthony, with love."

Again in each room he pulled off the lead-in to the heater and looked at the connection.

"All right, aren't they?" said the doctor.

"Quite all right. Tight fit. Good solid grey rubber."

"Well, then—"

Next on the left was an unused room, and opposite it, "Mr. H. J. Bannington." Neither of these rooms had gas fires. Mr. Bannington's dressing-table was littered with the usual array of greasepaint, the materials for his beard, a number of telegrams and letters, and several bills.

"About the body," the doctor began.

"We'll get a mortuary van from the Yard."

"But—Surely in a case of suicide—"

"I don't think this is suicide."

"But, good God!—D'you mean there's been an accident?"

"No accident," said Alleyn.

At midnight, the dressing-room lights in the Jupiter Theatre were brilliant, and men were busy there with the tools of their trade. A constable stood at the stage-door and a van waited in the yard. The front of the house was dimly lit and there, among the shrouded stalls, sat Coralie Bourne, Basil Gosset, H. J. Bannington, Dendra Gay, Anthony Gill, Reynolds, Katie the dresser, and the call-boy. A constable sat behind them and another stood by the doors into the foyer. They stared across the backs of seats at the fire curtain. Spirals of smoke rose from their cigarettes and about their feet were discarded programs. "Basil Gosset presents I CAN FIND MY WAY OUT by Anthony Gill."

In the manager's office Alleyn said: "You're sure of your facts, Mike?"

"Yes, sir. Honestly. I was right up against the entrance into the passage. They didn't see me because I was in the shadow. It was very dark offstage."

"You'll have to swear to it."

"I know."

"Good. All right, Thompson. Miss Gay and Mr. Gosset may go home. Ask Miss Bourne to come in."

When Sergeant Thompson had gone Mike said: "I haven't had a chance to say I know I've made a perfect fool of myself. Using your card and everything."

"Irresponsible gaiety doesn't go down very well in the service, Mike. You behaved like a clown."

"I *am* a fool," said Mike wretchedly.

The red beard was lying in front of Alleyn on Gosset's desk. He picked it up and held it out. "Put it on," he said.

"She might do another faint."

"I think not. Now the hat: yes—yes, I see. Come in."

Sergeant Thompson showed Coralie Bourne in and then sat at the end of the desk with his notebook.

Tears had traced their course through the powder on her face, carrying black cosmetic with them and leaving the greasepaint shining like snail-tracks. She stood near the doorway looking dully at Michael. "Is he back in England?" she said. "Did he tell you to do this?" She made an impatient movement. "Do take it off," she said, "it's a very bad beard. If Cann had only looked—" Her lips trembled. "Who told you to do it?"

"Nobody," Mike stammered, pocketing the beard. "I mean—As a matter of fact, Tony Gill—"

"*Tony?* But *he* didn't know. Tony wouldn't do it. Unless—"

"Unless?" Alleyn said.

She said frowning: "Tony didn't want Cann to play the part that way. He was furious."

"He says it was his dress for the Chelsea Arts Ball," Mike mumbled. "I brought it here. I just thought I'd put it on—it was idiotic, I know—for fun. I'd no idea you and Mr. Cumberland would mind."

"Ask Mr. Gill to come in," Alleyn said.

Anthony was white and seemed bewildered and helpless. "I've told Mike," he said. "It was my dress for the ball. They sent it round from the costume-hiring place this afternoon but I forgot it. Dendra reminded me and rang up the Delivery people—or Mike, as it turns out—in the interval."

"Why," Alleyn asked, "did you choose that particular disguise?"

"I didn't. I didn't know what to wear and I was too rattled to think. They said they were hiring things for themselves and would get something for me. They said we'd all be characters out of a Russian melodrama."

"Who said this?"

"Well—well, it was Barry George, actually."

"*Barry,*" Coralie Bourne said. "*It was Barry.*"

"I don't understand," Anthony said. "Why should a fancy dress upset everybody?"

"It happened," Alleyn said, "to be a replica of the dress usually worn by Miss Bourne's husband who also had a red beard. That was it, wasn't it, Miss Bourne? I remember seeing him—"

"Oh, yes," she said, "you would. He was known to the police." Suddenly she broke down completely. She was in an armchair near the desk but out of the range of its shaded lamp. She twisted and writhed, beating her hand against the padded arm of the chair. Sergeant Thompson sat with his head bent and his hand over his notes. Mike, after an agonized glance at Alleyn, turned his back. Anthony Gill leant over her: "Don't," he said violently. "Don't! For God's sake, stop."

She twisted away from him and, gripping the edge of the desk, began to speak to Alleyn; little by little gaining mastery of herself. "I want to tell you. I want you to understand. Listen." Her husband had been fantastically cruel, she said. "It was a kind of slavery." But when she sued for divorce he brought evidence of adultery with Cumberland. They had thought he knew nothing. "There was an abominable scene. He told us he was going away. He said he'd keep track of us and if I tried again for divorce, he'd come home. He was very friendly with Barry in those days." He had left behind him the first draft of a play he had meant to write for her and Cumberland. It had a wonderful scene for them. "And now you will never have it," he had said, "because there is no other playwright who could make this play for you but I." He was, she said, a melodramatic man but he was never ridiculous. He returned to the Ukraine where he was born and they had heard no more of him. In a little while she would have been able to presume death.

But years of waiting did not agree with Canning Cumberland. He drank consistently and at his worst used to imagine her husband was about to return. "He was really terrified of Ben," she said. "He seemed like a creature in a nightmare."

Anthony Gill said: "This play—was it—?"

"Yes. There was an extraordinary similarity between your play and his. I saw at once that Ben's central scene would enormously strengthen your piece. Cann didn't want me to give it to you. Barry knew. He said: 'Why not?' He wanted Cann's part and was furious when he didn't get it. So you see, when he suggested you should dress and make-up like Ben—" She turned to Alleyn. "You see?"

"What did Cumberland do when he saw you?" Alleyn asked Mike.

"He made a queer movement with his hands as if—well, as if he expected me to go for him. Then he just bolted into his room."

"He thought Ben had come back," she said.

"Were you alone at any time after you fainted?" Alleyn asked.

"I? No. No, I wasn't. Katie took me into my dressing-room and stayed with me until I went on for the last scene."

"One other question. Can you, by any chance, remember if the heater in your room behaved at all oddly?"

She looked wearily at him. "Yes, it did give a sort of plop, I think. It made me jump. I was nervy."

"You went straight from your room to the stage?"

"Yes. With Katie. I wanted to go to Cann. I tried the door when we came out. It was locked. He said: 'Don't come in.' I said: 'It's all right. It wasn't Ben,' and went on to the stage."

"I heard Miss Bourne," Mike said.

"He must have made up his mind by then. He was terribly drunk when he played his last scene." She pushed her hair back from her forehead. "May I go?" she asked Alleyn.

"I've sent for a taxi. Mr. Gill, will you see if it's there? In the meantime, Miss Bourne, would you like to wait in the foyer?"

"May I take Katie home with me?"

"Certainly. Thompson will find her. Is there anyone else we can get?"

"No, thank you. Just old Katie."

Alleyn opened the door for her and watched her walk into the foyer. "Check up with the dresser, Thompson," he murmured, "and get Mr. H. J. Bannington."

He saw Coralie Bourne sit on the lower step of the dress-circle stairway and lean her head against the wall. Nearby, on a gilt easel, a huge photograph of Canning Cumberland smiled handsomely at her.

H. J. Bannington looked pretty ghastly. He had rubbed his hand across his face and smeared his makeup. Florid red paint from his lips had stained the crêpe hair that had been gummed on and shaped into a beard. His monocle was still in his left eye and gave him an extraordinarily rakish look. "See here," he complained, "I've about *had* this party. When do we go home?"

Alleyn uttered placatory phrases and got him to sit down. He checked over H.J.'s movements after Cumberland left the stage and found that his account tallied with Mike's. He asked if H.J. had visited any of the other dressing-rooms and was told acidly that H.J. knew his place in the company. "I remained in my unheated and squalid kennel, thank you very much."

"Do you know if Mr. Barry George followed your example?"

"Couldn't say, old boy. He didn't come near *me*."

"Have you any theories at all about this unhappy business, Mr. Bannington?"

"Do you mean, why did Cann do it? Well, speak no ill of the dead, but I'd have thought it was pretty obvious he was morbid-drunk. Tight as an owl when we finished the second act. Ask the great Mr. Barry George. Cann took the big scene away from Barry with both hands and left him looking pathetic. All wrong artistically, but that's how Cann was in his cups." H.J.'s wicked little eyes narrowed. "The great Mr. George," he said, "must be feeling very unpleasant by now. You might say he'd got a suicide on his mind, mightn't you? Or don't you know about that?"

"It was not suicide."

The glass dropped from H.J.'s eye. "God," he said. "God. I told Bob Reynolds! I told him the whole plant wanted overhauling."

"The gas plant, you mean?"

"Certainly. I was in the gas business years ago. Might say I'm in it still with a difference, ha-ha!"

"Ha-ha!" Alleyn agreed politely. He leaned forward. "Look here," he said: "We can't dig up a gas man at this time of night and may very likely need an expert opinion. You can help us."

"Well, old boy, I was rather pining for a spot of shut-eye. But, of course—"

"I shan't keep you very long."

"God, I hope not!" said H.J. earnestly.

Barry George had been made up pale for the last act. Colorless lips and shadows under his cheek bones and eyes had skilfully underlined his character as a repatriated but broken prisoner-of-war. Now, in the glare of the office lamp, he looked like a grossly exaggerated figure of mourning. He began at once to tell Alleyn how grieved and horrified he was. Everybody, he said, had their faults, and poor old

Cann was no exception but wasn't it terrible to think what could happen to a man who let himself go downhill? He, Barry George, was abnormally sensitive and he didn't think he'd ever really get over the awful shock this had been to him. What, he wondered, could be at the bottom of it? Why had poor old Cann decided to end it all?

"Miss Bourne's theory," Alleyn began. Mr. George laughed. "Coralie?" he said. "So she's got a theory! Oh, well. Never mind."

"Her theory is this. Cumberland saw a man whom he mistook for her husband and, having a morbid dread of his return, drank the greater part of a bottle of whiskey and gassed himself. The clothes and beard that deceived him had, I understand, been ordered by you for Mr. Anthony Gill."

This statement produced startling results. Barry George broke into a spate of expostulation and apology. There had been no thought in his mind of resurrecting poor old Ben, who was no doubt dead but had been, mind you, in many ways one of the best. They were all to go to the Ball as exaggerated characters from melodrama. Not for the world —he gesticulated and protested. A line of sweat broke out along the margin of his hair. "I don't know what you're getting at," he shouted. "What are you suggesting?"

"I'm suggesting, among other things, that Cumberland was murdered."

"You're mad! He'd locked himself in. They had to break down the door. There's no window. You're crazy!"

"Don't," Alleyn said wearily, "let us have any nonsense about sealed rooms. Now, Mr. George, you knew Benjamin Vlasnoff pretty well. Are you going to tell us that when you suggested Mr. Gill should wear a coat with a fur collar, a black sombrero, black gloves and a red beard, it never occurred to you that his appearance might be a shock to Miss Bourne and to Cumberland?"

"I wasn't the only one," he blustered. "H.J. knew. And if it had scared him off, *she* wouldn't have been so sorry. She'd had about enough of him. Anyway if this is murder, the costume's got nothing to do with it."

"That," Alleyn said, getting up, "is what we hope to find out."

In Barry George's room, Detective Sergeant Bailey, a fingerprint expert, stood by the gas heater. Sergeant Gibson, a police photographer, and a uniformed constable were near the door. In the centre of the room stood Barry George, looking from one man to another and picking at his lips.

"I don't know why he wants me to watch all this," he said. "I'm exhausted. I'm emotionally used up. What's he doing? Where is he?"

Alleyn was next door in Cumberland's dressing-room, with H.J., Mike and Sergeant Thompson. It was pretty clear now of fumes and the gas fire was burning comfortably. Sergeant Thompson sprawled in the armchair near the heater, his head sunk and his eyes shut.

"This is the theory, Mr. Bannington," Alleyn said. "You and Cumberland have made your final exits; Miss Bourne and Mr. George and Miss Gay are all on the stage. Lord Michael is standing just outside the entrance to the passage. The dressers and stage-staff are watching the play from the side. Cumberland has locked himself in this room. There he is, dead drunk and sound asleep. The gas fire is burning, full pressure. Earlier in the evening he powdered himself and a thick layer of the powder lies undisturbed on the tap. Now."

He tapped on the wall.

The fire blew out with a sharp explosion. This was followed by the hiss of escaping gas. Alleyn turned the taps off. "You see," he said, "I've left an excellent print on the powdered surface. Now, come next door."

Next door, Barry George appealed to him stammering: "But I didn't know. I don't know anything about it. I don't *know*."

"Just show Mr. Bannington, will you, Bailey?"

Bailey knelt down. The lead-in was disconnected from the tap on the heater. He turned on the tap in the pipe and blew down the tube.

"An air lock, you see. It works perfectly."

H.J. was staring at Barry George. "But I don't know about gas, H.J., H.J., tell them—"

"One moment." Alleyn removed the towels that had been spread over the dressing-shelf, revealing a sheet of clean paper on which lay the rubber push-on connection.

"Will you take this lens, Bannington, and look at it. You'll see that it's stained a florid red. It's a very slight stain but it's unmistakably greasepaint. And just above the stain you'll see a wiry hair. Rather like some sort of packing material, but it's not that. It's crêpe hair, isn't it?"

The lens wavered above the paper.

"Let me hold it for you," Alleyn said. He put his hand over H.J.'s shoulder and, with a swift movement, plucked a tuft from his false moustache and dropped it on the paper. "Identical, you see, ginger. It seems to be stuck to the connection with spirit-gum."

The lens fell. H.J. twisted round, faced Alleyn for a second, and then struck him full in the face. He was a small man but it took three of them to hold him.

"In a way, sir, it's handy when they have a smack at you," said Detective Sergeant Thompson half an hour later. "You can pull them in nice and straightforward without any 'will you come to the station and make a statement' business."

"Quite," said Alleyn, nursing his jaw.

Mike said: "He must have gone to the room after Barry George and Miss Bourne were called."

"That's it. He had to be quick. The call-boy would be round in a minute and he had to be back in his own room."

"But look here—what about motive?"

"That, my good Mike, is precisely why, at half-past one in the morning, we're still in this miserable theatre. You're getting a view of the duller aspect of homicide. Want to go home?"

"No. Give me another job."

"Very well. About ten feet from the prompt-entrance, there's a sort of garbage tin. Go through it."

At seventeen minutes to two, when the dressing-rooms and passage had been combed clean and Alleyn had called a spell, Mike came to him with filthy hands. *"Eureka,"* he said, "I hope."

They all went into Bannington's room. Alleyn spread out on the dressing-table the fragments of paper that Mike had given him.

"They'd been pushed down to the bottom of the tin," Mike said.

Alleyn moved the fragments about. Thompson whistled through his teeth. Bailey and Gibson mumbled together.

"There you are," Alleyn said at last.

They collected round him. The letter that H. J. Bannington had opened at this same table six hours and forty-five minutes earlier, was pieced together like a jig-saw puzzle.

Dear H.J.
  Having seen the monthly statement of my account, I called at my bank this morning and was shown a check that is undoubtedly a forgery. Your histrionic versatility, my dear H.J., is only equalled by your audacity as a calligraphist. But fame has its disadvantages. The teller has recognized you. I propose to take action.

"Unsigned," said Bailey.

"Look at the card on the red roses in Miss Bourne's

room, signed C.C. It's a very distinctive hand." Alleyn turned to Mike. "Do you still want to be a policeman?"

"Yes."

"Lord help you. Come and talk to me at the office tomorrow."

"Thank you, sir."

They went out, leaving a constable on duty. It was a cold morning. Mike looked up at the façade of the Jupiter. He could just make out the shape of the neon sign: I CAN FIND MY WAY OUT *by Anthony Gill.*

Chapter and Verse: The Little Copplestone Mystery

When the telephone rang, Troy came in, sun-dazzled, from the cottage garden to answer it, hoping it would be a call from London.

"Oh," said a strange voice uncertainly. "May I speak to Superintendent Alleyn, if you please?"

"I'm sorry. He's away."

"Oh, dear!" said the voice, crestfallen. "Er—would that be—am I speaking to Mrs. Alleyn?"

"Yes."

"Oh. Yes. Well, it's Timothy Bates here, Mrs. Alleyn. You don't know me," the voice confessed wistfully, "but I had the pleasure several years ago of meeting your husband. In New Zealand. And he did say that if I ever came home I was to get in touch, and when I heard quite by accident that you were here—well, I *was* excited. But, alas, no good after all."

"I *am* sorry," Troy said. "He'll be back, I hope, on Sunday night. Perhaps—"

"Will he! Come, *that's* something! Because here I am at the Star and Garter, you see, and so—" The voice trailed away again.

"Yes, indeed. He'll be delighted," Troy said, hoping that he would.

"I'm a bookman," the voice confided. "Old books, you

know. He used to come into my shop. It was always such a pleasure."

"But, of course!" Troy exclaimed. "I remember perfectly now. He's often talked about it."

"*Has* he? Has he, really! Well, you see, Mrs. Alleyn, I'm here on business. Not to *sell* anything, please don't think that, but on a voyage of discovery; almost, one might say, of detection, and I think it might amuse him. He has such an eye for the curious. Not," the voice hurriedly amended, "in the trade sense. I mean curious in the sense of mysterious and unusual. But I mustn't bore you."

Troy assured him that he was not boring her and indeed it was true. The voice was so much colored by odd little overtones that she found herself quite drawn to its owner. "I know where you are," he was saying. "Your house was pointed out to me."

After that there was nothing to do but ask him to visit. He seemed to cheer up prodigiously. "May I? May I, really? Now?"

"Why not?" Troy said. "You'll be here in five minutes."

She heard a little crow of delight before he hung up the receiver.

He turned out to be exactly like his voice—a short, middle-aged, bespectacled man, rather untidily dressed. As he came up the path she saw that with both arms he clutched to his stomach an enormous Bible. He was thrown into a fever over the difficulty of removing his cap.

"How ridiculous!" he exclaimed. "Forgive me! One moment."

He laid his burden tenderly on a garden seat. "There!" he cried. "Now! How do you do!"

Troy took him indoors and gave him a drink. He chose sherry and sat in the window seat with his Bible beside him. "You'll wonder," he said, "why I've appeared with this unusual piece of baggage. I *do* trust it arouses your curiosity."

He went into a long excitable explanation. It appeared that the Bible was an old and rare one that he had picked up in a job lot of books in New Zealand. All this time he kept it under his square little hands as if it might open of its own accord and spoil his story.

"Because," he said, "the *really* exciting thing to me is *not* its undoubted authenticity but—" He made a conspiratorial face at Troy and suddenly opened the Bible. "Look!" he invited.

He displayed the flyleaf. Troy saw that it was almost filled with entries in a minute, faded copperplate handwriting.

"The top," Mr. Bates cried. "Top left-hand. Look at *that.*"

Troy read: *"Crabtree Farm at Little Copplestone in the County of Kent.* Why, it comes from our village!"

"Ah, ha! So it does. Now, the entries, my dear Mrs. Alleyn. The entries."

They were the recorded births and deaths of a family named Wagstaff, beginning in 1705 and ending in 1870 with the birth of William James Wagstaff. Here they broke off but were followed by three further entries, close together.

Stewart Shakespeare Hadet. Died: Tuesday, 5th April, 1779. 2nd Samuel 1.10.

Naomi Balbus Hadet. Died: Saturday, 13th August, 1779. Jeremiah 50.24.

Peter Rook Hadet. Died: Monday, 12th September, 1779. Ezekiel 7.6.

Troy looked up to find Mr. Bates's gaze fixed on her. "And what," Mr. Bates asked, "my dear Mrs. Alleyn, do you make of *that?*"

"Well," she said cautiously, "I know about Crabtree

Farm. There's the farm itself, owned by Mr. De'ath, and there's Crabtree House, belonging to Miss Hart, and—yes, I fancy I've heard they both belonged originally to a family named Wagstaff."

"You are perfectly right. Now! What about the Hadets? What about *them?*"

"I've never heard of a family named Hadet in Little Copplestone. But—"

"Of course you haven't. For the very good reason that there never have been any Hadets in Little Copplestone."

"Perhaps in New Zealand, then?"

"The dates, my dear Mrs. Alleyn, the dates! New Zealand was not colonized in 1779. Look closer. Do you see the sequence of double dots—ditto marks—under the address? Meaning, of course, 'also of Crabtree Farm at Little Copplestone in the County of Kent'."

"I suppose so."

"Of course you do. And how right you are. Now! You have noticed that throughout there are biblical references. For the Wagstaffs they are the usual pious offerings. You need not trouble yourself with them. But consult the text awarded to the three Hadets. Just you look *them* up! I've put markers."

He threw himself back with an air of triumph and sipped his sherry. Troy turned over the heavy bulk of pages to the first marker. "Second of Samuel, one, ten," Mr. Bates prompted, closing his eyes.

The verse had been faintly underlined.

"So I stood upon him," Troy read, *"and slew him."*

"That's Stewart Shakespeare Hadet's valedictory," said Mr. Bates. "Next!"

The next was at the 50th chapter of Jeremiah, verse 24: *"I have laid a snare for thee and thou are taken."*

Troy looked at Mr. Bates. His eyes were still closed and he was smiling faintly.

"That was Naomi Balbus Hadet," he said. "Now for Peter Rook Hadet. Ezekiel, seven, six."

The pages flopped back to the last marker.

"An end is come, the end is come: it watcheth for thee; behold it is come."

Troy shut the Bible.

"How very unpleasant," she said.

"And how very intriguing, don't you think?" And when she didn't answer, "Quite up your husband's street, it seemed to me."

"I'm afraid," Troy said, "that even Rory's investigations don't go back to 1779."

"What a pity!" Mr. Bates cried gaily.

"Do I gather that you conclude from all this that there was dirty work among the Hadets in 1779?"

"I don't know, but I'm dying to find out. *Dying* to. Thank you, I should enjoy another glass. Delicious!"

He had settled down so cosily and seemed to be enjoying himself so much that Troy was constrained to ask him to stay to lunch.

"Miss Hart's coming," she said. "She's the one who bought Crabtree House from the Wagstaffs. If there's any gossip to be picked up in Copplestone, Miss Hart's the one for it. She's coming about a painting she wants me to donate to the Harvest Festival raffle."

Mr. Bates was greatly excited. "Who knows!" he cried. "A Wagstaff in the hand may be worth two Hadets in the bush. I am your slave forever, my dear Mrs. Alleyn!"

Miss Hart was a lady of perhaps sixty-seven years. On meeting Mr. Bates she seemed to imply that some explanation should be advanced for Troy receiving a gentleman caller in her husband's absence. When the Bible was produced, she immediately accepted it in this light, glanced with professional expertise at the inscriptions and fastened on the Wagstaffs.

"No doubt," said Miss Hart, "it was their family Bible and much good it did them. A most eccentric lot they were. Very unsound. Very unsound, indeed. Especially Old Jimmy."

"Who," Mr. Bates asked greedily, "was Old Jimmy?"

Miss Hart jabbed her forefinger at the last of the Wagstaff entries. "William James Wagstaff. Born 1870. And died, although it doesn't say so, in April, 1921. Nobody was left to complete the entry, of course. Unless you count the niece, which I don't. Baggage, if ever I saw one."

"The niece?"

"Fanny Wagstaff. Orphan. Old Jimmy brought her up. Dragged would be the better word. Drunken old reprobate he was and he came to a drunkard's end. They said he beat her *and* I daresay she needed it." Miss Hart lowered her voice to a whisper and confided in Troy. "Not a *nice* girl. You know what I mean."

Troy, feeling it was expected of her, nodded portentously.

"A drunken end, did you say?" prompted Mr. Bates.

"Certainly. On a Saturday night after Market. Fell through the top-landing stair rail in his nightshirt and split his skull on the flagstoned hall."

"And your father bought it, then, after Old Jimmy died?" Troy ventured.

"Bought the house and garden. Richard De'ath took the farm. He'd been after it for years—wanted it to round off his own place. He and Old Jimmy were at daggers-drawn over *that* business. And, of course, Richard being an atheist, over the Seven Seals."

"I beg your pardon?" Mr. Bates asked.

"Blasphemous!" Miss Hart shouted. "That's what it was, rank blasphemy. It was a sect that Wagstaff founded. If the rector had known his business he'd have had him excommunicated for it."

Miss Hart was prevented from elaborating this theory by the appearance at the window of an enormous woman, stuffily encased in black, with a face like a full moon.

"Anybody at home?" the newcomer playfully chanted. "Telegram for a lucky girl! Come and get it!"

It was Mrs. Simpson, the village postmistress. Miss Hart said, "Well, *really!*" and gave an acid laugh.

"Sorry, I'm sure," said Mrs. Simpson, staring at the Bible which lay under her nose on the window seat. "I didn't realize there was company. Thought I'd pop it in as I was passing."

Troy read the telegram while Mrs. Simpson, panting, sank heavily on the window ledge and eyed Mr. Bates, who had drawn back in confusion. "I'm no good in the heat," she told him. "Slays me."

"Thank you so much, Mrs. Simpson," Troy said. "No answer."

"Righty-ho. Cheerie-bye," said Mrs. Simpson and with another stare at Mr. Bates and the Bible, and a derisive grin at Miss Hart, she waddled away.

"It's from Rory," Troy said. "He'll be home on Sunday evening."

"As that woman will no doubt inform the village," Miss Hart pronounced. "A busybody of the first water and ought to be taught her place. Did you ever!"

She fulminated throughout luncheon and it was with difficulty that Troy and Mr. Bates persuaded her to finish her story of the last of the Wagstaffs. It appeared that Old Jimmy had died intestate, his niece succeeding. She had at once announced her intention of selling everything and had left the district to pursue, Miss Hart suggested, a life of freedom, no doubt in London or even in Paris. Miss Hart wouldn't, and didn't want to, know. On the subject of the

Hadets, however, she was uninformed and showed no inclination to look up the marked Bible references attached to them.

After luncheon Troy showed Miss Hart three of her paintings, any one of which would have commanded a high price at an exhibition of contemporary art, and Miss Hart chose the one that, in her own phrase, really did look like something. She insisted that Troy and Mr. Bates accompany her to the parish hall where Mr. Bates would meet the rector, an authority on village folklore. Troy in person must hand over her painting to be raffled.

Troy would have declined this honor if Mr. Bates had not retired behind Miss Hart and made a series of beseeching gestures and grimaces. They set out therefore in Miss Hart's car which was crammed with vegetables for the Harvest Festival decorations.

"And if the woman Simpson thinks she's going to hog the lectern with *her* pumpkins," said Miss Hart, "she's in for a shock. Hah!"

St. Cuthbert's was an ancient parish church round whose flanks the tiny village nestled. Its tower, an immensely high one, was said to be unique. Nearby was the parish hall where Miss Hart pulled up with a masterful jerk.

Troy and Mr. Bates helped her unload some of her lesser marrows to be offered for sale within. They were observed by a truculent-looking man in tweeds who grinned at Miss Hart. "Burnt offerings," he jeered, "for the tribal gods, I perceive." It was Mr. Richard De'ath, the atheist. Miss Hart cut him dead and led the way into the hall.

Here they found the rector, with a crimson-faced elderly man and a clutch of ladies engaged in preparing for the morrow's sale.

The rector was a thin gentle person, obviously frightened of Miss Hart and timidly delighted by Troy. On being shown the Bible he became excited and dived at once into the story of Old Jimmy Wagstaff.

"Intemperate, I'm afraid, in everything," sighed the rector. "Indeed, it would not be too much to say that he both preached and drank hellfire. He *did* preach, on Saturday nights at the crossroads outside the Star and Garter. Drunken, blasphemous nonsense it was and although he used to talk about his followers, the only one he could claim was his niece, Fanny, who was probably too much under his thumb to refuse him."

"Edward Pilbrow," Miss Hart announced, jerking her head at the elderly man who had come quite close to them. "Drowned him with his bell. They had a fight over it. Deaf as a post," she added, catching sight of Mr. Bates's startled expression. "He's the verger now. *And* the town crier."

"What!" Mr. Bates exclaimed.

"Oh, yes," the rector explained. "The village is endowed with a town crier." He went over to Mr. Pilbrow, who at once cupped his hand round his ear. The rector yelled into it.

"When did you start crying, Edward?"

"Twenty-ninth September, 'twenty-one," Mr. Pilbrow roared back.

"I thought so."

There was something in their manner that made it difficult to remember, Troy thought, that they were talking about events that were almost fifty years back in the past. Even the year 1779 evidently seemed to them to be not so long ago, but, alas, none of them knew of any Hadets.

"By all means," the rector invited Mr. Bates, "consult the church records, but I can assure you—no Hadets. Never any Hadets."

Troy saw an expression of extreme obstinacy settle round Mr. Bates's mouth.

The rector invited him to look at the church and as they

both seemed to expect Troy to tag along, she did so. In the lane they once more encountered Mr. Richard De'ath out of whose pocket protruded a paper-wrapped bottle. He touched his cap to Troy and glared at the rector, who turned pink and said, "Afternoon, De'ath," and hurried on.

Mr. Bates whispered imploringly to Troy, "*Would* you mind? I *do* so want to have a word—" and she was obliged to introduce him. It was not a successful encounter. Mr. Bates no sooner broached the topic of his Bible, which he still carried, than Mr. De'ath burst into an alcoholic diatribe against superstition, and on the mention of Old Jimmy Wagstaff, worked himself up into such a state of reminiscent fury that Mr. Bates was glad to hurry away with Troy.

They overtook the rector in the churchyard, now bathed in the golden opulence of an already westering sun.

"There they all lie," the rector said, waving a fatherly hand at the company of headstones. "All your Wagstaffs, right back to the sixteenth century. But no Hadets, Mr. Bates, I assure you."

They stood looking up at the spire. Pigeons flew in and out of a balcony far above their heads. At their feet was a little flagged area edged by a low coping. Mr. Bates stepped forward and the rector laid a hand on his arm.

"Not there," he said. "Do you mind?"

"Don't!" bellowed Mr. Pilbrow from the rear. "Don't you set foot on them bloody stones, Mister."

Mr. Bates backed away.

"Edward's not swearing," the rector mildly explained. "He is to be taken, alas, literally. A sad and dreadful story, Mr. Bates."

"Indeed?" Mr. Bates asked eagerly.

"Indeed, yes. Some time ago, in the very year we have been discussing—1921, you know—one of our girls, a very beautiful girl she was, named Ruth Wall, fell from the balcony of the tower and was, of course, killed. She used to go up there to feed the pigeons and it was thought that in leaning over the low balustrade she overbalanced."

"Ah!" Mr. Pilbrow roared with considerable relish, evidently guessing the purport of the rector's speech. "Terrible, terrible! And 'er sweetheart after 'er, too. Terrible!"

"Oh, no!" Troy protested.

The rector made a dabbing gesture to subdue Mr. Pilbrow. "I wish he wouldn't," he said. "Yes. It was a few days later. A lad called Simon Castle. They were to be married. People said it must be suicide but—it may have been wrong of me—I couldn't bring myself—in short, he lies beside her over there. If you would care to look."

For a minute or two they stood before the headstones.

"Ruth Wall. Spinster of this Parish. 1903–1921. *I will extend peace to her like a river.*"

"Simon Castle. Bachelor of this Parish. 1900–1921. *And God shall wipe away all tears from their eyes.*"

The afternoon having by now worn on, and the others having excused themselves, Mr. Bates remained alone in the churchyard, clutching his Bible and staring at the headstones. The light of the hunter's zeal still gleamed in his eyes.

Troy didn't see Mr. Bates again until Sunday night service when, on her way up the aisle, she passed him, sitting in the rearmost pew. She was amused to observe that his gigantic Bible was under the seat.

"*We plow the fields,*" sang the choir, "*and scatter—*" Mrs. Simpson roared away on the organ, the smell of assorted greengrocery rising like some humble incense. Everybody in Little Copplestone except Mr. Richard De'ath was there for the Harvest Festival. At last the rector stepped over Miss Hart's biggest pumpkin and ascended the pulpit, Edward Pilbrow switched off all the lights except one and they settled down for the sermon.

"A sower went forth to sow," announced the rector. He spoke simply and well but somehow Troy's attention wandered. She found herself wondering where, through the centuries, the succeeding generations of Wagstaffs had sat until Old Jimmy took to his freakish practices; and whether Ruth Wall and Simon Castle, poor things, had shared the same hymnbook and held hands during the sermon; and whether, after all, Stewart Shakespeare Hadet and Peter Rook Hadet had not, in 1779, occupied some dark corner of the church and been unaccountably forgotten.

Here we are, Troy thought drowsily, and there, outside in the churchyard, are all the others going back and back—

She saw a girl, bright in the evening sunlight, reach from a balcony toward a multitude of wings. She was falling—dreadfully—into nothingness. Troy woke with a sickening jerk.

"—on stony ground," the rector was saying. Troy listened guiltily to the rest of the sermon.

Mr. Bates emerged on the balcony. He laid his Bible on the coping and looked at the moonlit tree tops and the churchyard so dreadfully far below. He heard someone coming up the stairway. Torchlight danced on the door jamb.

"You were quick," said the visitor.

"I am all eagerness and, I confess, puzzlement."

"It had to be here, on the spot. If you *really* want to find out—"

"But I do, I do!"

"We haven't much time. You've brought the Bible?"

"You particularly asked—"

"If you'd open it at Ezekiel, chapter twelve. I'll shine my torch."

Mr. Bates opened the Bible.

"The thirteenth verse. There!"

Mr. Bates leaned forward. The Bible tipped and moved. "Look out!" the voice urged.

Mr. Bates was scarcely aware of the thrust. He felt the page tear as the book sank under his hands. The last thing he heard was the beating of a multitude of wings.

"—and forevermore," said the rector in a changed voice, facing east. The congregation got to its feet. He announced the last hymn. Mrs. Simpson made a preliminary rumble and Troy groped in her pocket for the collection plate. Presently they all filed out into the autumnal moonlight.

It was coldish in the churchyard. People stood about in groups. One or two had already moved through the lych-gate. Troy heard a voice, which she recognized as that of Mr. De'ath. "I suppose," it jeered, "you all know you've been assisting at a fertility rite."

"Drunk as usual, Dick De'ath," somebody returned without rancor. There was a general laugh.

They had all begun to move away when, from the shadows at the base of the church tower, there arose a great cry. They stood, transfixed, turned toward the voice.

Out of the shadows came the rector in his cassock. When Troy saw his face she thought he must be ill and went to him.

"No, no!" he said. "Not a woman! Edward! Where's Edward Pilbrow?"

Behind him, at the foot of the tower, was a pool of darkness; but Troy, having come closer, could see within it a figure, broken like a puppet on the flagstones. An eddy of night air stole round the church and fluttered a page of the giant Bible that lay pinned beneath the head.

It was nine o'clock when Troy heard the car pull up outside the cottage. She saw her husband coming up the path and ran to meet him, as if they had been parted for months.

He said, "This is mighty gratifying!" And then, "Hullo, my love. What's the matter?"

As she tumbled out her story, filled with relief at telling him, a large man with uncommonly bright eyes came up behind them.

"Listen to this, Fox," Roderick Alleyn said. "We're in demand, it seems." He put his arm through Troy's and closed his hand round hers. "Let's go indoors, shall we? Here's Fox, darling, come for a nice bucolic rest. Can we give him a bed?"

Troy pulled herself together and greeted Inspector Fox. Presently she was able to give them a coherent account of the evening's tragedy. When she had finished, Alleyn said, "Poor little Bates. He was a nice little bloke." He put his hand on Troy's. "You need a drink," he said, "and so, by the way, do we."

While he was getting the drinks he asked quite casually, "You've had a shock and a beastly one at that, but there's something else, isn't there?"

"Yes," Troy swallowed hard, "there is. They're all saying it's an accident."

"Yes?"

"And, Rory, I don't think it is."

Mr. Fox cleared his throat. "Fancy," he said.

"Suicide?" Alleyn suggested, bringing her drink to her.

"No. Certainly not."

"A bit of rough stuff, then?"

"You sound as if you're asking about the sort of weather we've been having."

"Well, darling, you don't expect Fox and me to go into hysterics. Why not an accident?"

"He knew all about the other accidents, he *knew* it was dangerous. And then the oddness of it, Rory. To leave the

Harvest Festival service and climb the tower in the dark, carrying that enormous Bible!"

"And he was hell-bent on tracing these Hadets?"

"Yes. He kept saying you'd be interested. He actually brought a copy of the entries for you."

"Have you got it?"

She found it for him. "The selected texts," he said, "are pretty rum, aren't they, Br'er Fox?" and handed it over.

"Very vindictive," said Mr. Fox.

"Mr. Bates thought it was in your line," Troy said.

"The devil he did! What's been done about this?"

"The village policeman was in the church. They sent for the doctor. And—well, you see, Mr. Bates had talked a lot about you and they hope you'll be able to tell them something about him—whom they should get in touch with and so on."

"Have they moved him?"

"They weren't going to until the doctor had seen him."

Alleyn pulled his wife's ear and looked at Fox. "Do you fancy a stroll through the village, Foxkin?"

"There's a lovely moon," Fox said bitterly and got to his feet.

The moon was high in the heavens when they came to the base of the tower and it shone on a group of four men—the rector, Richard De'ath, Edward Pilbrow, and Sergeant Botting, the village constable. When they saw Alleyn and Fox, they separated and revealed a fifth, who was kneeling by the body of Timothy Bates.

"Kind of you to come," the rector said, shaking hands with Alleyn. "And a great relief to all of us."

Their manner indicated that Alleyn's arrival would remove a sense of personal responsibility. "If you'd like to have a look—?" the doctor said.

The broken body lay huddled on its side. The head

rested on the open Bible. The right hand, rigid in cadaveric spasm, clutched a torn page. Alleyn knelt and Fox came closer with the torch. At the top of the page Alleyn saw the word Ezekiel and a little farther down, Chapter 12.

Using the tip of his finger Alleyn straightened the page. "Look," he said, and pointed to the thirteenth verse. *"My net also will I spread upon him and he shall be taken in my snare."*

The words had been faintly underlined in mauve.

Alleyn stood up and looked round the circle of faces.

"Well," the doctor said, "we'd better see about moving him."

Alleyn said, "I don't think he should be moved just yet."

"Not!" the rector cried out. "But surely—to leave him like this—I mean, after this terrible accident—"

"It has yet to be proved," Alleyn said, "that it was an accident."

There was a sharp sound from Richard De'ath.

"—and I fancy," Alleyn went on, glancing at De'ath, "that it's going to take quite a lot of proving."

After that, events, as Fox observed with resignation, took the course that was to be expected. The local Superintendent said that under the circumstances it would be silly not to ask Alleyn to carry on, the Chief Constable agreed, and appropriate instructions came through from Scotland Yard. The rest of the night was spent in routine procedure. The body having been photographed and the Bible set aside for fingerprinting, both were removed and arrangements put in hand for the inquest.

At dawn Alleyn and Fox climbed the tower. The winding stair brought them to an extremely narrow doorway through which they saw the countryside lying vaporous in the faint light. Fox was about to go through to the balcony when Alleyn stopped him and pointed to the door jambs. They were covered with a growth of stonecrop.

About three feet from the floor this had been brushed off over a space of perhaps four inches and fragments of the microscopic plant hung from the scars. From among these, on either side, Alleyn removed morsels of dark-colored thread. "And here," he sighed, "as sure as fate, we go again. O Lord, O Lord!"

They stepped through to the balcony and there was a sudden whirr and beating of wings as a company of pigeons flew out of the tower. The balcony was narrow and the balustrade indeed very low. "If there's any looking over," Alleyn said, "you, my dear Foxkin, may do it."

Nevertheless he leaned over the balustrade and presently knelt beside it. "Look at this. Bates rested the open Bible here—blow me down flat if he didn't! There's a powder of leather where it scraped on the stone and a fragment where it tore. It must have been moved—outward. Now, why, why?"

"Shoved it accidentally with his knees, then made a grab and overbalanced?"

"But why put the open Bible there? To read by moonlight? *My net also will I spread upon him and he shall be taken in my snare.* Are you going to tell me he underlined it and then dived overboard?"

"I'm not going to tell you anything," Fox grunted and then: "That old chap Edward Pilbrow's down below swabbing the stones. He looks like a beetle."

"Let him look like a rhinoceros if he wants to, but for the love of Mike don't leer over the edge—you give me the willies. Here, let's pick this stuff up before it blows away."

They salvaged the scraps of leather and put them in an envelope. Since there was nothing more to do, they went down and out through the vestry and so home to breakfast.

"Darling," Alleyn told his wife, "you've landed us with a snorter."

"Then you *do* think—?"

"There's a certain degree of fishiness. Now, see here, wouldn't *somebody* have noticed little Bates get up and go out? I know he sat all alone on the back bench, but wasn't there *someone?*"

"The rector?"

"No. I asked him. Too intent on his sermon, it seems."

"Mrs. Simpson? If she looks through her little red curtain she faces the nave."

"We'd better call on her, Fox. I'll take the opportunity to send a couple of cables to New Zealand. She's fat, jolly, keeps the shop-cum-postoffice, and is supposed to read all the postcards. Just your cup of tea. You're dynamite with postmistresses. Away we go."

Mrs. Simpson sat behind her counter doing a crossword puzzle and refreshing herself with licorice. She welcomed Alleyn with enthusiasm. He introduced Fox and then he retired to a corner to write out his cables.

"What a catastrophe!" Mrs. Simpson said, plunging straight into the tragedy. "Shocking! As nice a little gentleman as you'd wish to meet, Mr. Fox. Typical New Zealander. Pick him a mile away and a friend of Mr. Alleyn's, I'm told, and if I've said it once I've said it a hundred times, Mr. Fox, they ought to have put something up to prevent it. Wire netting or a bit of ironwork; but, no, they let it go on from year to year and now see what's happened —history repeating itself and giving the village a bad name. Terrible!"

Fox bought a packet of tobacco from Mrs. Simpson and paid her a number of compliments on the layout of her shop, modulating from there into an appreciation of the village. He said that one always found such pleasant com-

pany in small communities. Mrs. Simpson was impressed
and offered him a piece of licorice.

"As for pleasant company," she chuckled, "that's as may
be, though by and large I suppose I mustn't grumble. I'm a
cockney and a stranger here myself, Mr. Fox. Only twenty-
four years and that doesn't go for anything with this lot."

"Ah," Fox said, "then you wouldn't recollect the former
tragedies. Though to be sure," he added, "you wouldn't do
that in any case, being much too young, if you'll excuse the
liberty, Mrs. Simpson."

After this classic opening Alleyn was not surprised to
hear Mrs. Simpson embark on a retrospective survey of life
in Little Copplestone. She was particularly lively on Miss
Hart, who, she hinted, had had her eye on Mr. Richard
De'ath for many a long day.

"As far back as when Old Jimmy Wagstaff died, which
was why she was so set on getting the next-door house; but
Mr. De'ath never looked at anybody except Ruth Wall, and
her head-over-heels in love with young Castle, which together with her falling to her destruction when feeding
pigeons led Mr. De'ath to forsake religion and take to
drink, which he has done something cruel ever since.

"They do say he's got a terrible temper, Mr. Fox, and it's
well known he give Old Jimmy Wagstaff a thrashing on
account of straying cattle and threatened young Castle, saying if he couldn't have Ruth, nobody else would, but fair's
fair and personally I've never seen him anything but nice-
mannered, drunk or sober. Speak as you find's my motto
and always has been, but these old maids, when they take a
fancy they get it pitiful hard. You wouldn't know a word of
nine letters meaning 'pale-faced lure like a sprat in a fishy
story,' would you?"

Fox was speechless, but Alleyn, emerging with his cables,
suggested "whitebait."

"Correct!" shouted Mrs. Simpson. "Fits like a glove. Although it's not a bit like a sprat and a quarter the size. Cheating, I call it. Still, it fits." She licked her indelible pencil and triumphantly added it to her crossword.

They managed to lead her back to Timothy Bates. Fox, professing a passionate interest in organ music, was able to extract from her that when the rector began his sermon she had in fact dimly observed someone move out of the back bench and through the doors. "He must have walked round the church and in through the vestry and little did I think he was going to his death," Mrs. Simpson said with considerable relish and a sigh like an earthquake.

"You didn't happen to hear him in the vestry?" Fox ventured, but it appeared that the door from the vestry into the organ loft was shut and Mrs. Simpson, having settled herself to enjoy the sermon with, as she shamelessly admitted, a bag of chocolates, was not in a position to notice.

Alleyn gave her his two cables: the first to Timothy Bates's partner in New Zealand and the second to one of his own colleagues in that country asking for any available information about relatives of the late William James Wagstaff of Little Copplestone, Kent, possibly resident in New Zealand after 1921, and of any persons of the name of Peter Rook Hadet or Naomi Balbus Hadet.

Mrs. Simpson agitatedly checked over the cables, professional etiquette and burning curiosity struggling together in her enormous bosom. She restrained herself, however, merely observing that an event of this sort set you thinking, didn't it?

"And no doubt," Alleyn said as they walked up the lane, "she'll be telling her customers that the next stop's bloodhounds and manacles."

"Quite a tidy armful of lady, isn't she, Mr. Alleyn?" Fox calmly rejoined.

The inquest was at 10:20 in the smoking room of the Star and Garter. With half an hour in hand, Alleyn and Fox visited the churchyard. Alleyn gave particular attention to the headstones of Old Jimmy Wagstaff, Ruth Wall, and Simon Castle. "No mention of the month or day," he said. And after a moment: "I wonder. We must ask the rector."

"No need to ask the rector," said a voice behind them. It was Miss Hart. She must have come soundlessly across the soft turf. Her air was truculent. "Though why," she said, "it should be of interest, I'm sure I don't know. Ruth Wall died on August thirteenth, 1921. It was a Saturday."

"You've a remarkable memory," Alleyn observed.

"Not as good as it sounds. That Saturday afternoon I came to do the flowers in the church. I found her and I'm not likely ever to forget it. Young Castle went the same way almost a month later. September twelfth. In my opinion there was never a more glaring case of suicide. I believe," Miss Hart said harshly, "in facing facts."

"She was a beautiful girl, wasn't she?"

"I'm no judge of beauty. She set the men by the ears. *He* was a fine-looking young fellow. Fanny Wagstaff did her best to get *him*."

"Had Ruth Wall," Alleyn asked, "other admirers?"

Miss Hart didn't answer and he turned to her. Her face was blotted with an unlovely flush. "She ruined two men's lives, if you want to know. Castle and Richard De'ath," said Miss Hart. She turned on her heel and without another word marched away.

"September twelfth," Alleyn murmured. "That would be a Monday, Br'er Fox."

"So it would," Fox agreed, after a short calculation, "so it would. Quite a coincidence."

"Or not, as the case may be. I'm going to take a gamble on this one. Come on."

They left the churchyard and walked down the lane,

overtaking Edward Pilbrow on the way. He was wearing his town crier's coat and hat and carrying his bell by the clapper. He manifested great excitement when he saw them.

"Hey!" he shouted, "what's this I hear? Murder's the game, is it? What a go! Come on, gents, let's have it. Did 'e fall or was 'e pushed? Hor, hor, hor! Come on."

"Not until after the inquest," Alleyn shouted.

"Do we get a look at the body?"

"Shut up," Mr. Fox bellowed suddenly.

"I got to know, haven't I? It'll be the smartest bit of crying I ever done, this will! I reckon I might get on the telly with this. 'Town crier tells old-world village death stalks the churchyard.' Hor, hor, hor!"

"Let us," Alleyn whispered, "leave this horrible old man."

They quickened their stride and arrived at the pub, to be met with covert glances and dead silence.

The smoking room was crowded for the inquest. Everybody was there, including Mrs. Simpson who sat in the back row with her candies and her crossword puzzle. It went through very quickly. The rector deposed to finding the body. Richard De'ath, sober and less truculent than usual, was questioned as to his sojourn outside the churchyard and said he'd noticed nothing unusual apart from hearing a disturbance among the pigeons roosting in the balcony. From where he stood, he said, he couldn't see the face of the tower.

An open verdict was recorded.

Alleyn had invited the rector, Miss Hart, Mrs. Simpson, Richard De'ath, and, reluctantly, Edward Pilbrow, to join him in the Bar-Parlor and had arranged with the landlord that nobody else would be admitted. The Public Bar, as a result, drove a roaring trade.

When they had all been served and the hatch closed,

Alleyn walked into the middle of the room and raised his hand. It was the slightest of gestures but it secured their attention.

He said, "I think you must all realize that we are not satisfied this was an accident. The evidence against accident has been collected piecemeal from the persons in this room and I am going to put it before you. If I go wrong I want you to correct me. I ask you to do this with absolute frankness, even if you are obliged to implicate someone who you would say was the last person in the world to be capable of a crime of violence."

He waited. Pilbrow, who had come very close, had his ear cupped in his hand. The rector looked vaguely horrified. Richard De'ath suddenly gulped down his double whiskey. Miss Hart coughed over her lemonade and Mrs. Simpson avidly popped a peppermint cream in her mouth and took a swig of her port-and-raspberry.

Alleyn nodded to Fox, who laid Mr. Bates's Bible, open at the flyleaf, on the table before him.

"The case," Alleyn said, "hinges on this book. You have all seen the entries. I remind you of the recorded deaths in 1779 of the three Hadets—Stewart Shakespeare, Naomi Balbus, and Peter Rook. To each of these is attached a biblical text suggesting that they met their death by violence. There have never been any Hadets in this village and the days of the week are wrong for the given dates. They are right, however, for the year 1921 and *they fit the deaths*, all by falling from a height, of William Wagstaff, Ruth Wall, and Simon Castle.

"By analogy the Christian names agree. William suggests Shakespeare. Naomi—Ruth; Balbus—a wall. Simon —Peter; and a Rook is a Castle in chess. And Hadet," Alleyn said without emphasis, "is an anagram of Death."

"Balderdash!" Miss Hart cried out in an unrecognizable voice.

"No, it's not," said Mrs. Simpson. "It's jolly good crossword stuff."

"Wicked balderdash. Richard!"

De'ath said, "Be quiet. Let him go on."

"We believe," Alleyn said, "that these three people met their deaths by one hand. Motive is a secondary consideration, but it is present in several instances, predominantly in one. Who had cause to wish the death of these three people? Someone whom old Wagstaff had bullied and to whom he had left his money and who killed him for it. Someone who was infatuated with Simon Castle and bitterly jealous of Ruth Wall. Someone who hoped, as an heiress, to win Castle for herself and who, failing, was determined nobody else should have him. Wagstaff's orphaned niece—Fanny Wagstaff."

There were cries of relief from all but one of his hearers. He went on. "Fanny Wagstaff sold everything, disappeared, and was never heard of again in the village. But twenty-four years later she returned, and has remained here ever since."

A glass crashed to the floor and a chair overturned as the vast bulk of the postmistress rose to confront him.

"Lies! *Lies!*" screamed Mrs. Simpson.

"Did you sell everything again, before leaving New Zealand?" he asked as Fox moved forward. "Including the Bible, Miss Wagstaff?"

"But," Troy said, "how could you be so sure?"

"She was the only one who could leave her place in the church unobserved. She was the only one fat enough to rub her hips against the narrow door jambs. She uses an indelible pencil. We presume she arranged to meet Bates on the balcony, giving a cock-and-bull promise to tell him something nobody else knew about the Hadets. She indicated the text with her pencil, gave the Bible a shove, and, as he leaned out to grab it, tipped him over the edge.

"In talking about 1921 she forgot herself and described the events as if she had been there. She called Bates a typical New Zealander but gave herself out to be a Londoner. She said whitebait are only a quarter of the size of sprats. New Zealand whitebait are—English whitebait are about the same size.

"And as we've now discovered, she didn't send my cables. Of course she thought poor little Bates was hot on her tracks, especially when she learned that he'd come here to see me. She's got the kind of crossword-puzzle mind that would think up the biblical clues, and would get no end of a kick in writing them in. She's overwhelmingly conceited and vindictive."

"Still—"

"I know. Not good enough if we'd played the waiting game. But good enough to try shock tactics. We caught her off her guard and she cracked up."

"Not," Mr. Fox said, "a nice type of woman."

Alleyn strolled to the gate and looked up the lane to the church. The spire shone golden in the evening sun.

"The rector," Alleyn said, "tells me he's going to do something about the balcony."

"Mrs. Simpson, née Wagstaff," Fox remarked, "suggested wire netting."

"And she ought to know," Alleyn said and turned back to the cottage.

OTHER STORIES

The Hand In The Sand

Truth may or may not be stranger than fiction. It is certainly less logical. Consider the affair of the severed hand at Christchurch, New Zealand, in 1885. Late in the afternoon of December 16th of that year, the sergeant on duty at the central police station was visited by two brothers and their respective small sons. They crowded into his office and, with an air of self-conscious achievement, slapped down a parcel, wrapped in newspaper, on his desk. Their name, they said, was Godfrey.

The sergeant unwrapped the parcel. He disclosed, nestling unattractively in folds of damp newsprint, a human hand. It was wrinkled and pallid like the hand of a laundress on washing day. On the third finger, left hand, was a gold ring.

The Godfreys, brothers and sons, made a joint announcement. "That's Howard's hand," they said virtually in unison and then added, in explanation, "bit off by a shark."

They looked significantly at a poster pasted on the wall of the police office. The poster gave a description of one Arthur Howard and offered a reward for information as to his whereabouts. The Godfreys also produced an advertisement in a daily paper of two months earlier:

Fifty Pounds Reward. Arthur Howard, drowned at Sumner on Saturday last. Will be given for the recovery of the body or the first portion received thereof recognizable. Apply Times Office.

The Godfreys were ready to make a statement. They had spent the day, it seemed, at Taylor's Mistake, a lonely bay not far from the seaside resort of Sumner, where Arthur Rannage Howard had been reported drowned on October 10th. At about two o'clock in the afternoon, the Godfreys had seen the hand lying in the sand below high-water mark.

Elisha, the elder brother, begged the sergeant to examine the ring. The sergeant drew it off the cold, wrinkled finger. On the inside were the initials A. H.

The Godfreys were sent away without a reward. From that moment they were kept under constant observation by the police.

A few days later, the sergeant called upon Mrs. Sarah Howard. At sight of the severed hand, she cried out—in tears—that it was her husband's.

Later, a coroner's inquest was held on the hand. Three insurance companies were represented. If the hand was Howard's hand, they were due to pay out, on three life policies, sums amounting to 2,400 pounds. The policies had all been transferred into the name of Sarah Howard.

The circumstances of what the coroner called "the alleged accident" were gone over at the inquest. On October 10, 1885, Arthur Howard, a railway workshop fitter, had walked from Christchurch to Sumner. On his way he fell in with other foot-sloggers who remembered his clothes and his silver watch on a gold chain and that he had said he meant to go for a swim at Sumner where, in those days, the waters were shark infested.

The next morning a small boy had found Howard's clothes and watch on the end of the pier at Sumner. A few days later insurance had been applied for and refused, the advertisement had been inserted in the paper and, as if in answer to the widow's prayer, the Godfreys, on December 16th, had discovered the hand.

But there also appeared the report of no less than ten

doctors who had examined the hand. The doctors, after the manner of experts, disagreed in detail but, in substance, agreed upon three points.

1) The hand had not lain long in the sea.

2) Contrary to the suggestions of the brothers Godfrey, it had not been bitten off by a shark but had been severed by the teeth of a hacksaw.

3) The hand was that of a *woman.*

This damaging report was followed by a statement from an engraver. The initials A. H., on the inside of the ring, had not been made by a professional's tool, said this report, but had been scratched by some amateur.

The brothers Godfrey were called in and asked whether, in view of the evidence, they would care to make a further statement.

Elisha Godfrey then made what must have struck the police as one of the most impertinently unlikely depositions in the annals of investigation.

Elisha said that in his former statement he had withheld certain information which he would now divulge. Elisha said that he and his brother had been sitting on the sands when from behind a boulder, there appeared a man wearing blue goggles and a red wig and saying, "Come here! There's a man's hand on the beach!"

This multi-colored apparition led Elisha and his brother to the hand, and Elisha had instantly declared, "That's Howard's hand."

The goggles and wig had then said, "Poor fellow . . . poor fellow."

"Why didn't you tell us before about this chap in the goggles and wig?" the police asked.

"Because," said Elisha, "he begged me to promise I wouldn't let anyone know he was there."

Wearily, a sergeant shoved a copy of this amazing deposition across to Elisha. "If you've still got the nerve, sign it."

The Godfreys read it through and angrily signed.

The police, in the execution of their duty, made routine inquiries for information about a gentleman in blue goggles and red wig in the vicinity of Sumner and Taylor's Mistake on the day in question.

To their intense astonishment they found what they were after.

Several persons came forward saying that they had been accosted by this bizarre figure, who excitedly showed them a paper with the Godfreys' name and address on it and told them that the Godfreys had found Howard's hand.

The police stepped up their inquiries and extended them the length and breadth of New Zealand. The result was a spate of information.

The wig and goggles had been seen on the night of the alleged drowning, going north in the ferry steamer. The man who wore them had been run in for insulting a woman, who had afterwards refused to press charges. He had taken jobs on various farms. Most strangely, he had appeared at dawn by the bedside of a fellow worker and had tried to persuade this man to open a grave with him. His name, he had said, was Watt. Finally, and most interesting of all, it appeared that on the 18th of December the goggles and wig had gone for a long walk with Mrs. Sarah Howard.

Upon this information, the police arrested the Godfrey brothers and Mrs. Howard on a charge of attempting to defraud the insurance companies.

But a more dramatic arrest was made in a drab suburb of the capital city. Here the police ran to earth a strange figure in clothes too big for him, wearing blue goggles and a red wig. It was the missing Arthur Howard.

At the trial, a very rattled jury found the Godfreys and Mrs. Howard "not guilty" on both counts and Howard guilty on the second count of attempting to obtain money by fraud.

So far, everything ties up quite neatly. What won't make sense is that Howard did his best to look like a disguised man, but came up with the most eye-catching "disguise" imaginable.

No clue has ever been produced as to the owner of the hand. Of eight graves that were subsequently opened in search for the body to match the hand, none contained a dismembered body. But the hand had been hacked off by an amateur. Could Howard have bribed a dissecting-room janitor or enlisted the help of some undertaker's assistant? And if, as seemed certain, it was a woman's hand, where was the rest of the woman?

Then there is Howard's extraordinary masquerade. Why make himself so grotesquely conspicuous? Why blaze a trail all over the country? Did his project go a little to his head? Was he, after all, a victim of the artistic temperament?

The late Mr. Justice Alper records that Howard's lawyer told him he knew the answer. But, soon after this, the lawyer died.

I have often thought I would like to use this case as the basis for a detective story, but the material refuses to be tidied up into fiction form. I prefer it as it stands, with all its loose ends dangling. I am loath to concoct the answers. Let this paradoxical affair retain its incredible mystery. It is too good to be anything but true.

The Cupid Mirror

"Bollinger '21," said Lord John Challis.

"Thank you, my lord," said the wine-waiter.

He retrieved the wine-list, bowed and moved away with soft assurance. Lord John let his eyeglass fall and gave his attention to his guest. She at once wrinkled her nose and parted her sealing-wax lips in an intimate smile. It was a pleasant and flattering grimace and Lord John responded to it. He touched his little beard with a thin hand.

"You look charming," he said, "and you dispel all unpleasant thoughts."

"Were they unpleasant?" asked his guest.

"They were uncomplimentary to myself. I was thinking that Benito—the wine-waiter, you know—had grown old."

"But why—?"

"I knew him when we were both young."

The head-waiter materialised, waved away his underlings, and himself delicately served the dressed crab. Benito returned with the champagne. He held the bottle before Lord John's eyeglass and received a nod.

"It is sufficiently iced, my lord," said Benito.

The champagne was opened, tasted, approved, poured out, and the bottle twisted down in the ice. Benito and the head-waiter withdrew.

"They know you very well here," remarked the guest.

"Yes. I dined here first in 1907. We drove from the station in a hansom cab."

"We?" murmured his guest.

"She, too, was charming. It is extraordinary how like the fashions of to-day are to those of my day. Those sleeves. And she wore a veil, too, and sat under the china cupid mirror as you do now."

"And Benito poured out the champagne?"

"And Benito poured out the champagne. He was a rather striking looking fellow in those days. Black eyes, brows that met over his nose. A temper, you'd have said."

"You seem to have looked carefully at him," said the guest lightly.

"I had reason to."

"Come," said the guest with a smile, "I know you have a story to tell and I am longing to hear it."

"Really?"

"Really."

"Very well, then."

Lord John leant forward a little in his chair.

"At the table where that solitary lady sits—yes—the table behind me—I am looking at it now in the cupid mirror—there sat in those days an elderly woman who was a devil. She had come for the cure and had brought with her a miserable niece whom she underpaid and bullied and humiliated after the manner of old devils all the world over. The girl might have been a pretty girl, but all the spirit was scared out of her. Or so it seemed to me. There were atrocious scenes. On the third evening—"

"The third?" murmured the guest, raising her thinned eyebrows.

"We stayed a week," explained Lord John. "At every meal that dreadful old woman, brandishing a repulsive ear-trumpet, would hector and storm. The girl's nerves had gone, and sometimes from sheer fright she was clumsy. Her mistakes were anathematised before the entire dining-room. She was reminded of her dependence and constantly of the circumstance of her being a beneficiary under the aunt's will. It was disgusting—abominable. They never sat through a meal without the aunt sending the niece on some errand, so that people began to wait for the moment when the girl, miserable and embarrassed, would rise and walk through the tables, pursued by that voice. I don't suppose that the other guests meant to be unkind but many of them were ill-mannered enough to stare at her and wait for her reappearance with shawl, or coat, or book, or bag, or medicine. She used to come back through the tables with increased gaucherie. Every step was an agony and then, when she was seated, there would be merciless criticism of her walk, her elbows, her colour, her pallor. I saw it all in the little cupid mirror. Benito came in for his share too. That atrocious woman would order her wine, change her mind, order again, say it was corked, not the vintage she ordered, complain to the head-waiter—I can't tell you what else. Benito was magnificent. Never by a hairsbreadth did he vary his courtesy."

"I suppose it is all in their day's work," said the guest.

"I suppose so. Let us hope there are not many cases as advanced as that harridan's. Once I saw him glance with a sort of compassion at the niece. I mean, I saw his image in the cupid mirror."

Lord John filled his guest's glass and his own.

"There was also," he continued, "her doctor. I indulge my hobby of speaking ill of the dead and confess that I did not like him. He was the local fashionable doctor of those days; a *soi-disant* gentleman with a heavy moustache and clothes that were just a little too immaculate. I was, and still am, a snob. He managed to establish himself in the good graces of the aunt. She left him the greater part of her very considerable fortune. More than she left the girl. There was never any proof that he was aware of this circumstance but I can find no other explanation for his extraordinary forbearance. He prescribed for her, sympathised, visited, agreed, flattered. God knows what he didn't do. And he dined. He dined on the night she died."

"Oh," said the guest lifting her glass in both hands, and staring at her lacquered fingertips, "she died, did she?"

"Yes. She died in the chair occupied at this moment by the middle-aged lady with nervous hands."

"You are very observant," remarked his companion.

"Otherwise I should not be here again in such delightful circumstances. I can see the lady with nervous hands in the cupid mirror, just as I could see that hateful old woman. She had been at her worst all day, and at luncheon the niece had been sent on three errands. From the third she returned in tears with the aunt's sleeping tablets. She always took one before her afternoon nap. The wretched girl had forgotten them and on her return must needs spill them all over the carpet. She and Benito scrambled about under the table, retrieving the little tablets, while the old woman gibed at the girl's clumsiness. She then refused to take one at all and the girl was sent off lunchless and in disgrace."

Lord John touched his beard with his napkin, inspected his half bird, and smiled reminiscently.

"The auguries for dinner were inauspicious. It began badly. The doctor heard of the luncheon disaster. The first dish was sent away with the customary threat of complaint to the manager. However, the doctor succeeded in pouring oil, of which he commanded a great quantity, on the troubled waters. He told her that she must not tire herself, patted her claw with his large white hand, and bullied the waiters on her behalf. He had brought her some new medicine which she was to take after dinner, and he laid the little packet of powder by her plate. It was to replace the stuff she had been taking for some time."

"How did you know all this?"

"Have I forgotten to say she was deaf? Not the least of that unfortunate girl's ordeals was occasioned by the necessity to shout all her answers down an ear-trumpet. The aunt had the deaf person's trick of speaking in a toneless yell. One lost nothing of their conversation. That dinner was quite frightful. I still see and hear it. The little white packet lying on the right of the aunt's plate. The niece nervously crumbling her bread with trembling fingers and eating nothing. The medical feller talking, talking, talking. They drank red wine with their soup and then Benito brought champagne. Veuve Clicquot, it was. He said, as he did a moment ago, 'It is sufficiently iced,' and poured a little into the aunt's glass. She sipped it and said it was not cold enough. In a second there was another formidible scene. The aunt screamed abuse, the doctor supported and soothed her, another bottle was brought and put in the cooler. Finally Benito gave them their Clicquot. The girl scarcely touched hers, and was asked if she thought the aunt had ordered champagne at thirty shillings a bottle for the amusement of seeing her niece turn up her nose at it. The girl suddenly drank half a glass at one gulp. They all drank. The Clicquot seemed to work its magic even on that appalling woman. She became quieter. I no longer looked into the cupid mirror but rather into the eyes of my vis-à-vis."

Lord John's guest looked into his tired amused old face and smiled faintly.

"Is that all?" she asked.

"No. When I next watched the party at that table a waiter had brought their coffee. The doctor feller emptied the powder from the packet into the aunt's cup. She drank it and made a great fuss about the taste. It looked as though we were in for another scene when she fell sound asleep."

"What!" exclaimed the guest.

"She fell into a deep sleep," said Lord John. "And died."

The lady with the nervous hands rose from her table and walked slowly past them out of the dining-room.

"Not immediately," continued Lord John, "but about two hours later in her room upstairs. Three waiters carried her out of the dining-room. Her mouth was open, I remember, and her face was puffy and had reddish-violet spots on it."

"What killed her?"

"The medical gentleman explained at the inquest that her heart had always been weak."

"But—you didn't believe that? You think, don't you, that the doctor poisoned her coffee?"

"Oh, no. In his own interest he asked that the coffee and the remaining powder in the paper should be analysed. They were found to contain nothing more dangerous than a very mild bromide."

"Then—? You suspected something I am sure. Was it the niece? The champagne—?"

"The doctor was between them. No. I remembered, however, the luncheon incident. The sleeping tablets rolling under the table."

"And the girl picked them up?"

"Assisted by Benito. During the dispute at dinner over the champagne, Benito filled the glasses. His napkin hid the aunt's glass from her eyes. Not from mine, however. You see, I saw his hand reflected from above in the little cupid mirror."

There was a long silence.

"Exasperation," said Lord John, "may be the motive of many unsolved crimes. By the way I was reminded of this story by the lady with the nervous hands. She has changed a good deal of course, but she still has that trick of crumbling her bread with her fingers."

The guest stared at him.

"Have we finished?" asked Lord John. "Shall we go?" They rose. Benito, bowing, held open the dining-room door.

"Good evening, Benito," said Lord John.

"Good evening, my lord," said Benito.

A Fool About Money

"Where money is concerned," Harold Hancock told his audience at the enormous cocktail party, "my poor Hersey —and she won't mind my saying so, will you, darling?—is the original dumbbell. Did I ever tell you about her trip to Dunedin?"

Did he ever tell them? Hersey thought. Wherever two or three were gathered did he ever fail to tell them? The predictable laugh, the lovingly coddled pause, and the punchline led into and delivered like an act of God—did he, for pity's sake, ever tell them!

Away he went, mock-serious, empurpled, expansive, and Hersey put on the comic baby face he expected of her. Poor Hersey, they would say, such a goose about money. It's a shame to laugh.

"It was like this—" Harold began. . . .

It had happened twelve years ago when they were first in New Zealand. Harold was occupied with a conference in Christchurch and Hersey was to stay with a friend in Dunedin. He had arranged that she would draw on his firm's Dunedin branch for money and take in her handbag no more than what she needed for the journey. "You know how you are," Harold said.

He arranged for her taxi, made her check that she had her ticket and reservation for the train, and reminded her that if on the journey she wanted cups of tea or synthetic coffee or a cooked lunch, she would have to take to her heels at the appropriate stations and vie with the competitive male. At this point her taxi was announced and Harold was summoned to a long-distance call from London.

"You push off," he said. "Don't forget that fiver on the dressing table. You won't need it but you'd better have it. Keep your wits about you. 'Bye, dear."

He was still shouting into the telephone when she left.

She had enjoyed the adventurous feeling of being on her own. Although Harold had said you didn't in New Zealand, she tipped the taxi driver and he carried her suitcase to the train and found her seat, a single one just inside the door of a Pullman car.

A lady was occupying the seat facing hers and next to the window.

She was well-dressed, middle-aged and of a sandy complexion with noticeably light eyes. She had put a snakeskin dressing case on the empty seat beside her.

"It doesn't seem to be taken," she said, smiling at Hersey.

They socialized—tentatively at first and, as the journey progressed, more freely. The lady (in his version Harold always called her Mrs. X) confided that she was going all the way to Dunedin to visit her daughter. Hersey offered reciprocative information. In the world outside, plains and mountains performed a grandiose kind of measure and telegraph wires leaped and looped with frantic precision.

An hour passed. The lady extracted a novel from her dressing case and Hersey, impressed by the handsome appointments and immaculate order, had a good look inside the case.

The conductor came through the car intoning, "Ten minutes for refreshments at Ashburton."

"Shall you join in the onslaught?" asked the lady. "It's a free-for-all."

"Shall you?"

"Well—I might. When I travel with my daughter we take turns. I get the morning coffee and she gets the afternoon. I'm a bit slow on my pins, actually."

She made very free use of the word "actually."

Hersey instantly offered to get their coffee at Ashburton and her companion, after a proper show of diffidence, gaily agreed. They explored their handbags for the correct amount. The train uttered a warning scream and everybody crowded into the corridor as it drew up to the platform.

Hersey left her handbag with the lady (an indiscretion heavily emphasized by Harold) and sprinted to the refreshment counter where she was blocked off by a phalanx of men. Train fever was running high by the time she was served and her return trip with brimming cups was hazardous indeed.

The lady was holding both their handbags as if she hadn't stirred an inch.

Between Ashburton and Oamaru, a long stretch, they developed their acquaintanceship further, discovered many tastes in common, and exchanged confidences and names. The lady was called Mrs. Fortescue. Sometimes they dozed. Together, at Oamaru, they joined in an assault on the dining room and together they returned to the carriage where Hersey scuffled in her stuffed handbag for a powder-compact. As usual it was in a muddle.

Suddenly a thought struck her like a blow in the wind and a lump of ice ran down her gullet into her stomach. She made an exhaustive search but there was no doubt about it.

Harold's fiver was gone.

Hersey let the handbag fall in her lap, raised her head, and found that her companion was staring at her with a very curious expression on her face. Hersey had been about to confide her awful intelligence but the lump of ice was exchanged for a coal of fire. She was racked by a terrible suspicion.

"Anything wrong?" asked Mrs. Fortescue in an artificial voice.

Hersey heard herself say, "No. Why?"

"Oh, nothing," she said rather hurriedly. "I thought—perhaps—like me, actually, you have bag trouble."

"I do, rather," Hersey said.

They laughed uncomfortably.

The next hour passed in mounting tension. Both ladies affected to read their novels. Occasionally one of them would look up to find the other one staring at her. Hersey's suspicions increased rampantly.

"Ten minutes for refreshments at Palmerston South," said the conductor, lurching through the car.

Hersey had made up her mind. "Your turn!" she cried brightly.

"Is it? Oh. Yes."

"I think I'll have tea. The coffee was awful."

"So's the tea actually. Always. Do we," Mrs. Fortescue swallowed, "do we really want anything?"

"I do," said Hersey very firmly and opened her handbag. She fished out her purse and took out the correct amount. "And a bun," she said. There was no gainsaying her. "I've got a headache," she lied. "I'll be glad of a cuppa."

When they arrived at Palmerston South, Hersey said, "Shall I?" and reached for Mrs. Fortescue's handbag. But Mrs. Fortescue muttered something about requiring it for change and almost literally bolted. "All that for nothing!" thought Hersey in despair. And then, seeing the elegant dressing case still on the square seat, she suddenly reached out and opened it.

On top of the neatly arranged contents lay a crumpled five-pound note.

At the beginning of the journey when Mrs. Fortescue

had opened the case, there had, positively, been no fiver stuffed in it. Hersey snatched the banknote, stuffed it into her handbag, shut the dressing case, and leaned back, breathing short with her eyes shut.

When Mrs. Fortescue returned she was scarlet in the face and trembling. She looked continuously at her dressing case and seemed to be in two minds whether or not to open it. Hersey died a thousand deaths.

The remainder of the journey was a nightmare. Both ladies pretended to read and to sleep. If ever Hersey had read guilt in a human countenance it was in Mrs. Fortescue's.

"I ought to challenge her," Hersey thought. "But I won't. I'm a moral coward and I've got back my fiver."

The train was already drawing into Dunedin station and Hersey had gathered herself and her belongings when Mrs. Fortescue suddenly opened her dressing case. For a second or two she stared into it. Then she stared at Hersey. She opened and shut her mouth three times. The train jerked to a halt and Hersey fled.

Her friend greeted her warmly. When they were in the car she said, "Oh, before I forget! There's a telegram for you."

It was from Harold.

It said: YOU FORGOT YOUR FIVER, YOU DUMB-BELL. LOVE HAROLD.

Harold had delivered the punchline. His listeners had broken into predictable guffaws. He had added the customary coda: "And she didn't know Mrs. X's address, so she couldn't do a thing about it. So of course to this day Mrs. X thinks Hersey pinched her fiver."

Hersey, inwardly seething, had reacted in the sheepish manner Harold expected of her when from somewhere at the back of the group a wailing broke out.

A lady erupted as if from a football scrimmage. She looked wildly about her, spotted Hersey, and made for her.

"At last, at last!" cried the lady. "After all these years!"

It was Mrs. Fortescue.

"It *was* your fiver!" she gabbled. "It happened at Ashburton when I minded your bag. It was, it was!"

She turned on Harold. "It's all your fault," she amazingly announced. "And mine of course." She returned to Hersey. "I'm dreadfully inquisitive. It's a compulsion. I—I —couldn't resist. I looked at your passport. I looked at everything. And my own handbag was open on my lap. And the train gave one of those recoupling jerks and both our handbags were upset. And I could see you," she chattered breathlessly to Hersey, "coming back with that ghastly coffee."

"So I shoveled things back and there was the fiver on the floor. Well, I had one and I thought it was mine and there wasn't time to put it in my bag, so I slapped it into my dressing case. And then, when I paid my luncheon bill at Oamaru, I found my own fiver in a pocket of my bag."

"Oh, my God!" said Hersey.

"Yes. And I couldn't bring myself to confess. I thought you might leave your bag with me if you went to the loo and I could put it back. But you didn't. And then, at Dunedin, I looked in my dressing case and the fiver was gone. So I thought you knew I knew." She turned on Harold.

"You must have left *two* fivers on the dressing table," she accused.

"Yes!" Hersey shouted. "You did, you did! There were two. You put a second one out to get change."

"Why the hell didn't you say so!" Harold roared.

"I'd forgotten. You know yourself," Hersey said with the glint of victory in her eye, "it's like you always say, darling, I'm such a fool about money."

Morepork

On the morning before he died, Caley Bridgeman woke to the smell of canvas and the promise of a warm day. Bell-birds had begun to drop their two dawn notes into the cool air and a native wood pigeon flopped onto the ridgepole of his tent. He got up and went outside. Beech bush, emerging from the night, was threaded with mist. The voices of the nearby creek and the more distant Wainui River, in endless colloquy with stones and boulders, filled the intervals between bird song. Down beyond the river he glimpsed, through shadowy trees, the two Land-Rovers and the other tents: his wife's; his stepson's; David Wingfield's, the taxidermist's. And Solomon Gosse's. Gosse, with whom he had fallen out.

If it came to that, he had fallen out, more or less, with all of them, but he attached little importance to the circumstance. His wife he had long ago written off as an unintelligent woman. They had nothing in common. She was not interested in bird song.

"Tink. Ding," chimed the bellbirds.

Tonight, if all went well, they would be joined on tape with the little night owl—*Ninox novaeseelandiae*, the ruru, the morepork.

He looked across the gully to where, on the lip of a cliff, a black beech rose high against paling stars. His gear was stowed away at its foot, well hidden, ready to be installed, and now, two hours at least before the campers stirred, was the time to do it.

He slipped down between fern, scrub and thorny undergrowth to where he had laid a rough bridge above a very deep and narrow channel. Through this channel flowed a creek which joined the Wainui below the tents. At that point the campers had dammed it up to make a swimming pool. He had not cared to join in their enterprise.

The bridge had little more than a four-foot span. It consisted of two beech logs resting on the verges and overlaid by split branches nailed across them. Twenty feet below, the creek glinted and prattled. The others had jumped the gap and goaded him into doing it himself. If they tried, he thought sourly, to do it with twenty-odd pounds of gear on their backs, they'd sing a different song.

He arrived at the tree. Everything was in order, packed in green waterproof bags and stowed in a hollow under the roots.

When he climbed the tree to place his parabolic microphone, he found bird droppings, fresh from the night visit of the morepork.

He set to work.

At half-past eleven that morning, Bridgeman came down from an exploratory visit to a patch of beech forest at the edge of the Bald Hill. A tui sang the opening phrase of "Home to Our Mountains," finishing with a consequential splutter and a sound like that made by someone climbing through a wire fence. Close at hand, there was a sudden flutter and a minuscule shriek. Bridgeman moved with the habitual quiet of the bird watcher into a patch of scrub and pulled up short.

He was on the lip of a bank. Below him was the blond poll of David Wingfield.

"What have you done?" Bridgeman said.

The head moved slowly and tilted. They stared at each other. "What have you got in your hands?" Bridgeman said. "Open your hands."

The taxidermist's clever hands opened. A feathered morsel lay in his palm. Legs like twigs stuck up their clenched feet. The head dangled. It was a rifleman, tiniest and friendliest of all New Zealand birds.

"Plenty more where this came from," said David Wingfield. "I wanted it to complete a group. No call to look like that."

"I'll report you."

"Balls."

"Think so? By God, you're wrong. I'll ruin you."

"Ah, stuff it!" Wingfield got to his feet, a giant of a man.

For a moment it looked as if Bridgeman would leap down on him.

"Cut it out," Wingfield said. "I could do you with one hand."

He took a small box from his pocket, put the strangled rifleman in it and closed the lid.

"Gidday," he said. He picked up his shotgun and walked away—slowly.

At noon the campers had lunch, cooked by Susan Bridgeman over the campfire. They had completed the dam, building it up with enormous turfs backed by boulders. Already the creek overflowed above its juncture with the Wainui. They had built up to the top of the banks on either side, because if snow in the back country should melt or torrential rain come over from the west coast, all the creeks and rivers would become torrents and burst through the foothills.

"Isn't he coming in for tucker?" Clive Grey asked his

mother. He never used his stepfather's name if he could avoid it.

"I imagine not," she said. "He took enough to last a week."

"I saw him," Wingfield offered.

"Where?" Solomon Gosse asked.

"In the bush below the Bald Hill."

"Good patch for tuis. Was he putting out his honey pots?"

"I didn't ask," Wingfield said, and laughed shortly.

Gosse looked curiously at him. "Like that, was it?" he said softly.

"Very like that," Wingfield agreed, glancing at Susan. "I imagine he won't be visiting us today," he said. "Or tonight, of course."

"Good," said Bridgeman's stepson loudly.

"Don't talk like that, Clive," said his mother automatically.

"Why not?" he asked, and glowered at her.

Solomon Gosse pulled a deprecating grimace. "This is the hottest day we've had," he said. "Shan't we be pleased with our pool!"

"I wouldn't back the weather to last, though," Wingfield said.

Solomon speared a sausage and quizzed it thoughtfully. "I hope it lasts," he said.

It lasted for the rest of that day and through the following night up to eleven o'clock, when Susan Bridgeman and her lover left their secret meeting place in the bush and returned to the sleeping camp. Before they parted she said, "He wouldn't divorce me. Not if we yelled it from the mountaintop, he wouldn't."

"It doesn't matter now."

The night owl, ruru, called persistently from his station in the tall beech tree.

"More-pork! More-pork!"

Towards midnight came a soughing rumour through the bush. The campers woke in their sleeping bags and felt cold on their faces. They heard the tap of rain on canvas grow to a downpour. David Wingfield pulled on his gum boots and waterproof. He took a torch and went round the tents, adjusting guy ropes and making sure the drains were clear. He was a conscientious camper. His torchlight bobbed over Susan's tent and she called out, "Is that you? Is everything O.K.?"

"Good as gold," he said. "Go to sleep."

Solomon Gosse stuck his head out from under his tent flap. "What a bloody bore," he shouted, and drew it in again.

Clive Grey was the last to wake. He had suffered a recurrent nightmare concerning his mother and his stepfather. It had been more explicit than usual. His body leapt, his mouth was dry and he had what he thought of as a "fit of the jimjams." Half a minute went by to the sound of water —streaming, he thought, out of his dream. Then he recognized it as the voice of the river, swollen so loud that it might be flowing past his tent.

Towards daybreak the rain stopped. Water dripped from the trees, clouds rolled away to the south and the dawn chorus began. Soon after nine there came tentative glimpses of the sun. David Wingfield was first up. He squelched about in gum boots and got a fire going. Soon the incense of wood smoke rose through the trees with the smell of fresh fried bacon.

After breakfast they went to look at the dam. Their pool had swollen up to the top of both banks, but the construction held. A half-grown sapling, torn from its stand, swept downstream, turning and seeming to gesticulate. Beyond their confluence the Wainui, augmented by the creek, thundered down its gorge. The campers were obliged to shout.

"Good thing," Clive mouthed, "we don't want to get out. Couldn't. Marooned. Aren't we?" He appealed to Wingfield and pointed to the waters. Wingfield made a dismissive gesture. "Not a hope," he signalled.

"How long?" Susan asked, peering into Wingfield's face. He shrugged and held up three and then five fingers. "My God!" she was seen to say.

Solomon Gosse patted her arm. "Doesn't matter. Plenty of grub," he shouted.

Susan looked at the dam where the sapling had jammed. Its limbs quivered. It rolled, heaved, thrust up a limb, dragged it under and thrust it up again.

It was a human arm with a splayed hand. Stiff as iron, it swung from side to side and pointed at nothing or everything.

Susan Bridgeman screamed. There she stood, with her eyes and mouth open. "Caley!" she screamed. "It's Caley!"

Wingfield put his arm round her. He and Solomon Gosse stared at each other over her head.

Clive could be heard to say: "It *is* him, isn't it? That's his shirt, isn't it? He's drowned, isn't he?"

As if in affirmation, Caley Bridgeman's face, foaming and sightless, rose and sank and rose again.

Susan turned to Solomon as if to ask him if it was true. Her knees gave way and she slid to the ground. He knelt and raised her head and shoulders.

Clive made some sort of attempt to replace Solomon, but David Wingfield came across and used the authority of the physically fit. "Better out of this," he could be heard to say. "I'll take her."

He lifted Susan and carried her up to her tent.

Young Clive made an uncertain attempt to follow. Solomon Gosse took him by the arm and walked him away from the river into a clearing in the bush where they could make themselves heard, but when they got there found nothing to say. Clive, looking deadly sick, trembled like a wet dog.

At last Solomon said, "I can't b-believe this. It simply isn't true."

"I ought to go to her. To Mum. It ought to be me, with her."

"David will cope."

"It ought to be me," Clive repeated, but made no move. Presently he said, "It can't be left there."

"David will cope," Solomon repeated. It sounded like a slogan.

"David can't walk on the troubled waters," Clive returned on a note of hysteria. He began to laugh.

"Shut up, for God's sake."

"Sorry. I can't help it. It's so grotesque."

"*Listen.*"

Voices could be heard, the snap of twigs broken underfoot and the thud of boots on soft ground. Into the clearing walked four men in single file. They had packs on their backs and guns under their arms and an air of fitting into their landscape. One was bearded, two clean-shaven, and the last had a couple of days' growth. When they saw Solomon and Clive they all stopped.

"Hullo, there! Good morning to you," said the leader. "We saw your tents." He had an English voice. His clothes, well-worn, had a distinctive look which they would have retained if they had been in rags.

Solomon and Clive made some sort of response. The man looked hard at them. "Hope you don't mind if we walk through your camp," he said. "We've been deer-stalking up at the head of Welshman's Creek but looked like getting drowned. So we've walked out."

Solomon said. "He's—we've both had a shock."

Clive slid to the ground and sat doubled up, his face on his arms.

The second man went to him. The first said, "If it's illness—I mean, this is Dr. Mark, if we can do anything."

Solomon said, "I'll tell you." And did.

They did not exclaim or overreact. The least talkative of them, the one with the incipient beard, seemed to be regarded by the others as some sort of authority and it turned out, subsequently, that he was their guide: Bob Johnson, a high-country man. When Solomon had finished, this Bob, with a slight jerk of his head, invited him to move away. The doctor had sat down beside Clive, but the others formed a sort of conclave round Solomon, out of Clive's hearing.

"What about it, Bob?" the Englishman said.

Solomon, too, appealed to the guide. "What's so appalling," he said, "is that it's there. Caught up. Pinned against the dam. The arm jerking to and fro. We don't know if we can get to it."

"Better take a look," said Bob Johnson.

"It's down there, through the b-bush. If you don't mind," said Solomon, "I'd—I'd be glad not to go b-back just yet."

"She'll be right," said Bob Johnson. "Stay where you are."

He walked off unostentatiously, a person of authority, followed by the Englishman and their bearded mate. The Englishman's name, they were to learn, was Miles Curtis-Vane. The other was called McHaffey. He was the local schoolmaster in the nearest township downcountry and was of a superior and, it would emerge, cantankerous disposition.

Dr. Mark came over to Solomon. "Your young friend's pretty badly shocked," he said. "Were they related?"

"No. It's his stepfather. His mother's up at the camp. She fainted."

"Alone?"

"Dave Wingfield's with her. He's the other member of our lot."

"The boy wants to go to her."

"So do I, if she'll see me. I wonder—would you mind taking charge? Professionally, I mean."

"If there's anything I can do. I think perhaps I should join the others now. Will you take the boy up? If his mother would like to see me, I'll come."

"Yes. All right. Yes, of course."

"Were they very close?" Dr. Mark asked. "He and his stepfather?"

There was a longish pause. "Not very," Solomon said. "It's more the shock. He's very devoted to his mother. We all are. If you don't mind, I'll—"

"No, of course."

So Solomon went to Clive and they walked together to the camp.

"I reckon," Bob Johnson said, after a hard stare at the dam, "it can be done."

Curtis-Vane said, *"They* seem to have taken it for granted it's impossible."

"They may not have the rope for it."

"We have."

"That's right."

"By Cripie," said Bob Johnson, "it'd give you the willies, wouldn't it? That arm. Like a bloody semaphore."

"Well," said Dr. Mark, "what's the drill, then, Bob? Do we make the offer?"

"Here's their other bloke," said Bob Johnson.

David Wingfield came down the bank sideways. He acknowledged Curtis-Vane's introductions with guarded nods.

"If we can be of any use," said Curtis-Vane, "just say the word."

Wingfield said, "It's going to be tough." He had not looked at the dam but he jerked his head in that direction.

"What's the depth?" Bob Johnson asked.

"Near enough five foot."

"We carry rope."

"That'll be good."

Some kind of reciprocity had been established. The two men withdrew together.

"What would you reckon?" Wingfield asked. "How many on the rope?"

"Five," Bob Johnson said, "if they're good. She's coming down solid."

"Sol Gosse isn't all that fit. He's got a crook knee."

"The bloke with the stammer?"

"That's right."

"What about the young chap?"

"All right normally, but he's—you know—shaken up."

"Yeah," said Bob. "Our mob's O.K."

"Including the pom?"

"He's all right. Very experienced."

"With me, we'd be five," Wingfield said.

"For you to say."

"She'll be right, then."

"One more thing," said Bob. "What's the action when we get him out? What do we do with him?"

They debated this. It was decided, subject to Solomon Gosse's and Clive's agreement, that the body should be carried to a clearing near the big beech and left there in a ground sheet from his tent. It would be a decent distance from the camp.

"We could build a bit of a windbreak round it," Bob
said.

"Sure."

"That's his tent, is it? Other side of the creek?"

"Yeah. Beyond the bridge."

"I didn't see any bridge."

"You must have," said Wingfield, "if you came that way.
It's where the creek runs through a twenty-foot-deep gut-
ter. Couldn't miss it."

"Got swept away, it might have."

"Has the creek flooded its banks, then? Up there?"

"No. No, that's right. It couldn't have carried away.
What sort of bridge is it?"

Wingfield described the bridge. "Light but solid," he
said. "He made a job of it."

"Funny," said Bob.

"Yeah. I'll go up and collect the ground sheet from his
tent. And take a look."

"We'd better get this job over, hadn't we? What about
the wife?"

"Sol Gosse and the boy are with her. She's O.K."

"Not likely to come out?"

"Not a chance."

"Fair enough," said Bob.

So Wingfield walked up to Caley Bridgeman's tent to
collect his ground sheet.

When he returned, the others had taken off their packs
and laid out a coil of climbers' rope. They gathered round
Bob, who gave the instructions. Presently the line of five
men was ready to move out into the sliding flood above the
dam.

Solomon Gosse appeared. Bob suggested that he take the
end of the rope, turn it round a tree trunk and stand by to
pay it out or take it up as needed.

And in this way and with great difficulty Caley

Bridgeman's body was brought ashore, where Dr. Mark examined it. It was much battered. They wrapped it in the ground sheet and tied it round with twine. Solomon Gosse stood guard over it while the others changed into dry clothes.

The morning was well advanced and sunny when they carried Bridgeman through the bush to the foot of the bank below that tree which was visited nightly by a morepork. Then they cut manuka scrub.

It was now that Bob Johnson, chopping through a stand of brushwood, came upon the wire, an insulated line, newly laid, running underneath the manuka and well hidden. They traced its course: up the bank under hanging creeper to the tree, up the tree to the tape recorder. They could see the parabolic microphone much farther up.

Wingfield said, "So that's what he was up to."

Solomon Gosse didn't answer at once, and when he did, spoke more to himself than to Wingfield. "What a weird bloke he was," he said.

"Recording bird song, was he?" asked Dr. Mark.

"That's right."

"A hobby?" said Curtis-Vane.

"Passion, more like. He's got quite a reputation for it."

Bob Johnson said, "Will we dismantle it?"

"I think perhaps we should," said Wingfield. "It was up there through the storm. It's a very high-class job—cost the earth. We could dry it off."

So they climbed the tree, in single file, dismantled the microphone and recorder and handed them down from one to another. Dr. Mark, who seemed to know, said he did not think much damage had been done.

And then they laid a rough barrier of brushwood over the body and came away. When they returned to camp, Wingfield produced a bottle of whisky and enamel mugs.

They moved down to the Land-Rovers and sat on their heels, letting the whiskey glow through them.

There had been no sign of Clive or his mother.

Curtis-Vane asked if there was any guessing how long it would take for the rivers to go down and the New Zealanders said, "No way." It could be up for days. A week, even.

"And there's no way out?" Curtis-Vane asked. "Not if you followed down the Wainui on this side, till it empties into the Rangitata?"

"The going's too tough. Even for one of these jobs." Bob indicated the Land-Rovers. "You'd never make it."

There was a long pause.

"Unpleasant," said Curtis-Vane. "Especially for Mrs. Bridgeman."

Another pause. "It is, indeed," said Solomon Gosse.

"Well," said McHaffey, seeming to relish the idea. "If it does last hot, it won't be very nice."

"Cut it out, Mac," said Bob.

"Well, you know what I mean."

Curtis-Vane said, "I've no idea of the required procedure in New Zealand for accidents of this sort."

"Same as in England, I believe," said Solomon. "Report to the police as soon as possible."

"Inquest?"

"That's right."

"Yes. You're one of us, aren't you? A barrister?" asked Curtis-Vane.

"And solicitor. We're both in this country."

"Yes, I know."

A shadow fell across the group. Young Clive had come down from the camp.

"How is she?" Wingfield and Gosse said together.

"O.K.," said Clive. "She wants to be left. She wants me

to thank you," he said awkwardly, and glanced at Curtis-
Vane, "for helping."

"Not a bit. We were glad to do what we could."

Another pause.

"There's a matter," Bob Johnson said, "that I reckon
ought to be considered."

He stood up.

Neither he nor Wingfield had spoken beyond the obliga-
tory mutter over the first drink. Now there was in his manner something that caught them up in a stillness. He did
not look at any of them but straight in front of him and at
nothing.

"After we'd finished up there I went over," he said, "to
the place where the bridge had been. The bridge that you"
—he indicated Wingfield—"talked about. It's down below,
jammed between rocks, half out of the stream."

He waited. Wingfield said, "I saw it. When I collected
the gear." And he, too, got to his feet.

"Did you notice the banks? Where the ends of the
bridge had rested?"

"Yes."

Solomon Gosse scrambled up awkwardly. "Look here,"
he said. "What is all this?"

"They'd overlaid the bank by a good two feet at either
end. They've left deep ruts," said Bob.

Dr. Mark said, "What about it, Bob? What are you
trying to tell us?"

For the first time Bob looked directly at Wingfield.

"Yes," Wingfield said. "I noticed."

"Noticed *what*, for God's sake!" Dr. Mark demanded.
He had been sitting by Solomon, but now moved over to
Bob Johnson. "Come on, Bob," he said. "What's on your
mind?"

"It'd been shifted. Pushed or hauled," said Bob. "So that
the end on this bank of the creek rested on the extreme

edge. It's carried away taking some of the bank with it and scraping down the face of the gulch. You can't miss it."

Clive broke the long silence. "You mean—he stepped on the bridge and fell with it into the gorge? And was washed down by the flood? Is that what you mean?"

"That's what it looks like," said Bob Johnson.

Not deliberately, but as if by some kind of instinctive compulsion, the men had moved into their original groups. The campers: Wingfield, Gosse and Clive; the deer-stalkers: Bob, Curtis-Vane, Dr. Mark and McHaffey.

Clive suddenly shouted at Wingfield, "What are you getting at! You're suggesting there's something crook about this? What the hell do you mean?"

"Shut up, Clive," said Solomon mildly.

"I won't bloody shut up. If there's something wrong I've a right to know what it is. She's my mother and he was—" He caught himself. "If there's something funny about this," he said, "we've a right to know. *Is* there something funny?" he demanded. "Come on. Is there?"

Wingfield said, "O.K. You've heard what's been suggested. If the bridge *was* deliberately moved—manhandled —the police will want to know who did it and why. And I'd have thought," added Wingfield, "you'd want to know yourself."

Clive glared at him. His face reddened and his mouth trembled. He broke out again: "Want to know! Haven't I said I want to know! What the hell are you trying to get at!"

Dr. Mark said, "The truth, presumably."

"Exactly," said Wingfield.

"Ah, stuff it," said Clive. "Like your bloody birds," he added, and gave a snort of miserable laughter.

"What can you mean?" Curtis-Vane wondered.

"I'm a taxidermist," said Wingfield.

"It was a flash of wit," said Dr. Mark.

"I see."

"You all think you're bloody clever," Clive began at the top of his voice, and stopped short. His mother had come through the trees and into the clearing.

She was lovely enough, always, to make an impressive entrance and would have been in sackcloth and ashes if she had taken it into her head to wear them. Now, in her camper's gear with a scarf round her head, she might have been ready for some lucky press photographer.

"Clive darling," she said, "what's the matter? I heard you shouting." Without waiting for his answer, she looked at the deer-stalkers, seemed to settle for Curtis-Vane, and offered her hand. "You've been very kind," she said. "All of you."

"We're all very sorry," he said.

"There's something more, isn't there? What is it?"

Her own men were tongue-tied. Clive, still fuming, merely glowered. Wingfield looked uncomfortable and Solomon Gosse seemed to hover on the edge of utterance and then draw back.

"Please tell me," she said, and turned to Dr. Mark. "Are you the doctor?" she asked.

Somehow, among them, they did tell her. She turned very white but was perfectly composed.

"I see," she said. "You think one of us laid a trap for my husband. That's it, isn't it?"

Curtis-Vane said, "Not exactly that."

"No?"

"No. It's just that Bob Johnson here and Wingfield do think there's been some interference."

"That sounds like another way of saying the same thing."

Solomon Gosse said. "Sue, if it has happened—"

"And it has," said Wingfield.

"—it may well have b-been some gang of yobs. They do

get out into the hills, you know. Shooting the b-birds. Wounding deer. Vandals."

"That's right," said Bob Johnson.

"Yes," she said, grasping at it. "Yes, of course. It may be that."

"The point is," said Bob, "whether something ought to be done about it."

"Like?"

"Reporting it, Mrs. Bridgeman."

"Who to?" Nobody answered. "Report it where?"

"To the police," said Bob Johnson flatly.

"Oh no! *No!*"

"It needn't worry you, Mrs. Bridgeman. This is a national park. A reserve. We want to crack down on these characters."

Dr. Mark said, "Did any of you see or hear anybody about the place?" Nobody answered.

"They'd keep clear of the tents," said Clive at last. "Those blokes would."

"You know," Curtis-Vane said, "I don't think this is any of our business. I think we'd better take ourselves off."

"No!" Susan Bridgeman said. "I want to know if you believe this about vandals." She looked at the deer-stalkers. "Or will you go away thinking one of us laid a trap for my husband? Might one of you go to the police and say so? Does it mean that?" She turned on Dr. Mark. "Does it?"

Solomon said, "Susan, my dear, *no,*" and took her arm.

"I want an answer."

Dr. Mark looked at his hands. "I can only speak for myself," he said. "I would need to have something much more positive before coming to any decision."

"And if you go away, what will you all do? I can tell you. Talk and talk and talk." She turned on her own men. "And so, I suppose, will we. Or won't we? And if we're penned up here for days and days and he's up there, wherever you've put him, not buried, not—"

She clenched her hands and jerked to and fro, beating the ground with her foot like a performer in a rock group. Her face crumpled. She turned blindly to Clive.

"I *won't*," she said. "I *won't* break down. Why should I? I won't."

He put his arms round her. "Don't you, Mum," he muttered. "You'll be all right. It's going to be all right."

Curtis-Vane said, "How about it?" and the deer-stalkers began to collect their gear.

"No!" said David Wingfield loudly. "No! I reckon we've got to thrash it out and you lot had better hear it."

"We'll only b-bitch it all up and it'll get out of hand," Solomon objected.

"No, it won't," Clive shouted. "Dave's right. Get it sorted out like they would at an inquest. Yeah! That's right. Make it an inquest. We've got a couple of lawyers, haven't we? They can keep it in order, can't they? Well, can't they?"

Solomon and Curtis-Vane exchanged glances. "I really don't think—" Curtis-Vane began, when unexpectedly McHaffey cut in.

"I'm in favour," he said importantly. "We'll be called on to give an account of the recovery of the body and that could lead to quite a lot of questions. How I look at it."

"Use your loaf, Mac," said Bob. "All you have to say is what you know. Facts. All the same," he said, "if it'll help to clear up the picture, I'm not against the suggestion. What about you, Doc?"

"At the inquest I'll be asked to speak as to"—Dr. Mark glanced at Susan—"as to the medical findings. I've no objection to giving them now, but I can't think that it can help in any way."

"Well," said Bob Johnson, "it looks like there's no objections. There's going to be a hell of a lot of talk and it might as well be kept in order." He looked round. "*Are* there any objections?" he asked. "Mrs. Bridgeman?"

She had got herself under control. She lifted her chin, squared her shoulders and said, "None."

"Fair enough," said Bob. "All right. I propose we appoint Mr. Curtis-Vane as—I don't know whether chairman's the right thing, but—well—"

"How about coroner?" Solomon suggested, and it would have been hard to say whether he spoke ironically or not.

"Well, C.-V.," said Dr. Mark, "what do you say about it?"

"I don't know what to say, and that's the truth. I—it's an extraordinary suggestion," said Curtis-Vane, and rubbed his head. "Your findings, if indeed you arrive at any, would, of course, have no relevance in any legal proceedings that might follow."

"Precisely," said Solomon.

"We appreciate that," said Bob.

McHaffey had gone into a sulk and said nothing.

"I second the proposal," said Wingfield.

"Any further objections?" asked Bob.

None, it appeared.

"Good. It's over to Mr. Curtis-Vane."

"My dear Bob," said Curtis-Vane, "what's over to me, for pity's sake?"

"Set up the program. How we function, like."

Curtis-Vane and Solomon Gosse stared at each other. "Rather you than me," said Solomon dryly.

"I suppose," Curtis-Vane said dubiously, "if it meets with general approval, we could consult about procedure?"

"Fair go," said Bob and Wingfield together, and Dr. Mark said, "By all means. Leave it to the legal minds."

McHaffey raised his eyebrows and continued to huff.

It was agreed that they should break up: the deer-stalkers would move downstream to a sheltered glade, where they would get their own food and spend the night in pup tents; Susan Bridgeman and her three would return to camp. They would all meet again, in the campers' large communal tent, after an early meal.

When they had withdrawn, Curtis-Vane said, "That young man—the son—is behaving very oddly."

Dr. Mark said, "Oedipus complex, if ever I saw it. Or Hamlet, which is much the same thing."

There was a trestle table in the tent and on either side of it the campers had knocked together two green-wood benches of great discomfort. These were made more tolerable by the introduction of bush mattresses—scrim ticking filled with brushwood and dry fern.

An acetylene lamp had been placed in readiness halfway down the table, but at the time the company assembled there was still enough daylight to serve.

At the head of the table was a folding camp stool for Curtis-Vane, and at the foot, a canvas chair for Susan Bridgeman. Without any discussion, the rest seated themselves in their groups: Wingfield, Clive and Solomon on one side; Bob Johnson, Dr. Mark and McHaffey on the other.

There was no pretence at conversation. They waited for Curtis-Vane.

He said, "Yes, well. Gosse and I have talked this over. It seemed to us that the first thing we must do is to define the purpose of the discussion. We have arrived at this conclusion: We hope to determine whether Mr. Caley Bridgeman's death was brought about by accident or by malpractice. To this end we propose to examine the circumstances preceding his death. In order to keep the proceedings as orderly as possible, Gosse suggests that I lead the inquiry. He also feels that as a member of the camping party, he himself cannot, with propriety, act with me. We both think that statements should be given without interruption and that questions arising out of them should be put with the same decorum. Are there any objections?" He waited. "No?" he said. "Then I'll proceed."

He took a pad of writing paper from his pocket, laid a pen beside it and put on his spectacles. It was remarkable how vividly he had established a courtroom atmosphere. One almost saw a wig on his neatly groomed head.

"I would suggest," he said, "that the members of my own party"—he turned to his left—"may be said to enact, however informally, the function of a coroner's jury."

Dr. Mark pulled a deprecating grimace, Bob Johnson looked wooden and McHaffey self-important.

"And I, if you like, an ersatz coroner," Curtis-Vane concluded. "In which capacity I put my first question. When was Mr. Bridgeman last seen by his fellow campers? Mrs. Bridgeman? Would you tell us?"

"I'm not sure, exactly," she said. "The day he moved to his tent—that was three days ago—I saw him leave the camp. It was in the morning."

"Thank you. Why did he make this move?"

"To record native bird song. He said it was too noisy down here."

"Ah, yes. And was it after he moved that he rigged the recording gear in the tree?"

She stared at him. "Which tree?" she said at last.

Solomon Gosse said, "Across the creek from his tent, Sue. The big beech tree."

"Oh. I didn't know," she said faintly.

Wingfield cut in. "Can I say something? Bridgeman was very cagey about recording. Because of people getting curious and butting in. It'd got to be a bit of an obsession."

"Ah, yes. Mrs. Bridgeman, are you sure you're up to this? I'm afraid—"

"Perfectly sure," she said loudly. She was ashen white.

Curtis-Vane glanced at Dr. Mark. "If you're quite sure. Shall we go on, then?" he said. "Mr. Gosse?"

Solomon said he, too, had watched Bridgeman take his final load away from the camp and had not seen him again. Clive, in turn, gave a similar account.

Curtis-Vane asked, "Did he give any indication of his plans?"

"Not to me," said Gosse. "I wasn't in his good b-books, I'm afraid."

"No?"

"No. He'd left some of his gear on the ground and I stumbled over it. I've got a dicky knee. I didn't do any harm, b-but he wasn't amused."

David Wingfield said, "He was like that. It didn't amount to anything."

"What about you, Mr. Wingfield? You saw him leave, did you?"

"Yes. Without comment."

Curtis-Vane was writing. "So you are all agreed that this was the last time any of you saw him?"

Clive said, "Here! Hold on. You saw him again, Dave. You know. Yesterday."

"That's right," Solomon agreed. "You told us at lunch, Dave."

"So I did. I'd forgotten. I ran across him—or rather he ran across me—below the Bald Hill."

"What were you doing up there?" Curtis-Vane asked pleasantly.

"My own brand of bird-watching. As I told you, I'm a taxidermist."

"And did you have any talk with him?"

"Not to mention. It didn't amount to anything."

His friends shifted slightly on their uneasy bench.

"Any questions?" asked Curtis-Vane.

None. They discussed the bridge. It had been built some three weeks before and was light but strong. It was agreed among the men that it had been shifted and that it would be just possible for one man to lever or push it into the lethal position that was indicated by the state of the ground. Bob Johnson added that he thought the bank might have been dug back underneath the bridge. At this point McHaffey was aroused. He said loftily, "I am not prepared to give an opinion. I should require a closer inspection. But there's a point that has been overlooked, Mr. Chairman," he added with considerable relish. "Has anything been done about footprints?"

They gazed at him.

"About footprints?" Curtis-Vane wondered. "There's scarcely been time, has there?"

"I'm not conversant with the correct procedure," McHaffey haughtily acknowledged. "I should have to look it up. But I do know they come into it early on or they go off colour. It requires plaster of Paris."

Dr. Mark coughed. Curtis-Vane's hand trembled. He blew his nose. Gosse and Wingfield gazed resignedly at McHaffey. Bob Johnson turned upon him. "Cut it out, Mac," he said wearily, and cast up his eyes.

Curtis-Vane said insecurely, "I'm afraid plaster of Paris is not at the moment available. Mr. Wingfield, on your return to camp, did you cross by the bridge?"

"I didn't use the bridge. You can take it on a jump. He built it because of carrying his gear to and fro. It was in place."

"Anybody else see it later in the day?"

"I did," said Clive loudly. As usual, his manner was hostile and he seemed to be on the edge of some sort of demonstration. He looked miserable. He said that yesterday morning he had gone for a walk through the bush and up the creek without crossing it. The bridge had been in position. He had returned at midday, passing through a patch of bush close to the giant beech. He had not noticed the recording gear in the tree.

"I looked down at the ground," he said, and stared at his mother, "not up."

This was said in such an odd manner that it seemed to invite comment. Curtis-Vane asked casually, as a barrister might at a tricky point of cross-examination: "Was there something remarkable about the ground?"

Silence. Curtis-Vane looked up. Clive's hand was in his pocket. He withdrew it. The gesture was reminiscent of a conjurer's: a square of magenta-and-green silk had been produced.

"Only this," Clive said, as if the words choked him. "On the ground. In the bush behind the tree."

His mother's hand had moved, but she checked it and an uneven blush flooded her face. "Is *that* where it was!" she said. "It must have caught in the bushes when I walked up there the other day. Thank you, Clive."

He opened his hand and the scarf dropped on the table. "It was on the ground," he said, "on a bed of cut fern."

"It would be right, then," Curtis-Vane asked, "to say that yesterday morning when Mr. Wingfield met Mr. Bridgeman below the Bald Hill, you were taking your walk through the bush?"

"Yes," said Clive.

"How d'you know that?" Wingfield demanded.

"I heard you. I was quite close."

"Rot."

"Well—not you so much as him. Shouting. He said he'd ruin you," said Clive.

Solomon Gosse intervened. "May I speak? Only to say that it's important for you all to know that B-B-Bridgeman habitually b-behaved in a most intemperate manner. He would fly into a rage over a chipped saucer."

"Thank you," said Wingfield.

Curtis-Vane said, "Why was he cross with you, Mr. Wingfield?"

"He took exception to my work."

"Taxidermy?" asked Dr. Mark.

"Yes. The bird aspect."

"I may be wrong," McHaffey said, and clearly considered it unlikely, "but I thought we'd met to determine when the deceased was last seen alive."

"And you are perfectly right," Curtis-Vane assured him. "I'll put the question: Did any of you see Mr. Bridgeman after noon yesterday?" He waited and had no reply. "Then I've a suggestion to make. If he was alive last evening there's a chance of proving it. You said when we found the apparatus in the tree that he was determined to record the call of the morepork. Is that right?"

"Yes," said Solomon. "It comes to that tree every night."

"If, then, there is a recording of the morepork, he had switched the recorder on. If there is no recording, of course nothing is proved. It might simply mean that for some reason he didn't make one. Can any of you remember if the morepork called last night? And when?"

"I do. I heard it. Before the storm blew up," said Clive. "I was reading in bed by torchlight. It was about ten o'clock. It went on for some time and another one, further away, answered it."

"In your opinion," Curtis-Vane asked the deer-stalkers, "should we hear the recording—if there is one?"

Susan Bridgeman said, "I would rather it wasn't played."

"But why?"

"It—it would be—painful. He always announced his recordings. He gave the date and place and the scientific name. He did that before he set the thing up. To hear his voice—I—I couldn't bear it."

"You needn't listen," said her son brutally.

Solomon Gosse said, "If Susan feels like that about it, I don't think we should play it."

Wingfield said, "But I don't see—" and stopped short. "All right, then," he said. "You needn't listen, Sue. You can go along to your tent, can't you?" And to Curtis-Vane: "I'll get the recorder."

McHaffey said, "Point of order, Mr. Chairman. The equipment should be handled by a neutral agent."

"Oh, for God's sake!" Wingfield exclaimed.

"I reckon he's right, though," said Bob Johnson.

Curtis-Vane asked Susan Bridgeman, very formally, if she would prefer to leave them.

"No. I don't know. If you must do it—" she said, and made no move.

"I don't think we've any right to play it if you don't want us to," Solomon said.

"That," said McHaffey pleasurably, "is a legal point. I should have to—"

"Mr. McHaffey," said Curtis-Vane, "there's nothing 'legal' about these proceedings. They are completely informal. If Mrs. Bridgeman does not wish us to play the record, we shall, of course, not play it."

"Excuse me, Mr. Chairman," said McHaffey, in high dudgeon. "That is your ruling. We shall draw our own conclusions. Personally, I consider Mrs. Bridgeman's attitude surprising. However—"

"Oh!" she burst out. "Play it, play it, play it. Who cares! I don't. Play it."

So Bob Johnson fetched the tape recorder. He put it on the table. "It may have got damaged in the storm," he said. "But it looks O.K. He'd rigged a bit of a waterproof shelter over it. Anyone familiar with the type?"

Dr. Mark said, "It's a superb model. With that parabolic mike, it'd pick up a whisper at ten yards. More than I could ever afford, but I think I understand it."

"Over to you, then, Doc."

It was remarkable how the tension following Susan Bridgeman's behaviour was relaxed by the male homage paid to a complicated mechanism. Even Clive, in his private fury, whatever it was, watched the opening up of the recorder. Wingfield leaned over the table to get a better view. Only Solomon remembered the woman and went to sit beside her. She paid no attention.

"The tape's run out," said Dr. Mark. "That looks promising. One moment; I'll rewind it."

There broke out the manic gibber of a reversed tape played at speed. This was followed by intervals punctuated with sharp dots of sound and another outburst of gibberish.

"Now," said Dr. Mark.

And Caley Bridgeman's voice, loud and pedantic, filled the tent.

"*Ninox novaeseelandiae.* Ruru. Commonly known as Morepork. Tenth January, 1977. Ten-twelve P.M. Beech bush. Parson's Nose Range. Southern Alps. Regarded by the Maori people as a harbinger of death."

A pause. The tape slipped quietly from one spool to the other.

"*More-pork!*"

Startling and clear as if the owl called from the ridgepole, the second note a minor step up from the first. Then a distant answer. The call and answer were repeated at irregular intervals and then ceased. The listeners waited for perhaps half a minute and then stirred.

"Very successful," said Dr. Mark. "Lovely sound."

"*But are you sure? Darling, you swear you're sure?*"

It was Susan Bridgeman. They turned, startled, to look at her. She had got to her feet. Her teeth were closed over the knuckles of her right hand. "No!" she whispered. "No, *no.*"

Solomon Gosse lunged across the table, but the tape was out of his reach and his own voice mocked him.

"Of course I'm sure, my darling. It's foolproof. He'll go down with the b-b-b-bridge."

A TELESCRIPT

Evil Liver

"Crown Court" was a popular British television series produced by Granada Television Limited. The program presented civil and criminal cases, with members of the audience chosen to act as the jury. Each script therefore gives brief alternate endings. Evil Liver was announced as "the first television play by distinguished crime thriller writer Dame Ngaio Marsh." It was recorded at the Granada studios in Manchester on July 23, 1975, and broadcast exactly a month later. It lasted an hour and fifteen minutes, including commercial breaks. Among its cast were William Mervyn as the Judge, Jonathan Elsom as the Prosecution Counsel, William Simons as the Defense Counsel, David Waller as Major Ecclestone, and Joan Hickson as Miss Freebody. Joan Hickson would later become famous for her role as Miss Marple in the British series which was broadcast in the United States on the Public Broadcasting System program Mystery and on the Arts and Entertainment cable network.

Although in line with the format of "Crown Court" the script of Evil Liver does not state who was guilty, Ngaio Marsh included clues which, I believe, point toward her solution. At the end of the play, I'll rejoin you to discuss the various possibilities.

We gratefully acknowledge Granada Television Limited for giving permission to print Evil Liver.

D. G. G.

Cast of Evil Liver:

MR. JUSTICE CAMPBELL
THE PROSECUTION COUNSEL, MARCUS GOLDING, QC
THE DEFENSE COUNSEL, MARTIN O'CONNOR
MARY FREEBODY
MAJOR BASIL ECCLESTONE
DR. STEPHEN SWALE
THOMAS TIDWELL
BARBARA ECCLESTONE
DR. ERNEST SMITHSON
GWENDOLINE MIGGS
WARDRESS
CLERK OF COURT
COURT USHER
JURY FOREMAN
COURT REPORTER

PART ONE

COURT REPORTER: The case you are about to see is fictional. But the jury is made up of members of the public, who will assess the evidence and deliver their own verdict at the end of the program.

(MAJOR ECCLESTONE *is called by the* PROSECUTION COUNSEL. *He takes the witness stand and takes the oath.)*

COURT REPORTER: On March 28th of this year, Miss Mary Freebody's cat was savaged and killed by Bang, an Alsatian dog belonging to her next-door neighbor, Major Basil Ecclestone. A week later, or the 4th April, meat ordered by the Ecclestones was delivered to the outside safe of their house. That evening Major Ecclestone took from the safe some liver for his dog. The dog ate a portion of the liver, was instantly thrown into violent convulsions, and died. The contents of its stomach were analyzed and found to contain a massive amount of cyanide-of-potassium. A tin of wasp exterminator containing a high proportion of cyanide was found in Miss Freebody's shrubbery, half empty. The Major made to the police an accusation of attempted murder against Miss Freebody maintaining that she had had the intention of killing not only his dog but himself. A police investigation has led to her being charged, and she now stands trial at the Crown Court in Fulchester.

GOLDING: . . . Now Major, if you would just describe the events leading to the—the tragedy. You were away from your house, were you not, during the afternoon of April 4th?

MAJOR: Club. Bridge. Every Friday. *(He gestures at the accused)* As was well-known to my neighbor.

GOLDING: Quite so. Your wife was at home, I think?

MAJOR: Migraine. In her room.

GOLDING: Yes. And you returned—when?

MAJOR: Six-thirty.

GOLDING: May we have the order of events from then on?

MAJOR: I—ah—I had a drink. Listened to the wireless. Seven o'clock, I went to the safe and got the dog's food.

GOLDING: Yes. The safe: where is it?

MAJOR: In the outside wall by the back door. It's a two-doored safe; you can open it inside from the pantry. The butcher uses the outside door. So could anyone else. *(At the prisoner)* It's opposite her bathroom window and her side door. And her gate onto the right-of-way. And my gate onto the right-of-way. She could get to it in a matter of seconds.

GOLDING: Quite so. We shall come to that presently, Major. Did you use the inside door of the safe into the pantry when you got the dog's liver?

MAJOR: I did.

GOLDING: Major, can you describe the wrapping at all? Did you happen to notice it?

MAJOR *(Pauses. Looks at prisoner):* Matter of fact I did. Two or three layers of the *Daily Telegraph.*

GOLDING: Good. So you removed the liver from the safe? And then?

MAJOR: I unwrapped the liver, put it in the dog's dish and took it out to the kennel.

GOLDING: The dog being tied up?

MAJOR: Certainly.

GOLDING: And then?

MAJOR: Put it in front of him.

GOLDING: How many pieces?

MAJOR: Two. All there was. Only gave him liver on Fridays. Other nights "Doggy Bits" or "Yaps." Sunday, a bone.

JUDGE: What are "Doggy Bits" and "Yaps"?

GOLDING: I understand they are proprietary canine food, my lord.

(The JUDGE *stares at the* MAJOR *and then nods to* PROSECUTION COUNSEL *to continue.)*

GOLDING: Yes, Major. So you put the dish before the dog. And?

MAJOR: He swallowed part of one piece.

GOLDING: Yes.

MAJOR: It happened at once. Frightful contortions. Convulsions. Agony. By Gad I've seen some terrible sights in my time, but never anything like that. And it was my dog, sir. It was Bang, my dog. My faithful old Bang. *(He breaks down, blows his nose and belches. The* JUDGE *contemplates him stonily.)*

GOLDING: A most painful experience and I am sorry to revive it. Mercifully it was soon over, was it not?

MAJOR: Nothing merciful about it. *(At the prisoner)* A fiendish, cold-blooded murder, deliberately brought about by a filthy-minded, vindictive old cat.

MISS FREEBODY *(standing):* Cat! Cat! You dare to utter the word!

MAJOR: I do so advisedly, madam. Cat. Cat is what I said and cat is what I meant . . .

MISS FREEBODY: Poor defenseless little thing. It was . . .

JUDGE: Silence. Silence. If there is any repetition of this grossly improper behavior I shall treat it as a contempt of court. *(Turning to the* MAJOR) You understand me?

MAJOR *(mumbling):* Great provocation. Regret—

JUDGE: What? Speak up.

MAJOR: I apologize, my lord.

JUDGE: So I should hope. *(He nods to* PROSECUTION COUNSEL)

GOLDING: My lord. Major Ecclestone, I want you to tell His Lordship and the jury what happened after the death of the dog.

MAJOR: My wife came down. At my suggestion, telephoned Dr. Swale.

JUDGE: Why not a veterinary surgeon?

MAJOR: I've no opinion of the local vet.

JUDGE: I see.

MAJOR: Besides, there was my wife.

JUDGE: Your wife, Major Ecclestone?

MAJOR: She was upset, my lord. He gave her a pill. I had a drink.

JUDGE: I see. Yes, Mr. Golding.

GOLDING: Go on please, Major.

MAJOR: Swale took away the remaining piece of liver to be analyzed and he also removed the—the body.

GOLDING: Was there any other event before or at about this time that seemed to you to have any bearing on the matter?

MAJOR: Certainly.

GOLDING: Please tell the court what it was.

MAJOR: That woman's *(The* JUDGE *looks at him)*—The accused's bathroom window overlooks my premises. It's got a venetian blind. She's in the habit of spying on us through the slats. I distinctly saw them—the slats, I mean—open in one place.

GOLDING: When did you see this?

MAJOR: Immediately after Swale left. She'd watched the whole performance. *And* gloated over it.

JUDGE: You are here to relate what you observed, Major, not what you may have conjectured.

GOLDING: Had anything occurred in the past to make bad blood between you and the defendant?

MAJOR: Yes.

GOLDING: What was it?

MAJOR: A cat.

JUDGE: What?

MAJOR: She had a cat, my lord. A mangy brute of a thing—

MISS FREEBODY: Lies! Lies! It was a beautiful little cat. *(The* WARDRESS *quells her.)*

GOLDING *(coughs)*: Never mind what sort of cat it was. Yes, Major?

MAJOR: About a week earlier it strayed into my garden at night. Not for the first time. Always doin' it. Yowlin' and diggin'. Drove my dog frantic. Naturally he broke his tether. Tore it away with a piece of the kennel.

GOLDING: And then?

MAJOR: Ask yourself.

GOLDING: But I'm asking you, you know.

MAJOR: Made short work of the poor pussy. *(He laughs shortly.)*

MISS FREEBODY: *Brute!*

JUDGE: Miss Freebody, you must be silent.

MISS FREEBODY: Pah!

JUDGE: Mr. O'Connor, will you speak to your client? Explain.

O'CONNOR: Certainly, my lord. *(He turns and speaks to the accused who stares over his head, biting her lip.)*

GOLDING: What were the results of the cat's demise?

MAJOR: She kicked up a dust.

GOLDING: In what way?

MAJOR: Waylaid my wife. Went to the police. Wrote letters. Threatened to do me in.

GOLDING: Did you keep any of these letters?

MAJOR: Last one. Burnt the others. About five of them.

GOLDING: May he be shown Exhibit Two?

(The letter is produced, identified, circulated to the JUDGE, *to* COUNSEL *and to the jury.)*

GOLDING: Is that the letter which you retained?

MAJOR: Yes.

GOLDING: It reads, members of the jury: "This is my final warning. Unless your brute is destroyed within the next three days, I shall take steps to insure that justice is done not only upon it but upon yourself. Neither you nor it is fit to live. Take warning. M. E. Freebody." *(To* MAJOR) You received this letter—when?

MAJOR: First of April.

(Laughter)

USHER: Silence in court.

GOLDING: Did you answer it?

MAJOR: Good God, no. Nor any of the others.

JUDGE: Why did you keep it, Major?

MAJOR: Thought of showing it to my lawyer. Decided to ignore it.

GOLDING *(quoting)*: "I shall take steps to see that justice is done not only upon it but upon yourself." Can you describe the nature of the letters you had received before this one?

MAJOR: Certainly. Same thing. Threats.

GOLDING: To you personally?

MAJOR: Saying that my dog ought to die and if I didn't act smartly we both would.

GOLDING: And it was after the death of the dog and in

consideration of all these circumstances, Major, that you decided to go to the police?

MAJOR: Precisely. Decided she meant business and that I was at risk personally. My wife urged me to act.

GOLDING: Thank you, Major Ecclestone.

(GOLDING *sits down.* DEFENSE COUNSEL *rises.*)

O'CONNOR: Major Ecclestone, would you describe yourself as a hot-tempered man?

MAJOR: I would not.

O'CONNOR: As an even-tempered man?

MAJOR: I consider myself to be a reasonable man, sir.

O'CONNOR: I said "even-tempered," Major.

MAJOR: Yes.

O'CONNOR: You get on well with your neighbors and tradesmen, for instance? Do you?

MAJOR: Depends on the neighbors and tradesmen. Ha!

O'CONNOR: Major Ecclestone, during the five years you have lived in Peascale you have quarreled violently with your landlord, your late doctor, the secretary of your club, your postman and your butcher, have you not?

MAJOR: I have not "quarreled violently" with anyone. Where I encounter stupidity, negligence and damned impertinence I made known my objections. That is all.

O'CONNOR: To the tune of threatening the postman with a horsewhip and the butcher's boy with your Alsatian dog?

MAJOR: I refuse to stand here and listen to all this nonsense. *(He pulls himself up, looks at his watch, takes a small container from his overcoat pocket, extracts a capsule and puts it in his mouth.)*

JUDGE: What is all this? Are you eating something, Major Ecclestone?

MAJOR: I suffer from duodenal ulcers, my lord. I have taken a capsule.

JUDGE *(after a pause)*: Very well. *(He nods to* DEFENSE COUNSEL.)

O'CONNOR: Major Ecclestone, was the liver the only thing in the safe that evening?

MAJOR: No, it wasn't. There was stuff for a mixed grill on Thursday. Chops, kidneys, sausages. That sort of thing.

O'CONNOR: And these had been delivered with the dog's meat that afternoon?

MAJOR: Yes.

O'CONNOR: Did you have your mixed grill?

MAJOR: No fear! Chucked it out. Destroyed it. Great mistake, as I now realize. Poisoned like the other. Not a doubt of it. Intended for me.

O'CONNOR: And what about Mrs. Ecclestone?

MAJOR: Vegetarian.

O'CONNOR: I see. Can I have a list of complaints, please? *(Solicitor gives him a paper.)* Major Ecclestone, is it true that, apart from my client, there have been five other complaints about the character and behavior of your dog?

MAJOR: The dog was perfectly docile. Unless provoked. They bated him.

O'CONNOR: And is it not the case that you have received

two warnings from the police to keep the dog under proper control?

MAJOR: Bah!

O'CONNOR: I beg your pardon.

MAJOR: Balderdash!

O'CONNOR: You are on oath, Major Ecclestone. Have you received two such warnings from the police?

MAJOR *(pause)*: Yes. *(Nods.)*

O'CONNOR: Thank you. *(He sits down)*

(DR. SWALE *is called to the stand.* PROSECUTION COUNSEL *rises.)*

GOLDING: Dr. Swale, you were called into The Elms on the evening of 4th April, were you not?

SWALE: Yes. Mrs. Ecclestone rang me up and sounded so upset I went round.

GOLDING: What did you find when you got there?

SWALE: Major Ecclestone was in the yard near the dog kennel with the Alsatian's body lying at his feet.

GOLDING: And Mrs. Ecclestone?

SWALE: She was standing nearby. She suffers from migraine and this business with the dog hadn't done anything to help her. I took her back to her room, looked at her and gave her one of the Sternetil tablets I'd prescribed.

GOLDING: And then?

SWALE: I went down to the Major.

GOLDING: Yes?

SWALE: He, of course, realized the dog had been poisoned and he asked me, as a personal favor, to get an analysis of what was left of the liver the dog had been eating and of the contents of the dog's stomach. I arranged this with the pathology department of the general hospital.

GOLDING: Ah yes. We've heard evidence of that. Massive quantities of potassium cyanide were found.

SWALE: Yes.

GOLDING: Did you, subsequently, discuss with Major Ecclestone the possible source of this cyanide?

SWALE: Yes.

GOLDING: Dr. Swale, were you shown any letters by Major Ecclestone?

SWALE: Yes. From the defendant.

GOLDING: Are you sure they were from the defendant?

SWALE: Oh yes. She had in the past written to me complaining about the National Health. It was her writing and signature.

GOLDING: What was the nature of the letters to Major Ecclestone?

SWALE: Threatening. I remember in particular the one that said his dog ought to die and if he didn't act smartly they both would.

GOLDING: What view did you take of these letters?

SWALE: A very serious one. They threatened his life.

GOLDING: Yes. Thank you, Dr. Swale. *(He sits.)*

(DEFENSE COUNSEL *rises.)*

O'CONNOR: Dr. Swale, you have known the Ecclestones for some time, haven't you?

SWALE: Yes.

O'CONNOR: In fact you are close friends?

SWALE *(after a slight hesitation)*: I have known them for some years.

O'CONNOR: Would you consider Major Ecclestone a reliable sort of man where personal judgments are concerned?

SWALE: I don't follow you.

O'CONNOR: Really? Let me put it another way. If antagonism has developed between himself and another person, would you consider his view of the person likely to be a sober, fair and balanced one?

SWALE: There are very few people, I think, of whom under such circumstances, that could be said.

O'CONNOR: I suggest that at the time we are speaking of, a feud developed between Major Ecclestone and the defendant and that his attitude towards her was intemperate and wholly biased. *(Pause)* Well, Dr. Swale?

SWALE *(unhappily)*: I think that's putting it a bit strong.

O'CONNOR: Do you indeed? Thank you, Dr. Swale. (DEFENSE COUNSEL *sits.)*

JUDGE: You may leave the witness box, Dr. Swale.

(THOMAS TIDWELL *is called to the stand.* PROSECUTION COUNSEL *rises.)*

GOLDING: You are Thomas Tidwell, butcher's assistant of the West End Butchery, 8 Park Street, Peascale, near Fulchester?

TIDWELL: Yar.

GOLDING: On Friday 4th April, did you deliver two parcels of meat at The Elms, No. 1 Sherwood Grove?

TIDWELL: Yar.

GOLDING: Would you describe them please?

TIDWELL: Aye?

GOLDING: How were they wrapped?

TIDWELL: In paper. (JUDGE *looks.*)

GOLDING: Yes, of course, but what sort of paper?

TIDWELL: Aye?

GOLDING: Were they wrapped in brown paper or in newspaper?

TIDWELL: One of each.

GOLDING: Thank you. Did you know, for instance, the contents of the newspaper parcel: what was in it?

TIDWELL: Liver.

GOLDING: How did you know that?

TIDWELL *(to* JUDGE): It was bloody, wannit? Liver's bloody. Liver'll bleed froo anyfink, won't it? I seen it, din' I? It'd bled froo the comics.

(MAJOR *half-rises.* PROSECUTION COUNSEL *checks him with a look.* MAJOR *signals to* USHER, *who goes to him.)*

JUDGE: Are you chewing something, Mr. Tidwell?

TIDWELL: Yar.

JUDGE: Remove it.

GOLDING: You're sure of this? The wrapping was a page from a comic publication, was it?

TIDWELL: That's what I said, din' I? I seen it, din' I?

GOLDING: If I tell you that Major Ecclestone says that the liver was wrapped in sheets from the *Daily Telegraph*, what would you say?

TIDWELL: 'E wants is 'ead read. Or else 'e was squiffy.

(The MAJOR rises and is restrained by the USHER.)

GOLDING *(glaring at the MAJOR, turning to TIDWELL)*: Yes. Yes. Very good. Now, will you tell the court how you put the parcels away?

TIDWELL: Like I always done. Opened the safe and bunged 'em in, din' I?

GOLDING: Anything at all unusual happen during this visit?

TIDWELL: Naow.

GOLDING: You left by the side gate into the right-of-way, didn't you?

TIDWELL: S'right.

GOLDING: This would bring you face to face with the side wall of Miss Freebody's house. Did you notice anything at all unusual about it?

TIDWELL: Nothin' unusual. What you might call a regular occurrence. She was snooping. Froo the blind. You know. Froo the slats—you know. Nosey. She's always at it.

GOLDING: Did you do anything about it?

TIDWELL *(Turns to accused, gives a wolf whistle and a sardonic salute. She is furious)*: Just for giggles. *(Whistles)*

GOLDING: Did Miss Freebody react in any way?

TIDWELL: Scarpered.

GOLDING: Why should she spy upon you, do you think?

TIDWELL: Me? Not me. I reckon she was waiting for the boyfriend.

MISS FREEBODY: How dare you say such things . . .

GOLDING: The boyfriend?

TIDWELL: S'right. *(He guffaws and wipes away the grin with his hand.)* Pardon me.

GOLDING *(He has been taken aback by this development but keeps his composure):* Yes. Well. I don't think we need concern ourselves with any visitor the accused may or may not have been expecting.

TIDWELL: Her? Not *her. Her.*

JUDGE: What *is* all this, Mr. Golding?

GOLDING: I'm afraid it's beyond me, my lord. Some sort of bucolic joke, I imagine.

*(*JUDGE *grunts.)*

GOLDING: That's all I have to ask this witness, my lord. *(He sits down.)*

*(*THOMAS TIDWELL *makes as if to leave the box.* DEFENSE COUNSEL *rises.)*

JUDGE: Stay where you are, Mr. Tidwell. *(He has decided to push this unexpected development a little further.)* Mr. Tidwell, when a moment ago you said "not *her*"—meaning the accused—but "*her*," to whom did you refer?

TIDWELL: It's well-known, innit? His missus.

JUDGE: Mrs. Ecclestone?

MAJOR: What the devil are you talking about?

TIDWELL: S'right. Every Friday, like I said, reg'lar as clockwork.

JUDGE: What is as regular as clockwork?

TIDWELL: 'E is. Droppin' in. On 'er.

JUDGE: Who is?

TIDWELL: 'Im. It's well-known. The doctor.

MAJOR: God damn it, I demand an explanation. Death and damnation—(USHER *moves to restrain the* MAJOR.)

MISS FREEBODY *(laughing)*: That's right. You tell them.

GOLDING: Major Ecclestone! Sit down.

USHER: Quiet!

(The commotion subsides.)

JUDGE: For the last time, Major Ecclestone, I warn you that unless you can behave yourself with propriety you will be held in contempt of court. Mr. Golding.

GOLDING: My lord, I do apologize. Major, stand up and apologize to his Lordship. *(The* MAJOR *mutters.)* Stand up then, and do it. Go on.

MAJOR *(He looks as if he will spontaneously combust. He rises, blows out his breath, comes to attention and bellows in court-martial tones):* Being under orders to do so, I tender my regrets for any apparently overzealous conduct of which I may appear to have been unwittingly guilty.

JUDGE: Very well. Sit down and—and—and imagine yourself to be gagged. *(The* MAJOR *sits. He is troubled with indigestion.)* Yes, Mr. O'Connor . . .

O'CONNOR: Now, Mr. Tidwell, you say, do you, that you know positively that Dr. Swale visited Major Ecclestone's house after you left it?

TIDWELL: 'Course I do.

O'CONNOR: How do you know?

TIDWELL: I seen 'im, din' I?

O'CONNOR: What time was this?

TIDWELL: Free firty.

O'CONNOR: Describe where you were and precisely how you saw Dr. Swale.

TIDWELL: I'm on me bike in the lane, arn' I, and I bike past 'is car and 'e's gettin' aht of it, inn'e? (O'CONNOR *signs for him to address the* JUDGE. *He does so.*) I turn the corner and I park me bike and come back and look froo the rear window of the car and see 'im turn into the right-of-way. *(He giggles.)*

O'CONNOR: Go on.

TIDWELL *(still vaguely to the* JUDGE*)*: Like I see 'im before. Other Fridays. "Ullo, ullo, ullo!" I says. "At it again?" So I nips back to the turning into the right-of-way, stroll up very natural and easy and see 'im go in at the garden gate. *And* let 'imself in by the back door, carryin' 'is little black bag. No excuse me's. *Very* much at 'ome. Oh dear!

O'CONNOR: And then?

TIDWELL: I return to bizzness, don' I? Back to the shop and first with the news.

O'CONNOR: Thank you.

(He sits. PROSECUTION COUNSEL *rises.)*

GOLDING: Did you notice the accused's bathroom window while you were engaged in this highly distasteful piece of espionage?

TIDWELL: 'Ow does the chorus go?

GOLDING: I beg your pardon?

TIDWELL: I don' get cher.

GOLDING: While you were spying on Dr. Swale, could you and did you see the accused's bathroom window?

TIDWELL: Oh, ar! I get cher. Yar. I seen it. And 'er, snooping as per, froo the blind.

GOLDING: Dr. Swale carried his professional bag, I think you said?

TIDWELL: S'right.

GOLDING: And he went straight into the house? Without pausing, for instance, by the safe?

TIDWELL: I couldn't see the safe, where I was, could I? But 'e went in.

GOLDING: Quite so. To his patient who was ill upstairs.

TIDWELL: Oh, yeah?

GOLDING: I have one more question. Do you deliver meat at the accused's house?

TIDWELL: Yar.

GOLDING: When was your last call there, previous to the 4th April?

TIDWELL: Free days before. She gets 'er order reg'lar on Wednesdays.

GOLDING: Do you remember what it was?

TIDWELL: Easy. Chops. Bangers. And—wait for it, *wait for it.*

GOLDING: Please answer directly. What else?

TIDWELL: Liver.

PART TWO

GOLDING: I call Mrs. Ecclestone.

USHER: Mrs. Ecclestone.

(MRS. ECCLESTONE *comes in with the* USHER. *Enters the box and takes the oath. While she is doing so we see* DR. SWALE *and the* MAJOR *and then the accused, leaning forward and staring at her.* MRS. ECCLESTONE *is a singularly attractive woman, beautifully dressed and aged about thirty-five. There is a slight stir throughout the court. At the end of the oath, she makes a big smile at the* JUDGE.)

GOLDING: You are Mrs. Ecclestone? *(She assents.)* What are your first names, please?

MRS. ECCLESTONE: Barbara Helen.

GOLDING: And you live at The Elms, No. 1 Sherwood Grove, Fulchester?

MRS. ECCLESTONE: Yes.

GOLDING: Thank you. Mrs. Ecclestone, I want you to tell his Lordship and the jury something of the relationship between you and the accused. Going back, if you will, to the time when you first came to live in your present house.

MRS. ECCLESTONE: We used to see her quite often in her garden and—and—

GOLDING: Yes?

MRS. ECCLESTONE: And in her house.

GOLDING: You visited her there?

MRS. ECCLESTONE: We could see her at the windows. Looking out.

GOLDING: Did you exchange visits?

MRS. ECCLESTONE: Not social visits. She came in not long after we arrived to—to—

GOLDING: Yes?

MRS. ECCLESTONE: Well, to complain about Bang.

GOLDING: The Alsatian?

MRS. ECCLESTONE: Yes. He'd found some way of getting into her garden.

GOLDING: Was that the only time she complained?

MRS. ECCLESTONE: No, it wasn't. She—well, really, she was always doing it. I mean—well, hardly a week went by. It was about then, I think, that she first complained to the police. They came to see us. After that we took every possible care. We put a muzzle on Bang when he wasn't tied up and made sure he never went near Miss Freebody's place. It made no difference to her behavior.

GOLDING: Would you say that the complaints remained at much the same level or that they increased in intensity?

MRS. ECCLESTONE: They became much more frequent. And vindictive. And threatening.

GOLDING: In what way threatening?

MRS. ECCLESTONE (to JUDGE, a nervous smile): Oh—notes in our letter box—waylaying us in the street—saying she would go to the police. That sort of thing. And when we were in the garden she would go close to her hedge and say things we could hear. Meaning us to hear them. Threats and abuse. *(The* JUDGE *is nodding.)*

GOLDING: What sort of threats?

MRS. ECCLESTONE: Well—actually to do my husband an injury. She said he wasn't fit to live and she said in so many words she'd see to it that he didn't. It was very frightening. We thought she must be—well, not quite right in the head.

GOLDING: Coming to Friday 28th March *(She looks uncertain)*—was there any further incident?

(Miss Freebody sits forward.)

MRS. ECCLESTONE: Oh—you mean the cat. I didn't remember the exact date.

GOLDING: But you remember the event?

MRS. ECCLESTONE: Oh yes, I do. It was dreadful. I was horrified. *(She puts her head in her hands)* I was—I was so deeply sorry and terribly upset. I wanted to go in and tell her so.

GOLDING: And did you do so?

MRS. ECCLESTONE: No. Basil—my husband—thought it better not.

GOLDING: And after this incident, what happened between you and the accused?

MRS. ECCLESTONE: It was worse than ever, of course. She complained again; she telephoned several times a day and wrote threatening letters. My husband burnt them but I remember one said something like vengeance being done not only on the dog but on himself.

GOLDING: Yes. And now, Mrs. Ecclestone, we come to the

4th April. The day when the dog was poisoned. *(Gestures to her)*

MRS. ECCLESTONE: I heard it happening—I was in my bedroom—and I got up and looked through the window. And saw. My husband shouted for me to come down. I went down and by then Bang was—dead. My husband told me to ring up Jim Swale—Dr. Swale—and ask him to come at once. And he did.

GOLDING: What happened then?

MRS. ECCLESTONE: They looked in the safe and Dr. Swale said we should destroy the rest of the meat in case it was contaminated. So we did. In the incinerator.

GOLDING: How was the other meat wrapped? In what sort of paper?

MRS. ECCLESTONE: Like the other—in newspaper.

GOLDING: You are sure? Not in brown paper?

MRS. ECCLESTONE: No—I'm sure I remember noticing when we burnt it. It was the front page of the *Telegraph*.

GOLDING: Thank you. And then?

MRS. ECCLESTONE: Dr. Swale suggested getting the vet, but my husband wanted *him* to cope and he very kindly said he would. I was feeling pretty ghastly by then *(smiles at Judge)*, so he asked me to go back to my room and I did. And he had a look at me before he left and gave me one of my pills. I didn't go downstairs again that evening. *(She hesitates.)* I think perhaps I ought to say that there was never any doubt in our minds—any of us—about who had put the poisoned meat in the safe.

O'CONNOR: My lord, I must object.

MRS. ECCLESTONE: After all, it was what had been threatened, wasn't it?

JUDGE: Yes, Mr. O'Connor. *(To* MRS. ECCLESTONE*)* You may not talk about what you think was in the minds of other persons, madam.

MRS. ECCLESTONE: I'm sorry.

GOLDING: When do you think the meat was poisoned?

MRS. ECCLESTONE: It must have been after the butcher delivered the order, of course.

GOLDING: Have you any idea of the time of the delivery?

MRS. ECCLESTONE: As it happens, I have. The church clock struck three just as he left.

GOLDING: Did you hear any sounds of later arrivals?

MRS. ECCLESTONE *(hesitating):* I—no—no, I didn't. *(Rapidly)* But of course it would be perfectly easy for somebody to watch their chance, slip across the right-of-way. Nobody would see. My bedroom curtains were closed because I darken my room when I have a migraine.

(Grin from TIDWELL *to* SWALE*)*

GOLDING: Yes. Had you seen anything of the accused during the day?

MRS. ECCLESTONE: Yes, indeed I had. That morning the paper boy delivered her *Telegraph* with our *Times.* I didn't want to see her; I slipped out by *our* front gate and up to *her* front door. I was going to put her *Telegraph* through the flap when the door opened and there she was. Stock still and sort of glaring over my head.

GOLDING: That must have been disconcerting.

MRS. ECCLESTONE: It was awful. It seemed to last for ages, and then I held out her paper and she snatched it.

GOLDING: Did she speak?

MRS. ECCLESTONE: She whispered.

GOLDING: What did she whisper?

MRS. ECCLESTONE: That I needn't imagine this would stop justice from taking its course. And then the door was slammed in my face.

MISS FREEBODY: Quite right.

GOLDING: And then?

MRS. ECCLESTONE: I went back. And my migraine started.

GOLDING: Mrs. Ecclestone, do you know what happened to the wrapping paper round the dog's liver?

MRS. ECCLESTONE: Yes. My husband had dropped it on the ground and Jim—Dr. Swale—said it shouldn't be left lying about and he put it into the incinerator.

GOLDING: Did you notice what paper it was?

MRS. ECCLESTONE: It was the same as the other parcel— the *Daily Telegraph.*

GOLDING: Thank you.

(He sits. DEFENSE COUNSEL *rises.)*

O'CONNOR: Mrs. Ecclestone, *anybody* could have come and gone through the right-of-way and through the garden gate and replaced one parcel of liver by another?

MRS. ECCLESTONE: I suppose they could have.

O'CONNOR: Your husband has a lot of enemies in the neighborhood apart from Miss Freebody, hasn't he?

MRS. ECCLESTONE *(deprecatingly):* Oh—enemies!

O'CONNOR: Let me put it another way. There had been a number of complaints about the dog from other neighbors, hadn't there?

MRS. ECCLESTONE: None of them threatened to kill my husband. Hers did.

O'CONNOR: Did other persons, apart from Miss Freebody, write letters and complain to the police?

MRS. ECCLESTONE: There were some, I think.

O'CONNOR: How many?

MRS. ECCLESTONE: I don't know.

O'CONNOR: Two? Three? Four? Half a dozen? More?

MRS. ECCLESTONE: No. No. I don't know. I don't remember.

O'CONNOR: How very odd. Had the dog ever attacked any of your friends? *(She is silent.)* Dr. Swale, for instance?

MRS. ECCLESTONE: Bang was rather jealous. Alsatians can be.

O'CONNOR: Jealous, Mrs. Ecclestone? Do you mean jealous of you? Did the dog resent anyone paying you particular attention, for example?

MRS. ECCLESTONE: He was rather a one—I mean a two-person—dog.

(MRS. ECCLESTONE *and* DR. SWALE *exchange a brief look.)*

O'CONNOR: Had Bang, in fact, ever attacked Dr. Swale?

MRS. ECCLESTONE: I think—once. Before he got to know him.

O'CONNOR: Because Dr. Swale was paying you "particular attention," Mrs. Ecclestone?

MRS. ECCLESTONE: No. I don't remember about it. It was nothing.

O'CONNOR: The dog did get to know Dr. Swale, didn't it?

MRS. ECCLESTONE: Well, yes, naturally.

O'CONNOR: Naturally, Mrs. Ecclestone?

MRS. ECCLESTONE: Dr. Swale is in our circle of friends.

O'CONNOR: Apart from being your doctor?

MRS. ECCLESTONE: Yes.

(She has become increasingly uneasy. MAJOR ECCLESTONE has been eyeing DR. SWALE with mounting distaste.)

O'CONNOR: On that Friday afternoon, Mrs. Ecclestone— earlier in the afternoon, when you were lying on your bed in your darkened room, did Dr. Swale come and see you?

MRS. ECCLESTONE: I—don't know who you—I—I— *(She looks at DR. SWALE. We see him very briefly close his eyes in assent.)* Why yes, as a matter of fact—I'd forgotten all about it, he did.

O'CONNOR: Thank you, Mrs. Ecclestone.

(DEFENSE COUNSEL sits. PROSECUTION COUNSEL rises.)

GOLDING: As this earlier visit of Dr. Swale's has been introduced, Mrs. Ecclestone, I think that perhaps, don't you, that we'd better dispose of it? Dr. Swale, you've told the court, is an old friend and a member of your social circle. Is that right?

MRS. ECCLESTONE *(she has pulled herself together):* Yes.

GOLDING: Was there anything at all out-of-the-way about his dropping in?

MRS. ECCLESTONE: No, of course not. He often looks in. He and my husband do crosswords and swop them over. I'd quite forgotten but I think that was what he'd come for— to collect the *Times* crossword and leave the *Telegraph* one. *(She catches her breath, realizing a possible implication.)*

GOLDING: Did you see him?

MRS. ECCLESTONE *(fractional hesitation):* I—think—yes, I remember I heard someone come in and I thought it was my husband, home early. So I called out. And Dr. Swale came upstairs—and knocked and said who it was.

GOLDING: Exactly. Thank you so much, Mrs. Ecclestone. *(He sits.)*

JUDGE: You may go and sit down, Mrs. Ecclestone.

MRS. ECCLESTONE: Thank you, my lord.

(She does so. As she goes to the witness seats, she and the accused look at each other. MRS. ECCLESTONE gets past the other witnesses, who leave room for her. She sits between DR. SWALE and her husband, looking at neither of them.)

GOLDING: That concludes the case for the prosecution, my lord.

(DEFENSE COUNSEL rises.)

O'CONNOR: I now call Mary Emmaline Freebody.

(The accused is escorted to the witness box and takes the oath. The CLERK asks her to remove her glove.)

O'CONNOR: You are Mary Emmaline Freebody of No. 2 Sherwood Grove, Peascale near Fulchester?

MISS FREEBODY: I am.

O'CONNOR: Miss Freebody, did you attempt to poison Major Ecclestone?

MISS FREEBODY: I did not.

O'CONNOR: You are a practicing Christian, are you not?

MISS FREEBODY: Certainly.

O'CONNOR: And you swear that you had no such intention?

MISS FREEBODY: I do.

O'CONNOR: Miss Freebody, I'm sorry to recall an extremely painful memory to you, but will you tell his Lordship and the jury how you first learnt of the death of your cat?

MISS FREEBODY *(breaking out):* Learnt of it! *Learnt* of it! I heard the screams. The screams. I still hear them. *(To* JUDGE) Still. All the time. Asleep and awake. I am haunted by them.

(MAJOR *snorts.)*

O'CONNOR: Where were you at the time of the cat's death?

MISS FREEBODY: Indoors. In my house.

O'CONNOR: What did you do when you heard the screams?

MISS FREEBODY: I rushed out. Of course. I thought he was in my garden. I hunted everywhere. The screams stopped but I hunted. And then I heard that man—that monster— that fiend—

O'CONNOR: Major Ecclestone?

MISS FREEBODY *(she gives a contemptuous assent):* Laughing. He was laughing. Devil! He was talking to it. To that *brute*. And do you know what he said?

GOLDING *(rising):* My lord! Really—

MISS FREEBODY *(shouting):* He said "Good dog." That's what he said: "Good dog." *(She bursts out crying.)*

JUDGE: If you would like to sit down, you may.

(The WARDRESS *moves to lower the flap-seat in the box.)*

MISS FREEBODY: I don't want to sit down. Go away. *(She blows her nose.)*

O'CONNOR: Miss Freebody, what happened after that? Please remember that you may tell the court if you heard people talking and you may say who they were and what you did but not what they said, unless they are going to give evidence or have done so.

MISS FREEBODY: Idiocy! Legal humbug! Balderdash!

JUDGE: *That will do.*

MISS FREEBODY: No, it won't. I won't be talked down. I won't be told what will do or won't do. I'll say what I've got to say and—

JUDGE: Be silent! Mr. O'Connor, I'm afraid that I am bound to agree with Miss Freebody that your exposition of the hearsay rules was so inaccurate as to amount to legal humbug. If you must tell witnesses what the law is, do at least try to get it right.

O'CONNOR: I'm sorry, my lord.

JUDGE: Miss Freebody, you will answer counsel's question: what happened after that?

(She stares at him and he at her.)

MISS FREEBODY *(suddenly and very rapidly):* "What happened after that?" He asks me, "What happened after that?" I'll tell you what happened after that. She talked and he talked and she talked and he talked and then—then —then—no, I can't. I can't.

O'CONNOR: Miss Freebody—however painful it is—please go on. Try to speak calmly.

MISS FREEBODY: Out of the air. At my feet. Wet. Bleeding. Torn to pieces. Dead.

O'CONNOR: You are telling the court, aren't you, that Major Ecclestone had thrown the body of the cat into your garden?

MISS FREEBODY: Cruel. *Cruel!* Horrible and wicked and cruel.

O'CONNOR: Please try to be calm. After that? Immediately after that and subsequently, what did you do?

MISS FREEBODY: I—I couldn't at first but then I did—I buried him. And then I—I went indoors and I felt desperately ill. I *was* ill and afterwards I lay on my bed.

O'CONNOR: Yes. You went to bed?

MISS FREEBODY: No. I lay there. As I was. All night. Sometimes I dozed off and then I had nightmares. I thought that brute was attacking *me* as it had my—my little cat. I thought it was coming at *me.* Here. *(She clasps her throat.)* And for night after night it was the same.

O'CONNOR: And during the daytime?

MISS FREEBODY: I kept thinking it was loose and outside my doors, snuffling at them. Scratching at them, trying to get at me. I telephoned the police. I was terrified.

O'CONNOR: Did you go out?

MISS FREEBODY: I was afraid to go out. I stayed indoors. Day after day.

O'CONNOR: But you sent letters, didn't you? To Major Ecclestone?

MISS FREEBODY: I gave them to my daily help to post. I was afraid to go out.

O'CONNOR: It has been suggested that you were spying upon Dr. Swale and his visits to The Elms.

MISS FREEBODY: Those two! I didn't care about *them*. I used to think they were wicked but they were against *him*, weren't they? They were making a fool of him. They wanted to be rid of him.

JUDGE: Miss Freebody, you must confine yourself to facts. You must not put forward your notions as to anybody's wishes or intentions.

(Pause. She sniffs.)

JUDGE: Very well.

O'CONNOR: On the morning of the dog's death, Mrs. Ecclestone called to give you your paper, didn't she?

MISS FREEBODY: I stood inside the door. I thought it was *him* with the dog. And then I heard her clear her throat. So I made myself open the door. And there she was! The adultress. Oh yes! She came.

O'CONNOR: Later in the day, did you see Dr. Swale go into The Elms?

MISS FREEBODY: Oh yes. I saw him. In at the side door as usual. He always does that. And upstairs in her bedroom she had the curtains drawn. All ready for him. As she always does on Fridays. And of course *he (She indicates the* MAJOR) was out playing bridge at his club, poor fool.

O'CONNOR: Did you see Dr. Swale enter the house?

MISS FREEBODY *(indifferent):* I can't see their side door. There's a tree and bushes.

O'CONNOR: And the outside safe? Can you see that?

MISS FREEBODY: Not that, either.

O'CONNOR: So you wouldn't know if Dr. Swale, for whatever purpose, paused by the safe before entering the house.

MISS FREEBODY *(her fingers at her lips, staring at him with growing excitement):* Paused? By the safe? For whatever purpose? But you're right. You're perfectly right. Fool that I am. Fool! Of course! That's how it was. He—the doctor—

(She points to DR. SWALE, *who stands.)*

DR. SWALE: My lord, I protest. This is outrageous.

JUDGE: You cannot address the court, sir. You must sit down.

DR. SWALE: My lord, this amounts to slander.

JUDGE: Be quiet, Dr. Swale. You must know very well that any such interruption is impermissible. Sit down, sir. (DR. SWALE *sits.)* Very well, Mr. O'Connor.

O'CONNOR: Miss Freebody, please answer the questions simply and without comment. I bring you to the death of the dog. Did you see anything or hear anything of that event?

MISS FREEBODY: I was upstairs. I heard a commotion—a howl and *his* voice shouting. So I went into the bathroom and looked. I saw the dog thrashing about and then I saw it was dead. And I was glad. *Glad.* I didn't know why it was dead. I thought at first that *he*—its owner—might have destroyed it at last but it was dead and I exulted and gave thanks and was joyful.

(She looks at the witnesses. Her gaze becomes riveted upon DR. SWALE and MRS. ECCLESTONE. She leans forward, apparently in the grip of some kind of revelation. We see them. They exchange a quick look. He briefly closes his hand over MRS. ECCLESTONE's. MISS FREEBODY licks her lips.)

O'CONNOR: Did you see the arrival of Dr. Swale? Miss Freebody!

(MISS FREEBODY is still gazing at DR. SWALE and MRS. ECCLESTONE.)

O'CONNOR: Miss Freebody, may I have your attention, please? *(She turns her head slowly and looks at him.)* Did you see the arrival of Dr. Swale?

MISS FREEBODY: Oh yes! Yes, I watched that. I watched him—the doctor. I saw how surprised and put out he was when they showed him the dog. Just like he is now. I saw them look at each other.

O'CONNOR: What happened next?

MISS FREEBODY: *She* went indoors and *he* followed. And he came back after a time and they carried away the carcass.

O'CONNOR: The two men did? *(She nods.)* Afterwards, when you heard about the poisoned meat, what then?

MISS FREEBODY: Ah! *Then* I didn't realize. But *now!* *(With an extraordinary sly look towards the witnesses' seats)* It could have been an accident, couldn't it? The dog, I mean.

O'CONNOR *(taken aback):* An *accident*, Miss Freebody?

MISS FREEBODY: *He* always has liver on Fridays. *She* is a vegetarian. They did it between them. They meant it for him. For him!

GOLDING: This is outrageous.

(GOLDING *is on his feet and so are* MAJOR ECCLESTONE *and* DR. SWALE. *They speak together.)*

MAJOR: My God, what's the woman saying? By God, she means me. She means—*(He turns on* SWALE.) By God, she means *you—*

SWALE: This must stop. I demand that she's stopped. Major, for God's sake, you can't think—

USHER: Silence. Silence in court.

JUDGE *(rapping)*: Silence! (ECCLESTONE *and* SWALE *subside.)* This is insupportable. If there is any more of it, I shall clear the court. *(Pause)* Yes, Mr. Golding.

GOLDING: Indeed, my lord. How much more of this *are* we to have? I protest most strongly, my lord.

JUDGE: Yes, Mr. Golding. You may well do so. Well, Mr. O'Connor?

O'CONNOR: My lord, I quite agree it is not for the witness to advance theories, but the point is not apparently without substance. I have no further questions.

JUDGE: Very will. In that case—Mr. Golding?

(PROSECUTION COUNSEL *rises.)*

GOLDING: Thank you, my lord. Now, Miss Freebody, we have heard a great deal about emotions and all the rest of it. Suppose for a change we get down to a few hard facts. You admit to writing a number of threatening letters the last of which includes the phrase "neither of you is fit to live, take warning." Do you agree?

MISS FREEBODY: Yes.

GOLDING: You have heard the police evidence. A container half-full of cyanide-of-potassium has been found in your shrubbery. You have heard the local chemist depose that he sold cyanide-of-potassium to the previous tenant of your house, who used it to exterminate wasps. The container, Exhibit One, is very clearly, even dramatically labelled. There it is. You see it there, don't you? On the clerk's desk?

MISS FREEBODY: For the first time.

GOLDING: What! You have never seen it before! Be careful, Miss Freebody. The chemist has identified the container and has told the court that he advised the purchaser to keep it in a conspicuous place. Had you never seen it in your garden shed?

MISS FREEBODY: My gardener saw that one.

GOLDING: Oh. The gardener saw it, did he? And reported it to you?

MISS FREEBODY: Yes. And I told him to get rid of it. So he did.

GOLDING: When was this?

MISS FREEBODY: Soon after I came. Five years ago.

GOLDING: Indeed. How did the gardener in fact "get rid of it," as you claim?

MISS FREEBODY: I have no idea.

GOLDING: You have no idea! Is the gardener going to give evidence on your behalf?

MISS FREEBODY: Can't. He's dead.

(Somebody laughs. DEFENSE COUNSEL *grins.)*

USHER: Silence in court.

GOLDING: And how do you account for its being discovered in your shrubbery in a perfectly clean condition three days after the dog was poisoned?

MISS FREEBODY: I repeat, the one in the shed had been destroyed. This was another one. Thrown there, of course, over the hedge.

GOLDING: We are to suppose, are we, that an unknown poisoner brought a second jar of cyanide with him or her, although he or she had already prepared the liver and wrapped it. Why on earth should anyone do that?

MISS FREEBODY: To incriminate me. Obviously.

GOLDING *(irritated):* Once more into the realms of fantasy! I put it to you that no shadow of a motive and no jot of evidence can be found to support such a theory.

MISS FREEBODY: Oh yes, it can. It can.

GOLDING: It can! Perhaps you will be good enough to explain—

JUDGE: Mr. Golding, you have very properly attempted to confine the witness to statements of fact. Are you now inviting her to expound a theory?

GOLDING: My lord, the accused, so far as one can follow her, appears to be advancing in her own defense a counter-accusation.

JUDGE: Mr. O'Connor, have you anything to say on this point?

O'CONNOR *(rising):* Yes, my lord, I have. I must say again at once, my lord, that I have received no instructions as to the positive identity of the person my client apparently believes—most ardently believes—to have—may I say "planted"?—the half-empty container of cyanide on her property. My instructions were simply that she herself is innocent and therefore the container *must* in fact have been planted. As a result of the way the evidence has developed, I'd be obliged for a short adjournment to see whether there are further enquiries that should be made.

(O'CONNOR *sits.* GOLDING *rises.)*

GOLDING: My lord, I submit that the antics, if I may so call them, of the accused in the witness box are completely irrelevant. If there were one jot of substance in this rigmarole, why on earth did she not advance it in the first instance?

MISS FREEBODY: And I can tell you why. It's because I've only now realized it—in this court. It's been borne in upon me. *(She points at* MRS. ECCLESTONE *and* DR. SWALE*)* Seeing those two together. Watching them. Hearing them! Knowing! Remembering! They're would-be murderers. That's what they are.

JUDGE: Be quiet, madam. I warn you that you do your own cause a great deal of harm by your extravagant and most improper behavior. For the last time, I order you to confine yourself to answering directly questions put by learned counsel. You may not, as you constantly have done, interrupt the proceedings and you may not, without permission, address the court. If you persist in doing so you will be held in contempt. Do you understand me?

(She makes no response.)

JUDGE: Mr. O'Connor, am I to understand that in view of the manner in which this case has developed and the introduction of elements—unanticipated, as you assure us, in your instructions—you would wish me to adjourn?

O'CONNOR: If your Lordship will.

JUDGE: Mr. Golding?

GOLDING: I have no objection, my lord.

JUDGE: Does an adjournment until ten o'clock tomorrow morning seem appropriate?

O'CONNOR: Certainly, my lord.

JUDGE: Very well. *(Generally)* The court is adjourned until ten o'clock tomorrow morning. *(He rises.)*

(The JUDGE goes out. COUNSEL gather up their papers and confer with their solicitor representatives. The accused is removed. The witnesses stand, and the CLERK issues instructions as to re-assembly. MAJOR ECCLESTONE confronts his wife and DR. SWALE. There is a momentary pause before she lifts her chin and goes out. The men remain face-to-face for a second or two, and then DR. SWALE follows and overtakes her in the doorway.)

(The court reassembles at 10:00 the next morning.)

(The JUDGE enters and takes his seat.)

JUDGE: Members of the jury, I am sure you apprehend the reasons for an adjournment in this, in many ways, somewhat eccentric case. I'm sorry if the delay has caused you inconvenience. Before we go on I would like to remind you that you are where you are for one purpose only: to decide whether accused, Mary Emmaline Freebody, is guilty of the attempted murder of Major Ecclestone. You are not concerned with anything that may have emerged outside the provenance of this charge unless it bears on the single question—the guilt or innocence of the accused.

(The accused is in the witness box. The ECCLESTONES *and* DR. SWALE *now sit apart from each other, separated by* TIDWELL *and the local chemist. They are shaken and anxious. They look straight in front of them. The* MAJOR *keeps darting glances at them. He withdraws a small plastic case from his pocket. He extracts a capsule and swallows it.)*

JUDGE: Mr. Golding, you may now wish to continue your cross-examination.

GOLDING: I have no further questions, my lord.

JUDGE: Very well. Mr. O'Connor, do you wish to re-examine the defendant, and may I say, Mr. O'Connor, that I trust there will be no repetition of yesterday's irregularities.

O'CONNOR *(rising):* My lord, I sincerely hope not. I have no further questions to put to the defendant.

JUDGE: You may go back to the dock, Miss Freebody.

(The WARDRESS *puts an arm on* MISS FREEBODY *who glares at her.* MISS FREEBODY *returns to the dock.* PROSECUTION COUNSEL *rises.)*

GOLDING: My lord, I must inform your Lordship that Major Ecclestone has waited upon me and has expressed a desire to amend some of his former evidence, and has asked me to put his request before your Lordship.

JUDGE: Did you anticipate anything of this sort, Mr. Golding?

GOLDING: Not I, my lord.

JUDGE *(after a long pause):* Very well.

GOLDING: I recall Major Basil Ecclestone.

(There is a general stir as the MAJOR goes back to the box. His manner is greatly changed. His animosity is now directed against DR. SWALE.)

GOLDING: May I remind you that you are still on oath. *(MAJOR grunts.)* Major Ecclestone, is it true that because of certain developments you now wish to amend some of the former evidence that you gave earlier in these proceedings?

MAJOR: I do.

GOLDING: And that evidence concerns the identity of the person you believe to have been responsible for poisoning the meat?

MAJOR: It does, sir.

GOLDING: And will you tell the court who—

(A cry from the MAJOR. The CLERK stands sharply. The MAJOR is in a sudden agony of convulsion. He struggles, jerks violently, falls, suffers a final galvanic spasm and is still. The USHER goes to the box. The body slides half down the steps. DR. SWALE hurries across and stoops over it.)

USHER: Quiet. Quiet! Silence in court. Silence.

(The JUDGE has risen. DR. SWALE looks up at him and with a slight gesture of bewilderment shakes his head.)

JUDGE: Clear the court! Usher. Clear the court.

(The accused is standing triumphant in the dock and pointing at the body.)

MISS FREEBODY: Justice. Justice.

(Reporters scramble for the door.)

PART THREE

O'CONNOR: . . . and I would submit, my lord, with respect that the evidence is admissable. My lord, may I very briefly review the somewhat macabre sequence of events?

JUDGE *(smiling):* Briefly, Mr. O'Connor? Very briefly?

O'CONNOR: My lord, I really am very much obliged. *Very* briefly then, my client is accused of putting cyanide-of-potassium into Major Ecclestone's meat. Major Ecclestone who laid the case against her has died and cyanide has been found in his body. There is a strong presumption—indeed an overwhelming probability—that cyanide was introduced into one of the capsules Major Ecclestone was in the habit of taking at stated intervals for a digestive disorder. He was seen to take one of these capsules immediately before his death. My lord, I shall, if permitted, call expert evidence to show that a capsule containing cyanide would only remain intact for an hour. After that, the poison would begin to seep through the container. Miss Freebody has not been left alone since the commencement of this trial. It is obvious, therefore, she cannot be held responsible for causing his death. Whoever murdered Major Ecclestone, it was certainly not Miss Freebody. So that if, as of course we most strenuously deny, she caused the death of the dog, we have to accept a grotesque coincidence of two persons independently attempting to kill Major Ecclestone. Thus, my lord, I submit that the circumstances leading to Major Ecclestone's death are admissable evidence.

(DEFENSE COUNSEL *sits down. A pause. The* JUDGE *has taken an occasional note during this submission. He now looks up and waits for a moment.)*

JUDGE: Yes. Thank you. *(He turns to* PROSECUTION COUNSEL.*)* Well, Mr. Golding?

GOLDING *(rising):* My lord, I shall oppose the introduction of any reference whatever to the death of Major Ecclestone. I submit that it would be grossly improper to confuse in the minds of the jury two entirely separate issues. The inquiry into Major Ecclestone's death is in the hands of the police. And if they make an arrest there will be a trial in another court under another jury. What will transpire on what accusations may be made is utterly irrelevant to these proceedings. I submit that it will be irregular in the highest degree to anticipate them. As far as this court is concerned, my lord, may I venture to remind my learned friend that "the dog it was that died" and not its master?

JUDGE: And what do you say to that, Mr. O'Connor?

O'CONNOR *(good-humoredly): Touché,* I suppose, my lord.

JUDGE: This is in more ways than one a most unusual case. The death in the witness box of the principal witness for the prosecution, the man who laid the accusation against the defendant, and the finding of cyanide in his body is an extraordinary circumstance. I may order the jury to dismiss all this from their minds, but gentlemen, I may do so until my wig turns black and falls off my head but they won't be able to do so. But to return to the argument. It would be remarkable if *two* people had independently desired to bring about the Major's death. Thus if the second, successful, attempt could not have been made by the accused, it seems to me to be relevant to the allegation that she made the first attempt. I therefore rule that evidence regarding the nature and characteristics of the poisoned capsule is admissable.

O'CONNOR: I am greatly obliged to your Lordship.

JUDGE: Very well. Here we go again, gentlemen. *(To the* USHER) The jury may come back.

(The court reassembles. The jury enters. MISS FREEBODY *returns to the dock.* DR. SWALE *now sits by himself in the witnesses' seats.* MRS. ECCLESTONE, *in mourning, hesitates and takes a seat removed from his. A pause and then he rises and goes to her. He bends over her for a moment and then offers his hand. After hesitating, she takes it. He then takes a seat behind hers.)*

JUDGE: Members of the jury. Your attendance in this case was interrupted by an extraordinary and most distressing event which in the interval has received a great deal of publicity and has acquired a considerable amount of notoriety. You are of course not here to try anyone for Major Ecclestone's death. You are here to decide whether Mary Emmaline Freebody is guilty or not guilty of attempted murder and that is your sole duty. Having said this I add one important qualification. If, during the continuation of the hearing, evidence is tendered that arises out of the circumstances attending upon Major Ecclestone's death and that evidence has a bearing upon the question of the defendant's guilt or innocence, then I will admit it for your consideration. Very well, Mr. O'Connor.

O'CONNOR *(rising):* You are Dr. Ernest Smithson, of 24 Central Square, Fulchester.

DR. SMITHSON: Yes.

O'CONNOR: You, Dr. Smithson, are consultant pathologist for the Fulchester Constabulary?

DR. SMITHSON: I am.

O'CONNOR: Did you carry out a post mortem on Major Ecclestone?

DR. SMITHSON: Yes. I found he had died of cyanide poisoning.

O'CONNOR: May he be shown Exhibit Six? Is that the bottle taken from the Major's body?

DR. SMITHSON: Yes. I found it myself in his pocket. It was a bottle of Duogastacone which contained capsules of potassium cyanide.

O'CONNOR: Which suggests that cyanide had been introduced into a bottle containing capsules of Duogastacone?

DR. SMITHSON: Yes.

O'CONNOR: Now will you please tell the court whether it would be possible to fill capsules of the sort commonly used in pharmaceutical dispensaries with cyanide-of-potassium?

DR. SMITHSON: It would be possible, yes.

O'CONNOR: In what form would the cyanide be?

DR. SMITHSON: In the form of powder.

O'CONNOR: And would the capsules be indistinguishable from those filled with a doctor's prescription?

DR. SMITHSON: If the prescribed powder was the same color, which it probably would be, yes. To begin with, that is.

JUDGE: To begin with, Dr. Smithson? Can you explain a little farther?

DR. SMITHSON: After about an hour, my lord, the cyanide would begin to seep through the capsule and this would become increasingly noticeable.

O'CONNOR: Let me get this quite clear. To escape detection the whole operation, filling the capsules with the lethal powder and conveying them to the intended victim, would have to be executed within an hour before one of the capsules was taken?

Dr. Smithson: Before they had begun to disintegrate, I would prefer to say.

O'Connor: Dr. Smithson, are you aware that from the day before the death of Major Ecclestone, my client has been under constant supervision?

Dr. Smithson: I have been so informed, yes.

O'Connor: And therefore could not, for instance, possibly have concocted lethal capsules of the sort we have been talking about and conveyed them to some person or place outside her own premises?

Dr. Smithson: Obviously not if she was under constant supervision.

O'Connor: Thank you.

(O'Connor *sits.* Golding *rises.*)

Golding: My lord.

Judge *(with a slight smile and an air of knowing what's coming):* Yes, Mr. Golding?

Golding: Well—yes, indeed, my lord. I merely beg to remind the jury of what your Lordship has already laid down. The defendant is not on trial for concocting lethal capsules and I submit that the evidence we have just heard is irrelevant. I have no questions to put to Dr. Smithson.

Judge *(to* Smithson): Thank you, Dr. Smithson. You may go if you wish.

Dr. Smithson: Thank you, my lord. *(He leaves the witness box.)*

O'Connor: My lord, in view of the development of this trial since Dr. Swale gave evidence and particularly in view of subsequent evidence, I ask for leave to re-open my cross-examination of him. I ask for him to be recalled.

JUDGE: What do you say to this, Mr. Golding? Do you object?

GOLDING: My lord, I can find no conceivable reason for this procedure, but—I do not object.

JUDGE *(after a moment's pause):* Very well, Mr. Defense Counsel. Go back to the witness box, please, Dr. Swale.

(DR. SWALE *takes the stand.)*

O'CONNOR: Dr. Swale, you realize that you are still on oath, do you not?

DR. SWALE: I do.

O'CONNOR: You heard the evidence given by the previous witness?

DR. SWALE: Yes.

O'CONNOR: Do you agree with it?

DR. SWALE: I am not a pathologist, but I would expect it to be correct.

O'CONNOR: With respect to the deterioration within an hour of a capsule containing cyanide?

DR. SWALE: I have had no experience of potassium cyanide, but yes, I would, of course, expect Dr. Smithson to be right.

O'CONNOR: Yes. Dr. Swale, I'm going to take you back if you please to April 4th, the evening when you were called in to the Ecclestones' and saw the dead Alsatian. You will remember that you removed what was left of the liver that had been fed to the dog and subsequently had it analyzed and that cyanide-of-potassium was found in massive quantities.

DR. SWALE: Yes.

O'CONNOR: There was also, in the same safe, the material for a mixed grill which was intended for the Major's dinner that night.

DR. SWALE: So I understand.

O'CONNOR: Did you do anything about this meat?

DR. SWALE: I have already deposed that I said it should be destroyed.

O'CONNOR: And was it destroyed?

DR. SWALE: It was. I have already said so.

O'CONNOR: By whom?

DR. SWALE: By Mrs. Ecclestone and myself. In their incinerator.

O'CONNOR: As she subsequently deposed. After you had given your evidence.

DR. SWALE: Quite.

O'CONNOR: Dr. Swale, did it not occur to you that this meat which was destined for the Major's dinner should also be analyzed?

DR. SWALE: No. I was simply concerned to get rid of it.

O'CONNOR: Upon further consideration would you now say it would have been better to have sent it, or a portion of it, for analysis?

DR. SWALE: Perhaps it might have been better. But the circumstances of the dog's death—their description of its symptoms and its appearance so strongly suggested a convulsive poison such as cyanide—I really didn't think.

O'CONNOR: I'm sorry, doctor, but you told us just now, you've had no experience of cyanide.

DR. SWALE: No experience in practice but naturally during the course of training I did my poisons.

O'CONNOR: Is Mrs. Ecclestone a vegetarian?

DR. SWALE *(a slight pause):* I believe so.

O'CONNOR: You believe so, Dr. Swale? But as Mrs. Ecclestone has told us, you are a member of their intimate circle. You are her doctor, are you not?

DR. SWALE *(less cool):* Yes, of course I am.

O'CONNOR: Surely, then, you know definitely whether or not she's a vegetarian?

DR. SWALE: Yes. All right. I simply said "I believe so" as one does in voicing an ordinary agreement. I know so, if you prefer it. She is a vegetarian.

O'CONNOR: Are you in the habit of visiting her on Friday afternoons?

DR. SWALE: Not "in the habit" of doing so. I sometimes used to drop in on Fridays to swop crosswords with the Major.

O'CONNOR: But Major Ecclestone was always at his club on Fridays.

DR. SWALE: He used to leave his crossword out for me. I visit The Hermitage private hospital on Fridays and it's close by. I did sometimes—quite often—drop in at The Elms.

O'CONNOR *(blandly):* For a cup of tea, perhaps?

DR. SWALE: Certainly. For a cup of tea.

O'CONNOR: You heard the evidence of Thomas Tidwell, didn't you?

DR. SWALE *(contemptuously):* If you can call it that.

O'CONNOR: What would you call it?

DR. SWALE: An example of small-town lying gossip dished out by a small-town oaf.

O'CONNOR: To what part of his evidence do you refer?

DR. SWALE: Clearly, since it concerns me, to the suggestion that I went to the house for any other purpose than the one I have given.

O'CONNOR: What do you say to Miss Freebody's views on the subject?

DR. SWALE: I would have thought it was obvious that they are those of a mentally disturbed spinster of uncertain age.

MISS FREEBODY *(sharply):* Libel! Cad! Murderer!

(The JUDGE *turns and stares at her. The* WARDRESS *admonishes her. She subsides.)*

O'CONNOR: You are not Miss Freebody's doctor, are you?

DR. SWALE: No, thank God.

(Laughter)

USHER: Silence in court.

O'CONNOR: When you paid your earlier visit to The Elms on the afternoon in question, did you carry your professional bag with you?

DR. SWALE *(after a pause):* I expect so.

O'CONNOR: Why? It was not a professional call.

DR. SWALE: I'm not in the habit of leaving it in the car.

O'CONNOR: What was in it?

DR. SWALE: You don't want an inventory, do you? The bag contains the normal impedimenta of a doctor in general practice.

O'CONNOR: And nothing else?

DR. SWALE: I'm not in the habit of using my case as a shopping bag.

O'CONNOR: Not for butcher's meat, for instance?

GOLDING: My lord, I do most strenuously object.

DR. SWALE: This is intolerable. Have I no protection against this sort of treatment?

JUDGE: No. Answer.

DR. SWALE: No. I do not and never have carried butcher's meat in my bag.

(DEFENSE COUNSEL sits.)

JUDGE *(to* GOLDING): Mr. Golding, do you wish to re-examine?

GOLDING: No, my lord.

JUDGE *(to* SWALE): Thank you, doctor.

DR. SWALE: My lord, may I speak to you?

JUDGE: No, Dr. Swale.

DR. SWALE: I demand to be heard.

JUDGE: You may do no such thing, you may—

DR. SWALE *(shouting him down):* My lord, it is perfectly obvious that counsel for the defense is trying to protect his client by throwing up a series of infamous suggestions intended to implicate a lady and myself in this miserable business.

JUDGE *(through this):* Be quiet, sir. Leave the witness box.

DR. SWALE: I refuse. I insist. We are not legally represented. I am a professional man who must be very gravely damaged by these baseless innuendoes.

JUDGE: For the last time I warn you—

DR. SWALE *(shouting him down):* I had nothing, I repeat, nothing whatever to do with the death of the Ecclestones' dog (JUDGE *gestures to* USHER), nor did I tamper with any of the meat in the safe. I protest, my lord. I protest.

(The USHER *and a police constable close in on him and the scene ends in confusion.)*

*(*GWENDOLINE MIGGS *is sworn in on the stand. She is a large, determined-looking woman of about sixty.)*

O'CONNOR: Your name is Sarah Gwendoline Miggs?

MIGGS: Yes.

O'CONNOR: And where do you live, Miss Miggs?

MIGGS: Flat 3, Flask Walk, Fulchester.

O'CONNOR: You are a qualified medical nurse, now retired?

MIGGS: I am.

O'CONNOR: Will you give us briefly an account of your professional experience?

MIGGS: Fifteen years in general hospital and twenty years in ten hospitals for the mentally disturbed.

O'CONNOR: The last one being at Fulchester Grange Hospital where you nursed for some two years before retiring?

MIGGS: Correct.

O'CONNOR: And have you, since the sitting of this court, been looking after the defendant, Miss Mary Emmaline Freebody?

MIGGS: Right.

O'CONNOR: Miss Miggs, will you tell his Lordship and the jury how the days are spent since you took this job?

MIGGS: I relieve the night nurse at 8:00 A.M. and am with the case until I'm relieved in the evening.

JUDGE: With the "case"?

O'CONNOR: Miss Freebody, my lord.

JUDGE (fretfully): Why can't we say so, for pity's sake? Very well.

O'CONNOR: Do you remain with Miss Freebody throughout the day?

MIGGS: Yes.

O'CONNOR: Never leave her?

MIGGS: Those are my instructions and I carry them out.

(DR. SWALE, *who has been looking fixedly at the witness, writes a note, signals to the* USHER *and gives him the note. The* USHER *takes it to* MR. GOLDING, *who reads it and shows it to his junior and the solicitor for the prosecution.*)

O'CONNOR: Do you find Miss Freebody at all difficult?

MIGGS: Not a bit.

O'CONNOR: She doesn't try to—to shake you off? She doesn't resent your presence?

MIGGS: Didn't like it at first. There was a slight resentment but we soon got over that. We're very good friends, now.

O'CONNOR: And you have never left her?

MIGGS: I said so, didn't I? Never.

O'CONNOR: Thank you, Miss Miggs.

(DEFENSE COUNSEL *sits.*)

GOLDING *(rising):* Yes. Nurse Miggs, you have told the court, have you not, that since you qualified as a mental nurse, you have taken posts in ten hospitals over a period of twenty years, the last appointment being of two years' duration at Fulchester Grange?

MIGGS: Correct.

GOLDING: Have you, in addition to these engagements, taken private patients?

MIGGS *(uneasily):* A few.

GOLDING: How many?

MIGGS: I don't remember offhand. Not many.

GOLDING: Nurse Miggs, have you ever been dismissed—summarily dismissed—from a post?

MIGGS: I didn't come here to be insulted.

JUDGE: Answer the question, nurse.

MIGGS: There's no satisfying some people. Anything goes wrong—blame the nurse.

GOLDING: Yes or no, Miss Miggs? *(He glances at the paper from* DR. SWALE.) In July 1969, were you dismissed by the doctor in charge of a case under suspicion of illegally obtaining and administering a drug and accepting a bribe for doing so?

MIGGS *(breaking in):* It wasn't true. It was a lie. I know where you got that from. *(She points to* DR. SWALE.) From him! He had it in for me. He couldn't prove it. He couldn't prove anything.

GOLDING: Come, Miss Miggs, don't you think you would be well advised to admit it at once?

MIGGS: He couldn't prove it. *(She breaks down.)*

GOLDING: Why did you leave Fulchester Grange?

MIGGS: I won't answer. It's all lies. Once something's said about you, you're done for.

GOLDING: Were you dismissed?

MIGGS: I won't answer.

GOLDING: Were you dismissed for illegally obtaining drugs and accepting a bribe for so doing?

MIGGS: It wasn't proved. They couldn't prove it. It's lies!

GOLDING: I have no further questions, my lord.

JUDGE: Mr. Defense Counsel? (O'CONNOR *shakes his head.)* Thank you, Miss Miggs. *(She leaves the witness box.)* Have you any further witnesses, Mr. Defense Counsel?

O'CONNOR: No, my lord.

JUDGE: Members of the jury, just let me tell you something about our function—yours and mine. I am here to direct you as to the law and to remind you of the salient features of the evidence. You are here as judges of fact; you and you alone have to decide, on the evidence you have heard, whether the accused is guilty or not of the charge of attempted murder. . . .

You may think it's plain that the liver which the dog ate was poisoned. The prosecution say that whoever poisoned that liver must have known that it might have been eaten by the late Major, and was only given to the dog by accident. The vital question, therefore, you may think, is who poisoned that liver. The prosecution say that Miss Freebody did. They say she had the opportunity to take the meat from the safe, poison it and replace it, having for some reason or other changed the paper in which it was wrapped. They say she had a motive—her antagonism to the Major as evidenced by the threatening letters which she wrote. But, say the defense, and you may think it is a point of some weight, the fact that the Major actually died before *your* eyes of cyanide poisoning at a time when the accused would have had no opportunity to administer the poison is evidence that someone else wanted to and *did* kill the Major. So if someone other than the accused did kill the Major in the second attempt on his life, how can you believe that the accused rather than the culprit of the second attempt was guilty of the first attempt?

Remember that before you can bring a verdict of guilty you must be satisfied beyond all reasonable doubt that the accused did make this attempt on the life of the late Major. Will you now retire, elect a foreman to speak for you when you return, and consider your verdict.

CLERK: All stand.

(The jury leave the room. Time passes, and the jury return to their seats.)

CLERK: Members of the jury, will your foreman stand. *(The* FOREMAN *rises.)* Just answer this question yes or no. Have you reached a verdict upon which you are all agreed?

FOREMAN: Yes.

CLERK: Do you find the accused, Mary Emmaline Freebody, guilty or not guilty on the charge of attempted murder?

FOREMAN *(answers either "guilty" or "not guilty."):*

CLERK *(if guilty):* Is that the verdict of you all?

JUDGE *(if not guilty):* Mary Emmaline Freebody, you are free to go.

COURT REPORTER *(if guilty):* Mary Freebody was remanded in custody for psychiatric reports.

The Case with Five Solutions

At the end of the broadcast of Evil Liver *the jury decided that Miss Freebody was not guilty, but nothing is recorded of their analysis of the prosecution's case or of their opinion about who in fact was guilty. But we can act as armchair detectives and examine the case against Miss Freebody as well as other possible solutions.*

SOLUTION 1

Miss Freebody poisoned the dog and, during the trial, murdered Major Ecclestone. The evidence supporting Miss Freebody's guilt in the poisoning of the dog is given in detail by the prosecution. Everything is circumstantial but nonetheless persuasive: she had threatened the Major and his dog because of the death of her cat; a tin of wasp exterminator containing cyanide was found on her property; and she could have poisoned the liver shortly after it was delivered. In short, motive, means, and opportunity. It might be argued that only a mentally disturbed person would so openly have warned her victim, but (if we can trust Dr. Swale) Miss Freebody was obviously mentally disturbed.

The jury found Miss Freebody not guilty probably because it seemed impossible for her to have killed Major Ecclestone during the trial. She could not have been near enough to him to have placed the cyanide capsule into his plastic medicine case. Not only did Nurse Miggs swear that Miss Freebody was constantly under observation, but common sense indicates that nothing like that could have happened without someone noticing. Is there any way that Miss Freebody could have gotten the capsule to the Major? First, it would have been necessary that someone be her agent. Second, the agent would have to have been someone with access to cyanide. Third, the agent must have been someone Miss Freebody could trust, either because she could exert pressure or because the agent had a motive for helping her. Is there anyone who fits those qualifications? Yes, indeed—Nurse Miggs is the obvious candidate. As a nurse she had access to cyanide. She worked for twenty years in a hospital for people with mental problems, and she also had private patients. Miss Freebody, we have noted, was certainly unbalanced and could well have been one of those patients. Perhaps Miss Freebody threatened to reveal Nurse Miggs's past. Or perhaps Nurse Miggs had a strong motive herself. She had a festering resentment against Dr. Swale, and having heard the testimony emerging against him saw her opportunity to make him a suspect in a murder. Is it any wonder that she and Miss Freebody became "good friends" during the trial? The murder of Major Ecclestone would avenge them both.

All of this seems a strong case until we look closely and see that there is little evidence. To take the successful murder first, no one testified that Nurse Miggs had gotten near enough to the Major to slip a capsule into his container; had she left Miss Freebody long enough to do so, someone surely would have seen her. As for most of the rest—Miss Freebody's being treated as a mental patient in the care of Nurse Miggs and so on—it's just unsubstantiated speculation. The evidence that Miss Freebody poisoned Bang, the Alsatian, is stronger, but I find it unconvincing, especially in regard to the tin of wasp exterminator. Even a slightly deranged person would have known better than to toss such an incriminating bit of evidence onto her own property. As Miss Freebody herself pointed out, it has all the indications of a plant. If it was not part of a frame-up, it must have been discarded by someone who wanted to get rid of it as quickly as possible.

SOLUTION 2

Dr. Swale and Mrs. Ecclestone poisoned the dog and killed the Major. We needn't go over this theory in as much detail, for perhaps even more obviously than in the case against Miss Freebody, Dr. Swale had motive, means, and opportunity in the poisoning of the liver. If Dr. Swale did the deed, the killing of the dog must have been accidental, or a preliminary to the Major's death when he ate the mixed grill, which we can assume was also poisoned. In regard to the successful attempt against the Major, we should note that Dr. Swale had access to cyanide and to capsules, and that Mrs. Ecclestone was sitting next to her husband and could have slipped the poisoned capsule into his medicine case. It's a bit harder to know why the poisoning was done in the courtroom, especially since it seemed to exonerate Miss Freebody. The Major was about to accuse his wife and Dr. Swale, but unless he had new evidence the accusation would not have meant much. But did he have new evidence? We don't know, though Dr. Swale may have feared that the Major could make the accusation stick.

Like the case against Miss Freebody, the above outline seems at first glance plausible, but it founders on a problem. Mrs. Ecclestone certainly and Dr. Swale probably knew that liver was always given to the dog. They also were familiar enough with the Major's character to know that he would have assumed that he was the target. Why, if they planned to murder the Major, did they devise a scheme by which the dog would die first? They could have made certain that the Major ate the poisoned food first—the mixed grill—then fed a bit to the dog so that Miss Freebody's threatening letters would make her the obvious suspect in both deaths. Moreover, if they did not poison the liver, they had no reason to fear any courtroom revelations from the Major, and therefore no reason to kill him during the trial.

SOLUTIONS 3 AND 4

Miss Freebody poisoned the dog, but Dr. Swale and Mrs. Ecclestone poisoned the Major. Solution 4 is the reverse: *Dr. Swale and Mrs. Ecclestone poisoned the dog, but Miss Freebody poisoned the Major.* As experienced mystery readers, we don't have to agree with the Judge's opinion that both crimes were the work of the same person, but in this case it's difficult to accept a Miss Freebody–Dr. Swale–Mrs. Ecclestone combination. This solution, no matter how the details are juggled about, combines the weaknesses of the previous solutions. In order to show why a Solution 5 is necessary, let's summarize the conclusions that seem to exonerate the obvious suspects:

The First Crime:

Miss Freebody probably did not poison the liver because she would not have left the tin of wasp exterminator in her own shrubbery.

Dr. Swale and Mrs. Ecclestone probably did not poison the liver because they would not have poisoned the dog first.

The Second Crime:

Miss Freebody probably did not murder the Major because she was watched at all times and her only possible agent, Nurse Miggs, could not have poisoned him without someone noticing that she was no longer guarding Miss Freebody.

Dr. Swale and Mrs. Ecclestone probably did not murder the Major because they would not have done it during the trial unless they were guilty of the first crime which, as we have pointed out, is unlikely.

Having finally eliminated these three suspects, we are left with—

SOLUTION 5

A person or persons previously unsuspected committed both crimes. Ngaio Marsh, like her contemporaries Agatha Christie, John Dickson Carr, and Ellery Queen, often used the least-likely-person gambit. Would Marsh have chosen someone like Miss Freebody, Mrs. Ecclestone, and Dr. Swale, who had such obvious motives? She carefully shows that others had less obvious but perhaps just as compelling motives to kill Major Ecclestone. The Major quarrelled with everyone he dealt with, including his landlord, his late doctor, the secretary of his club, the postman, and the butcher. In fact, he threatened the butcher's boy with his dog. Whether this boy was Thomas Tidwell or, more likely, a lad who worked with him, Tidwell had a motive to kill the dog and by extension the Major himself. But how could Tidwell have gotten the poison and the capsule in which to put it? Quite easily: he was apparently a friend of the local chemist, with whom he is sitting in the final scene. The tin of wasp exterminator came from the chemist. We recall that Mrs. Ecclestone testified that Tidwell delivered the meat shortly after 3:00, but that Tidwell himself said that he left at 3:30. What was he doing during that half hour? Though he probably did not know of Miss Freebody's motive, he knew that Dr. Swale was having an affair with Mrs. Ecclestone, and that Miss Freebody could swear to their frequent meetings. He must have been waiting for Dr. Swale's arrival so that an obvious suspect was present. He poisoned the liver, and then changed the wrappings to indicate that someone had opened the parcel after he had handled it. But he feared being caught with the tin of poison, so he simply threw it into the nearest shrubbery. During the trial, Miss Freebody seemed genuinely surprised by the evidence against Dr. Swale and Mrs. Ecclestone. Not only was Tidwell not surprised, but he carefully pointed it out.

To make his case against Dr. Swale and Mrs. Ecclestone complete and to make Major Ecclestone finally pay for his threats, Tidwell decided to poison the Major during the trial. Did he do it himself, or did his friend the chemist manage it? We don't know, for Ngaio Marsh's stage directions are a bit vague, but she points out that the two of them sat between the Ecclestones. In both the death of the dog and the murder of the Major, Thomas Tidwell had the most obvious opportunity, and when that is combined with his motive and, through the chemist, the means, it is clear that he should be the defendant in the next session of "Crown Court."

—Douglas G. Greene

The Figure Quoted

Mr. Batey (Batey and Burt, Auctioneers) stood in the middle of those ill-lit, indescribably dreary business premises of his and looked unenthusiastically at the "lots" which he hoped to sell in the course of the next two hours.

This was a remnant day. All the hopelessly impossible oddments of former sales were massed together, with one or two attractions thrown in to arouse the desirable gambling spirit in the heart of that peculiar public which waited upon Mr. Batey's arts as an auctioneer. There were neat little lots of china, three cotton gabardine dresses of no character, an ancient gramophone, which in response to the solicitations of Mr. Batey's clerk, was even now giving tongue to a hopelessly ancient fox-trot; there were piles of dreadful old music sheets and collections of second-hand books. Hanging disconsolately on the dirty wall were three oil-paintings. One of them presented some indecently-pink flamingos standing in a pool which at first glance appeared to be afflicted with floating kidneys. A closer examination showed these objects to be the leaves of water-lilies. The other two works were landscapes of terrifying gloom.

In the middle of all this decorous and depressing jumble stood the marble basin that was attracting Mr. Batey's attention at the moment. It was unbelievably lovely and Mr. Batey despised it from the depths of his heart. Its shape was perfect. The pure Greek outline of a shallow vessel with outward-curving, generous base and exquisitely-tilted lip. Beneath the rim was a band of fruit and leaves enclosed between two garlands that a Doric shepherd might have woven one day in spring. Inside the rim was a little flattened platform where once upon a time a stone nymph must have sat, dabbling her feet in the water and looking down slantways at the faun who still crouched on the pedestal. But the nymph had gone.

"What are you to do with a thing like that?" asked Mr. Batey of his assistant. "I dunno what you were thinking of, Ern . . . a good quid . . . and what I mean to say is . . . who's going to buy it?"

"I kind of liked it," said Ern.

"Well, I can't say I see what took your fancy."

If Ern had moved in other circles he might have returned the inevitable answer of the layman: "I don't know anything about it, but I do know what I like." However, he was unacquainted with this formula and merely said combatively: "What's wrong with it? It's pretty."

"It's that big you might have a bath in it," returned Mr. Batey inconsequentially, "and that affair sitting down at the bottom with sheep's legs . . . I mean to say!"

The customers began to drift in and inspect the lots. . . .

It would be difficult to say from what section of the public Mr. Batey drew his patrons. For the most part they were women in overcoats of varying degrees of dilapidation. Half a dozen men hung about the entrance and cracked a dispirited joke or two. It was the usual weekly afternoon auction and the usual crowd attended it, poking, examining . . . dubious faces thrust forward to reject, or to appraise with pursed lips of covetousness, some dingy object, which, heaven knows why, attracted their ineradicable acquisitiveness.

A little group collected round the stone basin.

"Look very nice in the front garden, Mrs. Clark," said Mr. Batey jovially.

"What's it for?" inquired the lady he had spoken to.

"It's . . . well, you see what it is . . . it's an ornamental urn, in a manner of speaking."

"Ow!"

"Very fine thing."

A dealer pushed his way through the crowd and looked at it disinterestedly.

"Didn't know you went in for that sort of thing," he remarked.

Mr. Batey detected a sneer, and without replying, majestically mounted his desk and, putting on his pince-nez, surveyed his audience with a practised eye. Suddenly and vehemently, he attacked it with his professional manner.

"Now then, ladies and gentlemen." He paused effectively, and the crowd settled itself on benches, chairs, packing-cases, and on the flight of stairs that ran up the back wall of the room. Mr. Batey, in a few well-chosen words, enlarged on the excellence of a coal-scuttle which Ern, cynically staring about him, held up for everyone to see.

"Now then," repeated Mr. Batey, "it's a beautiful thing. Good as new. Worth a couple of quid. How much have you got for it, ladies? Start me with something."

This phrase was a convention. Nobody ever started Mr. Batey with any bid, however lowly, but the use of the convention enabled him to proceed along the usual lines and in five minutes the coal-scuttle, "worth a couple of quid," was knocked down for eight shillings. It was quickly succeeded by a meat dish and a set of the works of Lord Byron.

Mr. Batey was apparently on the top of his form, attacking vigorously, uttering an occasional quip, and inquiring pathetically, "What's the matter with it, ladies?" yet, in his heart, he was ill at ease. That stone basin . . . ridiculously fancied by Ern . . . had really almost taken hold of Mr.

Batey's imagination; an experience which, as he himself would have said, was as unusual as it was "undesirable." He was not keen on his imagination at any time. It was a quality of his mind in which he was not interested, and to have it aroused by a tuppeny-ha'penny bit of masonry was very fidgeting. He wished that the long shaft of sunlight coming in at the top of the stairs had not fallen so exactly on the little stone faun as he crouched on his furry haunches at the foot of the pedestal. Mr. Batey's eyes, try as he would to fix them on his audience, would keep turning toward the empty platform inside the rim of the bowl, at which the faun so fixedly stared. Better put the thing up at once and get it off his mind. He knocked Lord Byron down to a dealer for three-and-six, and said hastily:

"Lot 5. Ornamental Urn."

At this flamboyant description of himself, Ern gave a sudden start.

" 'Ow much?" he ejaculated.

"Not you. That," said Mr. Batey.

Ern, covered in confusion, came down from his table to the accompaniment of a subdued titter from the crowd. Mr. Batey was glad of the laugh. It gave him time, like a comedian who is uncertain of his lines, to gather himself together for his opening sally. It was all very tiresome, though why he should be so fussed about it he could not have said.

Nobody would bid and the thing would fall back on his hands; which was exactly what he did not want. The fountain, basin, urn, whatever it was, was a "rum affair," and he wouldn't wonder if there wasn't something uncanny about it. Come, come.

"Now, ladies and gentlemen, I have got something particularly fine to offer you. A really classy bit of masonry. Put it on the front lawn and your residence would be at once exclusive and genteel. Now, how much will you start me at?"

He paused, entirely without expectation, when to his utter amazement a man's voice said very placidly:

"Three pounds."

Mr. Batey kept his head admirably. His eyes, perhaps, turned a little glassy, but he actually managed to ejaculate coldly:

"Well, ladies and gentlemen, I suppose I must start somewhere, so I'll take three pounds as a bid. Three pounds I've got . . ." and lowering his voice he went on quacking in the orthodox manner. "Three pounds I got—three pounds—three quid I got—three quid."

There was some sort of disturbance going on at the head of the stairs. That single shaft of sunlight prevented Mr. Batey from seeing clearly in this direction. Vague, drab figures jostled each other behind a screen of gold-dust. Suddenly a clear and extraordinary youthful voice called out something that he could not catch.

"Is that a bid up there?" asked Mr. Batey. The same voice made the same bird-like exclamation.

"Three-ten," said Mr. Batey on the off-chance, and not being contradicted drew breath to quack again.

"Four," said the man's voice. "Four," said Mr. Batey. A little pale hand and a bare arm shot up on the other side of the shaft of light. Odd!

"Five," said Mr. Batey.

"Ten," said the first bidder. The insane idea that Ern had taken it upon himself to "trot" his fancy visited Mr. Batey's confused and harried soul, but he held on nobly.

"That's better, gentlemen—thank you, sir. Ten quid I got. Ten for this highly-ornamental urn. Ten quid."

He turned his head automatically toward the spot from which the voice of his female bidder seemed to come . . . and nearly fainted.

From out of the confused jumble of vague figures at the head of the stairs, emerged, all too clearly to be seen, a lovely girl. She floated, rather than walked, to the banister head, which in area was about the same size as the empty platform inside the stone bowl. On this banister post she seated herself, cupping her chin in her hand and looking down slantways at the faun who was so far below. Mr. Batey's first wild desire was to heave in her direction one of his cotton gabardine dresses.

She was wearing nothing at all.

The grateful sun shone directly upon her, and so pale she was and so still she sat that she looked for all the world as if she were carved out of stone. Her appearance acted upon Mr. Batey exactly like a severe concussion following a blow on the head. His voice and limbs and even his brain went on functioning, but unnaturally . . . they were prone at any moment to peter out altogether. He continued to quack. She nodded. He took her bid and quacked again. He could now see the gentleman who had first called the running, a scholarly-looking, elderly person, leaning against the front door post. "Fifteen," said this man, calmly, without so much as glancing at the head of the stairs.

Mr. Batey glanced. Poor Mr. Batey, victim of circumstances and of his trade, continued to take bids from a completely-undressed lady whom nobody else appeared to notice. That was the queer part about it. There were all those elderly and respectable ladies round her, paying no more attention to her than if she had been as fully clad as they themselves. Was she a mad woman? Was everyone mad, wondered Mr. Batey, or was he himself insane? A cold sweat burst out on his brow.

"Twenty. Thank you, madam," he shouted, wildly averting his gaze from her as she gently inclined her head toward him. "Come on, sir, it's against you . . . twenty pounds . . . cheap y'know."

"Twenty-five."

"Twenty-five I've got." Gosh, there she was nodding at him again! "Thirty. Thirty pounds . . . thirty quid . . . come on, ladies and gentlemen, what's the matter with it?" (What, indeed!) "Thirty I've got!"

"Wait a moment," said the gentleman quietly. "Shouldn't there be a second figure?"

"Another!" screamed Mr. Batey, almost unmanned by this final irregularity. "*Another figure!* How many more?" He clutched at the rail of his desk and glared quite dreadfully into the middle distance.

"I believe there has been, at some time, a female figure seated on the platform inside the basin. Have you this figure? Is it detachable?

Mr. Batey had almost reached the end of his tether. The whole of his everyday business had become pagan and improper. What was all this chat about figures? This unblushing demand and all-too-ready supply? What were they taking him for?

"If you want figgers!" he suddenly bawled in the astonished gentleman's face—"'Ow abuut that!" and he pointed wildly but dramatically at his offensive visitor. The gentleman put up his glasses and gazed across the room.

"H'm," he said.

"What d'you mean, 'H'm'?" roared Mr. Batey. "I should think it was 'H'm.'"

"Before we go any further," said the gentleman, "I should like to look at this separate piece . . ."

" 'Piece' is right."

". . . presumably it goes with the fountain?"

"Perzoomably . . . !" Mr. Batey was inarticulate. The shameless man was now approaching the girl on the banister head. She took no notice of him, but remained as if frozen, her chin in her hand, a slanting smile on her lips. This smile, the gentleman's face, as if it were a mirror, faintly reflected. Then, glancing at Ern, who was looking a little dazed, he murmured, "May we not re-enthrone her?" and before Mr. Batey's galvanised eyes, they toppled her over, bore her down the stairs, and set her up inside the stone basin. There she sat, lost behind an age of antiquity, sun-warmed, but quite, quite still.

"Forty . . . for the whole thing," said the gentleman.

It was Mr. Batey's swan song, but he managed it.

"Any advance on forty for the whole concern?" he gabbled, insanely beating the air with his hammer. There was no advance. "Away she goes," gasped Mr. Batey. "That's all, thank you, ladies and gentlemen."

The crowd, surprised at the short duration of the sale, drifted away. The man who had bought . . . "goodness knows what he has bought," thought Mr. Batey . . . gave his cheque and address to Ern and with a nod towards Mr. Batey walked briskly away.

Mr. Batey and Ern behaved very much like simultaneous comedians. They watched the customer disappear; they turned their heads sharply toward each other, and in perfect unison asked each other:

"Where did it come from?"

"Where did it come from?"

"What!"

"What!"

"The figger."

"The figger."

"Don't *you* know!" gasped Mr. Batey.

"I thought you'd bought it," said Ern. Mr. Batey became glassy.

"Who run 'im up to forty?" asked Ern. "I couldn't see her. Who was she, anyway?"

"Not . . . not much to look at."

"Well-dressed sorter dame?"

"Dressed?" repeated Mr. Batey with extreme difficulty; "I wouldn't say well-dressed."

"Well, Mr. Batey, I wasn't so far wrong after all," suggested Ern, "when I said it was a bit of good stuff."

"I still consider it an unwarranted speculation," said Mr. Batey, "in . . . ah . . . in consideration of . . . the figure quoted."

"I don't get you," said Ern.

"You wouldn't," said Mr. Batey, profoundly.

Ngaio Marsh

Author of thirty-two classic English detective novels featuring Inspector Roderick Alleyn of Scotland Yard, **Edith Ngaio Marsh** in fact spent most of her life outside of England. She was born in New Zealand in 1895, and received her early training in the theater. It was, however, in England, where she lived from 1928 until the early 1930s, that she wrote her first novel, *A Man Lay Dead*. Soon she was recognized as probably the finest stylist of mystery writers, concerned not merely with dovetailing the plot but with creating believable characters. She explained that "I try to write with realism in the non-realistic convention of the detective story." Because of her respect for style, she sometimes took as long as two years to write a novel.

But her first love remained the stage. "I am a busy woman," she remarked when she was seventy years old, "and when I am not writing detective novels I am working in the theater." Much of her time was spent producing and directing, but she also wrote plays for children, adaptations of her own novels, a courtroom drama for British television, and a handbook on theatrical production. For her work in the theater, she was made Dame Commander of the British Empire by Queen Elizabeth II. For her contributions as a mystery novelist, she was recognized as Grand Master by the Mystery Writers of America. She died in Christchurch, New Zealand, in 1982.

Douglas G. Greene is a widely recognized expert on crime and mystery fiction. He has contributed articles to *The Armchair Detective, The Poisoned Pen, CADS: Crime and Detective Stories, The Baker Street Journal, The Thorndyke File, The Chesterton Review,* and *Critical Survey of Mystery and Detective Fiction.* He graduated from the University of South Florida in 1966, and after earning the degrees of Master of Arts and Doctor of Philosophy from the University of Chicago he joined the faculty of Old Dominion University in Norfolk, Virginia. He is currently Professor of History and Director of the Institute of Humanities. He has written or edited ten books, ranging from studies of seventeenth-century Britain to bibliographies of L. Frank Baum's *Oz* books. His most recent work is *Fell and Foul Play* by John Dickson Carr, published by International Polygonics, Ltd.